# Knightley & Son

## ROHAN GAVIN

BLOOMSBURY

LONDON  NEW DELHI  NEW YORK  SYDNEY

Bloomsbury Publishing, London, New Delhi, New York and Sydney

First published in Great Britain in January 2014 by Bloomsbury Publishing Plc
50 Bedford Square, London WC1B 3DP

www.bloomsbury.com

Bloomsbury is a registered trademark of Bloomsbury Publishing Plc

A CIP catalogue record for this book is available from the British Library

ISBN 978 1 4088 3891 4

Typeset by Hewer Text UK Ltd, Edinburgh
Printed and bound in Great Britain by CPI Group (UK) Ltd, Croydon CR0 4YY

3 5 7 9 10 8 6 4

*For my wife & son*

# Prologue
## THE CODE

He opened the cover and found the first page. The book felt substantial and had a good weight to it, despite being slim enough for the casual reader. The cover had a striking symbol and a catchy title: *The Code*. It felt both old and new. He rarely read outside of the classroom, but this book was strangely inviting. Besides, he'd heard it was good from all the buzz on the internet.

He traced his finger over the first sentence. It was clear and concise:

*Change your life now.*

Intrigued, he continued reading.

*You hold the key to unlocking your future, your power, your potential. 'The Code' has been handed down over thousands of years in order to find its way into your hands right now.*

Lee clamped his knees tightly around the school bag at his feet, and shuffled into a private corner between two book displays. He didn't want to be interrupted. He looked around, making a brief survey of the other customers. What if one of his classmates saw him? It was a self-help book after all. He could always blame it on his mum – and Christmas wasn't far away. She might want to read it too. He loosened the tie of his school uniform, twanged his dental braces and kept reading.

*The wise always listen to their inner voice, because it's the sound of the universe speaking to you. And it never lies. The voice is telling you that whatever you want can be yours, if you want it enough . . .*

Inner voice? His mum would have a fit if she found this on his bedside table. But it felt good. And as the book said, if it feels good, it must be right.

His eyes scanned over the sentences, faster and faster, flicking from left to right and back again. He could almost feel it working on him, sending tiny electrical charges around his head, unlocking his potential and delivering a pleasant shiver of excitement at the same time. He suddenly saw it all clearly: success, fame and his wildest dreams come true. This was the moment he would remember when he was lying on a beach somewhere, with perfect teeth. He kept reading voraciously, covering the first few pages in less than a minute, consuming every last piece of wisdom the text had to offer. Then he stopped.

'Ouch!'

He felt a sting as he turned the page. A paper cut? But there wasn't any blood.

Then he noticed it, crawling away from the spine, towards the corner of the page: a scorpion. Just like the one from biology class. He blinked. It couldn't be. But the black creature continued scuttling across the margin, making a clicking sound, and dropped over the edge.

He stared at the book, transfixed, as another bug emerged from behind the cover; then a centipede calmly headed in the opposite direction. A spider followed it: a big one, draped in brittle hair. And another insect he didn't even recognise. And another.

'Wha–?'

Lee dropped the book as a swarm of insects fell out of the pages, turning it into a black, moving mass. It hummed with activity, the chorus of a hundred tiny clicks, as all manner of creatures came spilling out of it.

'Someone . . . help!'

He backed away from the display stand, tripping over his school bag, splaying his arms to regain his balance.

He looked down at his hands and saw more insects appearing from his shirtsleeves, running up the arms of his school uniform.

'Help me!'

He half fell through another display, sending rows of new releases collapsing to the floor. His yells escalated to full-blown screams as the insects covered his whole body, racing up his tie, inside his collar, secreting themselves on his person, burrowing into every corner.

Other customers spun round, confused, awoken from their browsing.

A shop assistant quickly moved away from the cash register to locate the source of the disturbance.

Lee was writhing on the floor, surrounded by books, clawing at his clothes and kicking his legs in all directions, fighting off an unseen enemy. The shop assistant broke through the circle of onlookers, quickly assessed the situation, then knelt down and tried to place a book between the boy's teeth.

'G-get them off me!' Lee cried out, desperately pointing all round himself.

The onlookers stared down at him, baffled, then

exchanged concerned glances – because he was pointing into thin air. There was no enemy attacking him. There was nothing there.

Away from the gathering crowd and the overturned displays, a copy of *The Code* sat forgotten on the floor, clean and inviting, its glossy cover and symbol reflecting in the fluorescent lighting.

# Chapter 1
## THE KNIGHTLEYS

In a private room in a quiet garden suburb outside London, Alan Knightley slept a dreamless sleep. This condition was not unusual for a patient who had been asleep for over four years. Experts said he was somewhere between a coma and a trance. Some such patients dreamed and some did not – at least, that was according to the ones fortunate enough to wake up.

Although he was forty-eight years old, Knightley still had a freshness and youth about his face, with no grey hair to speak of. The doctors assumed this was due to the sheer amount of uninterrupted rest he'd enjoyed during his interminable stay at Shrubwoods Hospice. Despite an occasional flutter of the eyelids, or an even more occasional grunt, he showed no sign of waking up any time soon.

Several tubes and wires protruded from the sleeves of his gown, running along the side of the bed, connecting to an intravenous drip and an ECG machine, which displayed a pulsing green line resembling a distant mountain range. At the end of the bed, a clipboard read: *Knightley, Alan.*

His hair was neatly combed back to reveal sharp, if not conventionally handsome, features. He had a wide, knowledgeable brow; an angular nose interrupted by two slight bumps that indicated he had, on occasion, encountered opponents who could not be reasoned with; and a jaw that was proud and composed even while unconscious.

His room had an old TV angled the wrong way, and beyond that a window looked out over neatly manicured lawns, hedges and a dense outcrop of trees. There was only one picture on the wall: a child's painting of a father and son, which made up for its lack of formal skill with its bold use of colour and unusual attention to detail. Both figures wore a suit and tie: the father's suit was red and the son's green.

Darkus Knightley, the smaller figure from the picture, sat patiently by his father's bedside. He was older now, but he wasn't embarrassed by the painting that hung over him. It reminded him of how far he'd come in the past four years, leading up to his thirteenth birthday – a hollow affair that had taken place a month earlier. His father, on the other hand, was still lying in the exact same position he always did, impervious to the passage of time, hardly moving a muscle: the cause of his condition as yet unknown.

As chance would have it, Darkus was wearing green, just like in the picture; to be precise, it was a forest-green tweed waistcoat and jacket ensemble that was somewhat ahead of his years. His shoes were highly polished brogues. His sharp blue eyes, neatly parted hair and angular nose and ears also seemed in advance of his years – certainly different from your average thirteen-year-old.

Without warning, he began to speak aloud, apparently from memory, for there was no printed matter in evidence.

'Last week I examined the Curious Case of the Amber Necklace,' Darkus began. 'I found the line of reasoning clear and well laid out, but its conclusions were lacking.' He paused and watched his father's closed eyelids for any kind of response. Seeing none, he continued. 'If there *was* a larger organisation responsible for its disappearance, I see no hard evidence to prove it . . .' He paused again, watching his father the way a fisherman watches the still surface of a lake, waiting for a ripple that means the bait has been taken. He received no such ripple.

What he did receive, however, was an audible signal

from outside the door: a minute squeak from the linoleum, as if someone had been standing outside, possibly even eavesdropping on him. Darkus turned his head to the door and saw a small circle of mist on the porthole window. Someone had most certainly been watching him, but he told himself that in all likelihood it was only a concerned member of the nursing staff. He checked his simple Timex watch, which confirmed his time was up. Besides, he had an event to attend that evening.

'That concludes my report for today,' he announced. Then he added gently, 'Sleep tight, Dad.'

On cue, a female nurse opened the door with no attempt to be quiet. She had stopped bothering with details like that a few years ago.

'Same time next week then?' she asked Darkus.

'Yes-yes,' he answered softly, then collected his herringbone coat and Donegal tweed walking hat and quietly left the room.

# Chapter 2
## WORDPLAY

By that evening, a thick fog had rolled across the south-east, moving through the dense woodland and over the substantial grounds of Cranston School. The classrooms were empty, the rows of desks faintly lit by lamp posts standing along the perimeter. The fog gathered around the facade of the main building, creeping over the railings towards a modern structure set back from the rest.

The assembly hall stood out like a beacon, its windows giving off a good-natured glow. A murmur of activity came from inside as some two hundred pupils and parents sat facing a wide, raised stage. The pupils were all in civilian clothes, including a small group in designer hooded tops skulking near the back of the room.

A male teacher in a patterned sweater stood at the side of the stage holding a microphone. Behind the lectern, three teenage pupils sat waiting their turn: a boy in jeans and a T-shirt, a girl in leggings and a black leather jacket, and a familiar figure in a green tweed waistcoat and jacket ensemble.

'Darkus Knightley, prepare to spell,' the teacher announced.

Darkus stood up and approached the lectern. He looked upward and to the right, unconsciously holding the mic stand for moral support.

The teacher held his own microphone close. 'Your word is . . .' He paused enigmatically, then said, 'Zarzuela.'

The audience whispered the word to each other, exchanging glances.

The teacher repeated it once more for dramatic effect: 'Zarzuela.'

The audience went quiet.

Darkus focused his gaze on the upper right of the auditorium, briefly closed his eyes, then responded: 'Z-a-r-z-u-e-l-a. Zarzuela. A Spanish opera noted for its spoken dialogue and comic subject matter.'

The teacher nodded. 'Correct.'

The audience applauded, except for the hooded tops who remained indifferent near the back of the room.

The teacher added, 'The definition is not strictly necessary, Darkus, but I won't object. Thank you.'

Darkus nodded and returned to his seat, unmoved by the applause. He made brief eye contact with his mum and stepdad, who were seated in the middle of the audience, dressed in smart casual clothes. Darkus returned his attention to his waistcoat as the teacher announced the next name.

'Gary Evans, prepare to spell.' The boy in the jeans and T-shirt approached the microphone. 'Your word is . . . yosenabe,' said the teacher, then repeated the word for effect.

The boy gripped the mic stand and stared dead ahead into the crowd. 'Y-o-s- . . .' he stammered, 'e-n-a-b-y? Yosenaby?'

The teacher paused then shook his head. 'I'm afraid that is incorrect. The correct spelling is: y-o-s-e-n-a-b-e. A soup consisting of seafood and vegetables cooked in a broth. You can leave the stage, Gary.'

The audience clapped respectfully. Gary hung his head and exited the stage, avoiding the gaze of his parents huddled together applauding in the front row.

'Tilly Palmer, prepare to spell.'

The thirteen-year-old girl in the black leather jacket approached the microphone, and a murmur rippled through the crowd, as if her reputation preceded her. Her hair was jet black with blue lowlights – although it had a tendency to change colour dramatically and without warning, for no reason that Darkus could deduce, and to the consternation of the school authorities.

Darkus's relationship with Tilly was complicated for

several reasons. Firstly, she was the daughter of his father's former assistant, Carol. Secondly, Carol had died in a tragic car accident six years ago – a year before Darkus's own parents split up. Thirdly – and most unexpectedly – the world had conspired to bring together Darkus's divorced mum and Tilly's widowed father.

As a result, Tilly had become his stepsister.

'Tilly, your word is . . . logorrhoea,' the teacher announced. 'If you answer correctly, you're in with a chance to win the competition.'

Tilly narrowed her eyes in concentration.

Darkus watched from his seat, feeling no sense of competition – quite the opposite in fact. Tilly had performed admirably throughout the heats; she had a broad, often incisive knowledge of a variety of subjects, drawn from many long hours spent browsing the internet. This was partly down to the fact that her father had temporarily confined her to Cranston as a boarder after she ran away from home once too often. More than anyone, including himself, she deserved to win. Darkus interlaced his fingers and waited for her to answer.

'L-o-g-o-r- . . . r-h-o-e-a. Logorrhoea,' she recited. 'Pathologically incoherent and repetitious speech.'

The teacher nodded. 'Correct.'

The crowd rippled with applause, which was quickly overtaken by the customary murmuring that followed

Tilly like a shadow. She returned to her seat without expression, imperceptibly glancing at Darkus as she went.

'Darkus, prepare to spell. Your word is . . . abalone.'

Darkus arrived at the microphone, staring up and to the right again. Out of the corner of his eye he saw Tilly behind him, shifting in her seat.

The teacher repeated, 'Abalone.'

Darkus began, 'A-b-a-l-o-n. Abalon.' He turned to the teacher.

The teacher looked up, surprised. 'I'm afraid that is incorrect, Darkus. Abalone is A-b- . . .'

As the teacher correctly spelled the word, Darkus noticed Tilly react, bemused, from behind him. The teacher read the definition and Darkus unconsciously whispered the words along with him, for he was well aware of both the meaning and spelling of 'abalone'.

'A mollusc of the genus Haliotis with a bowl-like shell and a row of respiratory holes,' the teacher advised him.

Darkus nodded and returned to his seat, closely examined by Tilly.

'Tilly, prepare to spell for the competition. Your word is . . . vivisepulture . . .'

As Tilly approached the mic, Darkus's mind drifted off a bit. He knew she would get this one. Vivisepulture: the act of being buried alive. Hardly the most uplifting end to the competition, but a common occurrence in

14

the annals of crime, at least according to his research. In fact, he had only just read about the heinous custom in his father's account of the Incident of the Missing Headstone.

'V-i-v-i- . . .' she began, then glanced off at Darkus with some suspicion, then continued, '. . . s-e-p-u-l-t-u-r-e. Vivisepulture.'

Before the teacher could confirm the result, Darkus had already started clapping.

'That is correct,' the teacher announced.

The audience reluctantly broke into applause, temporarily drowning out the murmuring. Darkus quietly made his way offstage, away from the commotion.

Tilly squinted behind the lectern as flashbulbs captured the moment. A second teacher arrived carrying a trophy.

Audience members began filing out of the auditorium. Darkus made his way up the aisle towards the back of the room.

'Hey, Dorkus,' said one of the hooded tops, leering at him. 'Better luck next time.'

'Thanks,' he answered politely.

Unfortunately his name was perfectly suited to a number of less than flattering alterations and abbreviations. If it wasn't for this moniker he could have faded even further into the dull backdrop of school life, which was his preferred position: out of sight, out of mind. The name was by all accounts his father's idea, not his mother's – as she reminded him on a regular basis. Perhaps by way of apology, his father had abbreviated it to 'Doc', which was marginally less of a problem, although Darkus preferred to reserve that name as a term of endearment between him and his dad rather than share it with the school.

For that reason, he hadn't heard the name 'Doc' in almost four years.

'See you around,' the hooded top threatened.

'Not if I see you first,' Darkus whispered to himself, until a hand grabbed his shoulder.

'Hey –' A voice accompanied it.

He turned to find Tilly facing him.

'You let me win,' she said.

Darkus paused a moment, then shook his head. 'There's no empirical proof of that.'

'I don't need proof. I know you did.'

'You were an excellent competitor, Tilly. You won on your own merits.' He bowed his head a little. 'I for one am looking forward to half-term,' he embellished. 'How about you?'

She examined him with her overpoweringly dark eyes, unconvinced by his story.

'Kids . . . ?' A booming male voice broke the moment.

Darkus turned to see his stepdad, Clive, emerge from the crowd. The waist of Clive's jeans appeared to be even higher than usual, leaving a gap of several inches between the hem of his trouser leg and the tongue of his loafers. This being an occasion of sorts, the sock was an argyle. The outfit was completed by a silver nylon jacket that resembled something an astronaut might have worn during the early days of lunar exploration. Meeting Tilly's stare, Clive modified his tone a bit and unconsciously ran a hand through his nest of curly salt-and-pepper hair:

'Er, Darkus? Your mother wants to get back for the telly,' he lied. 'Unlucky on the spelling test,' he added with a shrug. 'Tilly, you've earned yourself some reward points. I'll reconsider my position on the Xbox.'

Tilly looked at him, unflinching, then reluctantly turned and followed Darkus out of the assembly hall.


At Shrubwoods Hospice, Alan Knightley's chest heaved and sank at long, excruciating intervals, while his eyelids remained defiantly and terminally closed. The female nurse rhythmically raised and lowered Knightley's feet at faster intervals, bending his legs at the knee joint with a loud clicking noise: a thankless ritual she had to perform several times a day to maintain adequate circulation to his extremities.

Behind her, a male doctor entered and examined the patient warily.

'Any improvement?' he asked.

'Nope.'

'Speech function?'

'Not a word.'

The doctor watched the patient, then shook his head. 'Let me know if anything changes.'

'Will do.'

The doctor exited, walking down the corridor.

The nurse waited for her superior's footsteps to recede into the distance, then roughly dropped Knightley's feet on to the bed and checked her watch. Without looking, her hand quickly located the remote control on the side table and pointed it at the TV set. She sat on the lone chair, leaned back and stared up.

The TV flickered to life, showing a panel of judges sitting under a row of spotlights. One by one they rose up in a standing ovation. The nurse lowered the volume, so as not to be heard. On the screen, music reverberated through the studio, only to be drowned out by the cheers of the audience.

'Congratulations,' the first judge announced.

The female contestant shrugged modestly.

The second judge paused for effect. 'I think . . . you might have just the right combination to win this competition.' The applause got louder.

The nurse's eyes glittered as she watched the screen,

as if the praise was for her. Behind her, Knightley's eyelids appeared to flutter, as if he was aware of the commotion. The fingers on his right hand tensed up, seemed to make a gesture for a second, then relaxed.

On TV, the third judge took over: 'I agree. The *combination* of that voice and that performance could take you all the way.' The crowd erupted into applause again.

The nurse shifted on her chair, excited.

Behind her, Knightley flinched. Something the judge had said was having an effect on him. One eye seemed to open, then closed again. His mouth started gaping, as if trying to say something. 'Coh . . .' he whispered, unheard. 'Coh . . .'

On TV, the music started up again as the contestant left the stage. The nurse watched, entranced.

Behind her, Knightley's hand moved again. It was more extreme this time, pointing into space, his mouth clearly trying to articulate a word.

On TV, the music began to die down.

'Coh . . . mm . . .' Knightley's lips jutted out, taking all his effort. 'Combi–'

Suddenly the nurse's pager beeped loudly, startling her. She quickly raised the remote control, clicked off the TV and marched to the door, her white shoes squeaking across the floor.

She did not notice Knightley behind her, now

gesturing wildly with both hands, his tubes getting crossed, straining at their moorings. As she slammed the door behind her, Knightley sat bolt upright in bed and managed to get the word out in one go.

'The Combination!' he said, sounding strangely surprised.

He opened his eyes – or tried to. His left eyelid was sealed shut, giving a sort of pirate impression, the eyelashes bound together by hundreds of hours of sleep. He rubbed them impatiently then both eyes opened, looking alarmed, taking in their surroundings.

'What . . . ?' He inspected the tubes running from his arms and chest. Without thinking, he quickly tore them out. 'Ouch!!' he screamed, and looked around to see if anyone had heard him, but apparently no one had. The ECG machine was flashing an error, but as yet no one seemed to have noticed.

He tried to move but found more tubes under the sheets, rooting him in place. He winced as he disconnected them, then smiled, relieved, and managed to swing his legs out of bed. His toes touched the cold linoleum and flinched slightly. Unperturbed, he adjusted his gown, pressed his soles to the floor and took his first steps.

Knightley's knees buckled and he fell flat on his face. He breathed slowly, performing a series of mental diagnostics on his body. His hands were functioning, his arms were passable, but his legs were basically useless. There was adequate feeling, but no muscle mass.

He reached out for the foot of the cupboard and used it to drag himself along the floor, creating a deafening squeaking noise of bare skin against linoleum. His features set into a look of grim determination as he reached the cupboard and then stretched out his hand to find purchase on a wall socket. He continued traversing the room like a rock climber, only he was climbing across the floor.

In a nearby corridor, the nurse's pager beeped again. She looked down at it, annoyed. Then a much louder beeping echoed through the whole building. She could not ignore this sound because it was the alarm. She took off down the corridor at a brisk clip, turned the corner and was confronted by something so inexplicable that it momentarily took her breath. The door to Alan Knightley's room was hanging ajar. She had not left it that way. She raced towards it, breaking into a sprint.

She burst into the room to find the bed empty, tubes discarded on the floor, a puddle of intravenous liquid gathering under the bed. The nurse stood gaping as the doctor burst through the door behind her.

'What happened? Where is he?!' The doctor gripped the nurse's arm, breaking her trance.

'I don't know . . .' she responded.

In another wing of the hospice, Knightley staggered down a corridor bow-legged, his limbs barely supporting his body. At the end of the corridor, a walking frame stood discarded outside a recreation room and Knightley grabbed hold of the handlebars. With a lurch, he accelerated down another corridor, wheels rattling.

He reached a staircase and paused, his legs wobbling uncontrollably. He heard voices from the bottom of the stairs.

'He's not in his room? Well, he's not down here.'

The voices were getting closer. Knightley saw a private room on his right and ducked inside. An elderly male patient reclining in the bed looked up from behind an oxygen mask.

'And how are we doing today, Mr . . . ?' Knightley cleared his throat and glanced at the man's clipboard. 'Jones?'

Mr Jones looked up at him, alarmed: this was most certainly *not* his doctor. He moaned loudly, trying to alert the nurses. Knightley spotted a pair of slippers by the bed.

'Mind if I borrow these?' he asked.

The patient groaned in complaint.

'Thanks.' Knightley put them on and raised the sash window behind the bed. With some difficulty he used both hands to lift his leg on to the mattress, stepped over Mr Jones and slid himself on to the window ledge.

Outside, a strong wind gusted through the trees, lifting Knightley's gown, which he held firmly in place. He stupidly looked down, seeing the manicured lawns and hedges some six or seven metres below. He shivered, feeling goose pimples popping up over his entire body. He willed his slippered feet to inch along the parapet ledge towards a rusted fire escape at the corner of the building. His feet shuffled obediently as the wind kept up, ruffling his hair.

He reached the fire escape, swung his legs over the railing and awkwardly backed down the ladder towards a row of flower beds.

Floodlights flicked on across the grounds. The doctor and several nurses ran out of the main entrance, scanning the area.

'Mr Knightley! Mr Knightley, come back!'

At the edge of the lawn, just beyond the large circles of electric light, a white shape disappeared into a hedge.

Knightley careered headlong through the undergrowth, tearing his gown. The heavens opened up, drenching him in heavy rain. Undaunted, he swung himself over a perimeter fence and found himself on a dimly lit local road. He stumbled along the grassy verge towards a row of neon lamps in the distance.

# Chapter 3

## THE CASE OF THE
## SCRATCHED QUARTER PANEL

Clive pressed his face against the misted windscreen, peering through the fog as they drove home from the competition. Jackie, Darkus's mum, fiddled with the heating controls. She was still attractive, even under a layer of sensible woollies, with her hair in a more conservative style than in her younger days.

'I can't get the demister to work,' she complained softly.

'The climate control in this thing is pretty much non-existent,' Clive muttered.

'In your review you called it "absolutely spectacular",' said Darkus from the back seat, attempting light conversation.

'That was TV – this is reality. Big difference,' replied Clive. 'Besides, they gave us a deal on *this*!' he said, gesturing dismissively at the car.

'Well, it's lucky you've got your new jacket,' Jackie reminded him. 'That'll keep out the cold.'

'It'll keep out a nuclear winter,' remarked Tilly from beside Darkus, then returned to staring sullenly into the soupy darkness.

Clive glanced at his daughter in the rear-view mirror. 'Well, if I wanted fashion advice, Tilly, you wouldn't be the first person I'd ask, that is unless I was going to a funer—'

'Clive,' Jackie interrupted him.

'Sorry, love.' He guided the estate car into a bend.

Tilly smiled privately, shook her head and continued watching the trees go by. Her dad would feel worse about this last comment than she would.

Darkus considered giving her a sympathetic glance, then thought better of it. He and his stepsister kept a safe distance; it was easier that way.

They emerged from the mist on to a quiet residential street, signposted Wolseley Close, and pulled up to a neat, detached mock-Tudor house. A large Jaguar coupe took up one side of the driveway.

Clive switched off the car and Tilly was first up the path and into the house, using her own keys. Jackie gave Clive a look and he returned his customary shrug. They continued up the driveway after her, with Darkus in tow, until Clive came to an abrupt halt.

'I don't *believe* it . . .' Clive froze, then crouched down like a Neanderthal, approaching the Jaguar almost on all fours. He peered over at the neighbouring house whose garden was adjacent to theirs. 'That son of a –'

'Clive,' Jackie interrupted him.

'Well, look!' He gesticulated towards the back of the car.

A thin silver line defiled the perfect midnight-blue paintwork of the Jaguar's rear quarter panel.

Clive stared at the scratch in a stunned trance. 'It must've been the wheelie bins. He's always moving those ruddy bins around.' He took out his mobile phone and marched after Jackie into the house, angrily dialling a number.

Darkus watched him go, then returned to the scene. He knelt down by the Jaguar and examined the scratch, slowly running his finger over it. Then he glanced at the grass around the edge of the driveway. Satisfied that he'd observed everything he needed to, he walked into the house and closed the front door behind him.

Clive was striding around the kitchen on the phone while Jackie stood patiently by the kettle.

'He's not picking up. Typical.' Clive waved the phone in the air, awaiting an acknowledgement from Jackie, who instead set about making the tea.

'Well, we've all had a difficult day,' she said, nodding at Darkus, who had appeared from the other room and sat down at the kitchen table. 'Jam sandwich, sweetie?' she asked him.

'Yes-yes. Triangles not squares,' Darkus answered automatically, nodded appreciatively and sat silent for a moment. Then he added, as if in passing, 'Er, Clive?'

'Yes . . . ?' he hissed impatiently.

'I think you'll find it wasn't him,' Darkus stated frankly, then turned his attention to the cup of tea his mum had just set before him. He sipped it and raised his eyebrows. 'Perfect, thank you.'

'What do you *mean*, it wasn't *him?*' Clive demanded.

'It wasn't Mr Hanson, or his bins.'

'Jackie, tell the boy to speak English, for crying out loud.' Jackie and Clive watched Darkus, awaiting an explanation. 'Well . . . ?' Clive implored.

'Judging by the slightly deeper incision on the right side, you'll find that the scratch moved from right to left, indicating that the perpetrator was moving in the direction of the house. That fact discounts the possibility of the wheelie bins being the weapon, as Mr Hanson's bins are still in the road and haven't been brought in yet.'

Clive gawped at Darkus, astounded. Behind him, Jackie carefully applied jam to four pieces of buttered white bread, sandwiched them together and cut them into triangles.

Darkus watched her do this, took another sip of tea, then continued. 'I also noted only one set of footprints on that side of the car, and those are consistent with a

27

casual loafer, not the more formal shape of Mr Hanson's business shoe.'

Darkus refreshed himself once more with some tea before carrying on.

'Finally, I observed that the scratch was uniformly level at one metre from the ground. So I conclude that the only possibility is that you were in fact the culprit, Clive, by accident or misadventure of course. And I will hazard a guess that if you measure the position of the zip on your fashionable new coat, in all probability you will find it's approximately one metre from the ground.'

Clive looked down at the oversized zip on his jacket – which was positioned exactly as described – then erupted: 'That's it! I've had it with this detective stuff –'

'Clive, control yourself,' Jackie admonished.

Darkus selected a jam sandwich and took a bite, nodding his satisfaction. 'Excellent.'

'You'd better be careful he doesn't turn out like his father!' Clive warned. 'I mean, he *talks* like Alan, he *dresses* like Alan. And look what happened to *him* . . .'

Jackie set down her cup of tea in protest.

'I think I'll retire to my room,' said Darkus politely.

'Me too,' said Jackie, glaring at Clive before following her son upstairs.

Darkus's bedroom was simple and well appointed. A heavy oak bureau desk faced the window with a comfortable office chair behind it. Beyond the window was a view of the street and a single lamp post. Against the bedroom wall were a series of bookshelves and a filing cabinet, overshadowing a single bed. No posters were in evidence, only a whiteboard neatly arranged with handwritten Post-its.

Darkus entered his room, placed a coaster on the desk and set his cup of tea on it. Jackie watched him, concerned, closing the door behind them.

'Sweetie,' she said.

'Yes, Mum?'

'Clive . . .' she began, 'well, he just never understood your father. For that matter, neither did I. Alan's . . . complicated.'

'He's not crazy,' Darkus responded.

'Sweetie, your dad saw the world differently from the rest of us. He looked at things more closely than the rest of us. He often mistook fantasy for reality. That's why it didn't make sense to live together any more.'

'He'll prove you all wrong when he wakes up.'

'The doctors don't know when that'll be,' Jackie explained gently, 'or if he'll even remember anything from before his . . .' she chose her words carefully, 'from before his episode.'

'I know what they said,' Darkus replied, 'but they're wrong,' he stated without anxiety.

Jackie sat on the bed, facing him. 'Look, I know you miss your dad, and, believe it or not, sometimes so do I.' Darkus looked up hopefully for a moment, until Jackie qualified her last statement. 'Not enough to ever consider turning back the clock, obviously.'

Darkus frowned and sipped his tea.

'And Tilly misses her mum . . .' Jackie continued, 'and she'll *never* get her back.' Darkus nodded solemnly. 'We may not be perfect, sweetie, but we're still a family,' she concluded, 'and Clive and me are doing the best we can to make it a happy one.'

'I know, Mum,' said Darkus, hoping this awkward conversation was drawing to a close.

'And I'm always here for you, Doc,' she said, using his father's nickname. Her eyes unexpectedly welled up. 'Always.'

'Thanks, Mum,' replied Darkus sincerely.

She stood up and gave him a brief hug. 'Don't stay up here all evening, OK?'

'OK.'

Jackie smiled and closed the door behind her.

Darkus watched the door for a moment, then rolled his office chair towards the filing cabinet. He took a key from his waistcoat pocket and unlocked one of the metal drawers. He slid it open and reached inside.

His fingers found a small leather case, secured with a

strap. He took it out, unfastened the buckle and slid out a computer hard drive. He rolled back over to the desk, opened his laptop, connected the hard drive with a USB cable, then clicked on the icon and brought up a series of files.

He began to scroll through hundreds of pages of text, images and diagrams, all heavily annotated, with time stamps dating back to the 1980s. The file headings bore names like *The Haverstock Hill Murders* and *The Salamander Incident*. Photographs showed streets and buildings, and blurred faces that were obviously captured covertly. From the changing appearance of the buildings' facades, and the style and dress of the characters, the document contained well over twenty years of detective work. Strangely, Darkus found that reading his father's macabre case studies made him feel closer to him, even if he didn't fully understand everything he was reading about.

Darkus clicked through the pages, past detailed drawings of a lock barrel and the blueprint of a building, arriving at a sketch of an open hand with its palm up, and another with an extended fist.

The bluish glow of the computer screen cast a reflection of him in the front window. He glanced at his image, then peered through it to the outside. The fog was still rolling in around the neighbouring houses. The single lamp post produced a small circle of light in the murk, illuminating what Darkus realised was a shape standing underneath it. He drew closer to the window-pane, looking out.

A massive bulky man in a long coat and a homburg hat stood beneath the lamp post, watching their house. A tiny red ember flashed from under the brim of his hat and a plume of cigar smoke billowed up, commingling with the fog.

Darkus closed his laptop to watch unobserved. But the man had already seen him, for he turned and walked away from the circle of light with a heavy, waddling gait. Darkus quickly opened the window, letting in the cold, and poked his head out for a better look.

But the stranger had already vanished into the gloom.

# Chapter 4
## UNCLE BILL

The following day proceeded without incident, but Darkus couldn't shake the feeling that all was not as it should be. He did not have the empirical data to know if the massive man in the homburg hat was in fact staking out the house, or if there was a more innocent explanation for what he'd seen.

Darkus had a tendency to filter everything he saw through what he called his 'catastrophiser'. It was a mental device that had announced itself quite out of the blue, at the exact moment he first heard his father had entered the coma. For Darkus, the catastrophiser was both a gift and a burden, his protector and his enemy. In the absence of certainty, the world provided only signs of what might be: signs that indicated a possible explanation for a particular question. Every sign the world provided him with, whether visual, aural or otherwise, was fed into the catastrophiser, which always produced the worst-case scenario. Of course the worst-case scenario was often *not* the case, but on the occasion that it was, it gave Darkus an almost clairvoyant ability to detect trouble. For the rest of the time, the catastrophiser was a nagging machine running in the background of his mind, giving him little chance to be an ordinary child.

For example, on his customary walk to the corner shop, Darkus observed the local assembly of hoodies waiting across the road. Their leader always had his hands buried in the pockets of his sweatshirt, and sometimes Darkus thought he saw an angular shape through the fabric. The catastrophiser said it was a knife. Rationally, based on the statistics of his quiet neighbourhood, Darkus knew it was more likely to be a mobile phone. But when the catastrophiser spoke, Darkus had to listen. He knew it wasn't exactly a positive device, but he couldn't seem to switch it off.

He never spoke to anyone about the engine running in his head – except his dad, who, in his current state, was a great listener, but clearly wasn't in a position to give much advice. He visited his dad every Saturday, travelling by bus to the hospice and spending several hours with him, telling him details of his life in no particular order. At first it had felt sad and forced, but after a few visits Darkus overcame his embarrassment and found himself having better conversations with him while he was unconscious than he'd ever managed to have with him when he was awake. Then, after discovering the hard drive, the conversation had progressed to a more professional level, with Darkus commenting on each case as he read it, often in great detail, harbouring the secret hope that some keyword or phrase might dislodge something in his father's mind and wake him from his coma.

Today, although it was Sunday and Darkus had been at the hospice only the previous day, he felt an especially strong urge to see his dad again. Something about the bulky man's surveillance of the house unnerved him, and his father was the only one he could talk to about it. Darkus felt that if he didn't see him, something bad might happen.

As he returned home from the corner shop his train of thought was interrupted by a familiar figure in a black leather jacket with a rucksack, blocking his path. Only now her hair was a violent shade of pink.

'Hey, Darkus,' Tilly announced.

'Hello, Tilly –'

'You *cheated*. You knew the spelling of abalone.'

'There's no way you could possibly prove that.'

'Miss Khan videoed the whole contest and uploaded it to YouTube,' she declared victoriously. 'I saw your lips moving.'

'Ah.' Darkus fell silent, finding himself caught bang to rights.

'If you're lying about that, what else are you lying about? Huh? What've you got to hide?'

Darkus blinked. 'I'm flattered you think I have anything worth hiding. But I can assure you, I'm an open book.' He sidestepped her. 'Now, if you'll excuse me —' Then he stopped in his tracks, seeing a massive figure further down the road, approaching them slowly but steadily, with a waddling gait: the man in the homburg hat. 'I really must go now,' he added quickly, then ducked down a side street in the opposite direction.

Tilly watched him, baffled, then continued on her way.

Darkus turned back to see the man in the homburg hat crossing the street, now clearly zeroing in on him, with ghoulish determination.

Darkus increased his pace to a fast walk, not wanting to betray his fear by actually running. Although the man in the homburg had a lumbering step, his legs were long enough to effortlessly reduce the distance between them with each stride.

On reaching the main road, Darkus found cars barrelling past in both directions. He pressed the 'Wait' button at the traffic lights, but the signals weren't changing. Seeing no other option, he turned to face his pursuer, who was by this time towering over him.

'Darkus? Darkus Knightley?' his pursuer wheezed in a thick Scottish accent, clutching at his chest. Under the hat was a heavyset man in his fifties, the remains of a lit cigar balanced in the corner of his mouth, his plump cheeks puffing smoke, his eyes concealed behind them. His florid complexion and the billowing fumes gave the impression that he was almost on fire.

'What do you want?' demanded Darkus.

'Just a wee chat,' said the man, gasping for breath.

'I don't talk to strangers,' answered Darkus. The traffic lights finally changed, and as the pedestrian tone started beeping he prepared to cross, until the man said something that stopped him.

'I'm a friend ay yer father, a'right?' he blurted in his near-incomprehensible accent. Surely no one, not even the oldest Scottish Highland clans, could have such heavy intonation.

Darkus turned to face him. 'What's your name?'

'I'm Uncle Bill,' the man said, doffing his hat.

His face seemed familiar somewhere in the deep recesses of Darkus's memory, but beyond that he had no reference. 'I don't have an uncle,' he said suspiciously.

'Not technically, nae, laddie. But I've known yer father since our university days. Been through a lot together, him and me. Seen a lot of exciting and sometimes unbelievable things. And if you're anything like Alan used tae describe ye, well, I'm sure you've grown tae be a rather special lad yerself.'

37

Darkus examined him sceptically. 'What do you want?' he repeated.

Bill looked around. 'This is nae the sort of place for this sort of conversation. If ye'd feel more comfortable, we could gab at Jackie and Clive's place?'

Darkus examined the mountain of a man once more, then reluctantly nodded. 'If we keep to the main road, where everyone can see us.'

'Auld ah th' horn choice,' said Bill.

Darkus had no idea what that meant. But his catastrophiser had stopped whirring for the first time that day, so he decided to trust his instincts.

The unlikely pair made their way to Wolseley Close in plain view, and when Jackie saw the bulky figure beside her son on the doorstep, she retreated in surprise.

'Uncle Bill . . . ?' she faltered, her eyes flicking between him and Darkus.

'Thought I'd drop in for a cuppa,' he announced. 'If you're nae too busy of course.'

'Of course. But it's been . . .' she stammered.

'How long *has* it been? Four years, nearly fife?' he mumbled, doffing his hat and bowing his head a little to enter the house. Once inside, the full size of the man became apparent. 'Nou, how about that tea . . .' he said cheerfully, attaching his heavy coat and homburg hat to a hanger in the hallway.

She forced a smile and headed for the kitchen. 'I'll go and put the kettle on.'

Clive emerged from another part of the house. 'Jackie . . . ? Where's all that smoke coming from . . . ?' Then he also recognised the visitor. 'Oh . . .'

'A'right, Clive.'

'Uncle Bill,' recited Clive, looking a bit pale. 'Er . . . what can we do for you?'

'Just a social call,' Bill explained, and followed Jackie through the house, trailing cigar smoke. He took a seat at the head of the table while Jackie took up position by the kettle.

'Milk and sugar?' she asked.

'Swit 'n' law, if ye have it,' replied Bill. 'I'm watchin' mah weecht.'

Jackie wasn't exactly sure what he'd said, but dug around in the cupboard for a sweetener.

Clive shifted on his feet near the corner of the room, his hands thrust in his pockets. Darkus couldn't remember seeing either of them like this. He'd never known Clive tolerate even the slightest inconvenience, let alone an impromptu visit from a giant Scotsman; and Jackie guarded her territory fiercely. And yet, for some reason, they couldn't seem to refuse this Uncle Bill.

Darkus took a seat opposite their visitor, wasting no time. '*Where* exactly did you meet my father?'

'Freshers' week at Oxford,' mused Bill. 'Course I was a lot younger, and lighter, than I am nou. Would ye be so kind . . . ?' He extended his cigar in Clive's direction, caked in ash.

Clive located an ashtray and placed it in front of him.

'Happier days, better days,' Bill said, ashing his cigar.

Jackie and Clive exchanged a worried glance.

'Do ye have onie biscuits by chance?' Bill asked. Clive sighed and reached into another cupboard. Bill waited patiently for what he would find. Clive set the packet on the table grimly. Bill shrugged. 'Ginger nuts – that'll dae.'

'Darkus, maybe you should go upstairs,' Jackie suggested. 'I'm worried about the second-hand smoke.'

Bill stubbed out his cigar. 'On the contrary, I'd like him tae hear this.'

Clive looked at Jackie, confused.

'Hear what?' said Darkus.

'What d'ye know about yer father, Darkus?' Bill enquired.

Darkus thought about it for a moment. 'He was the most caring and generous dad anyone could ask for . . .' He paused, then added, 'And he solved problems for people.'

Jackie swallowed hard.

'Aye, that's the Alan I know,' said Bill.

Jackie and Clive remained tactfully silent.

Bill took his time, then continued. 'He also solved problems for people who . . . shaa we say, people with . . . less than ordinary problems.'

'Meaning?' asked Darkus.

'Yer father was a dick. A private dick. A detective. The best there is.'

Darkus listened, impassive. He knew full well what his father did for a living, but this was the first time he'd had it independently confirmed.

'It was his blessing and his curse,' Bill went on.

'Has this got something to do with why he's unconscious?' said Darkus.

'Nae one knows why Alan entered that state. What I dae know is yer father's mind was playing tricks on him. His investigations were becoming more bizarre, more outlandish. He'd gone too deep intae the realm of possibility . . . far from the safe haven of reality.' Bill sighed heavily. 'Everything became a sign tae him. Everyone was tae be suspected and mistrusted. Facts only colluded with each other tae support his hysterical visions.' Bill massaged the smooth pate of his head. 'Alan came tae believe evil resides around us all the time, lurking in every shadow. I believe it drove him tae the edge of sanity, and ultimately tae his . . . episode.'

There was that word again. The one everybody used.

'It's a documented medical condition,' insisted Darkus.

'Somewhere between a coma and a narcoleptic trance.'

'Documented, aye, laddie, but never explained.' Bill dunked his biscuit, took a bite, then washed it down with more tea. 'When Alan was found at his office there was nae sign of blunt trauma, nae sign of intoxication. Nae obvious reason at all why he entered this state . . .' Bill slowly set down his cup. 'But what I dae know is, for some reason, at approximately 7.30 p.m. last night, he woke up and left the hospice.'

'What?!' Clive burst out.

'I knew it . . .' said Jackie, betraying herself with a smile for a second.

Darkus suddenly felt nauseous and faint. His head began to spin from a cocktail of emotions that was part excitement, part disbelief. 'Where is he now?' he demanded.

'That's what I'm trying tae find oot,' Bill replied. 'I figured he'd show up here first. But it seems I was wrong.'

Clive cleared his throat nervously. 'Is he considered . . . dangerous?'

Jackie glared. 'Alan's never hurt anyone.'

'Nae one appears tae have been harmed during his departure from Shrubwoods,' explained Bill. 'However, I strongly suggest ye inform me if he attempts tae contact ye.' He slid a card across the table, showing simply a phone number, nothing else.

'Why are you so interested?' asked Darkus.

'I'm a colleague and a friend,' said Bill. 'Yer father's welfare is of great importance tae me and many others.'

'Which others?' said Darkus.

Bill got to his feet. 'Be a good lad and dae as I ask. I have other rocks tae turn over. Thank ye for the tea, and the rather disappointing biscuits.'

Clive twitched. Jackie ushered Bill towards the door.

As Bill hoisted his coat and hat on, Darkus appeared behind him, impatient.

'What if Dad was right?' Darkus asked.

Bill looked down at him and slowly removed a fresh cigar from his top pocket. 'Aboot . . . ?' he said, striking a match and lighting up.

'About evil lurking in every shadow . . .' said Darkus, holding his stare.

'Then we'd better hope there's enough good to go aroond,' said Bill, puffing a particularly large cloud of smoke. 'Cheerio for nou.'

He ambled off down the driveway, noting the scratch on Clive's Jaguar. He shook his head and continued on to the street, watched by Clive, Jackie and Darkus forming a row on the doorstep. As if on cue, a silver Ford saloon car pulled up and Bill opened the rear passenger door. The driver paused as Bill slid himself into the back seat, then the Ford pulled away.

43

# Chapter 5
## THE UNUSUAL COMBINATION

Despite Darkus's best efforts at interrogation, Clive and Jackie refused to elaborate on Uncle Bill or what business he had with his father. Darkus found himself tantalised by the prospect that his dad was actually awake and very much alive somewhere, but troubled by the fact that he hadn't thought to contact him, his only son. The evening passed heavily with the weight of so many unanswered questions.

Tilly returned home briefly without saying a word, then went out again. During dinner, Clive appeared to be watching the street a lot more than usual. Jackie appeared to be watching the phone a lot more than usual. Eventually they distracted themselves by watching TV even more than usual.

The ten o'clock news reported that a growing number of apparently ordinary citizens – all with no previous criminal record – were committing bank robberies, presumably as a result of the gloomy economic outlook.

'Probably on benefits too,' declared Clive ungenerously.

In other news, there was a special report on customers suffering seizures at bookshops around the country. A medical expert blamed it on the difference in temperature between the cold weather outside and the overly warm shop floors. That, combined with long hours spent browsing, was evidently proving too much for some customers.

Darkus found the news pieces a little stranger than usual – and the official explanations oddly unsatisfactory – but he had bigger things on his mind.

He retired to his bedroom, where he was unable to read or sleep. Finding his mind whirring mechanically, he unlocked the filing cabinet and reconnected the hard drive. He clicked to open its contents.

Picking up from where he had left off, Darkus examined a diagram of what appeared to be a circular chamber surrounded by tunnels and a series of numbers that seemed to bear no relation to each other. Eventually the random arrangement of shapes and numbers lulled him to sleep, and he flopped in his chair with the computer screen on.

At some point, he heard Tilly arrive home. She ignored Clive's muttered protests from the master bedroom and vanished into her quarters. Somehow Darkus found the energy to crawl into bed, still fully clothed. His head rested on the pillow, which muted the ticking of the clock on his dresser.

The world descended into complete silence . . .

. . . until a light scratching noise intruded on the uppermost frequencies of his hearing, followed by a barely discernible click.

Darkus opened his eyes, staring into the pitch blackness, seeing only the weird, random shapes his retinas were creating in the absence of any light. He concentrated his mind on the aural spectrum instead of the visual. And he heard it again. A clearly audible click, followed by the faint sound of something softly crushing the fabric of the carpeted stairs.

Darkus swung his legs out of bed, aware of the minute sonic vibrations his own movements would create. He stepped lightly towards his bedroom door and turned the handle as slowly and quietly as he could. The door didn't make a noise as it opened – he kept the hinges well oiled for that very reason. He crept out on to the landing and heard a different kind of fabric sound: a faint brushing noise, accompanied by the clink of what sounded like metal hangers.

He moved across the landing towards a cupboard located outside Clive and Jackie's bedroom. Barely lit, kneeling by the drawers at the base of the cupboard, was a ghostly human form. A familiar one.

'Dad,' Darkus whispered, his heart beating in his throat.

The shape stopped what it was doing.

'Darkus?' the shape said.

'What are you *doing?*'

'Looking for something to wear. Doesn't he have anything that isn't nylon?' A cigarette lighter flicked to life, illuminating Alan Knightley wearing an ill-fitting shell suit clearly belonging to Clive. Darkus couldn't quite believe his eyes: his father looked different now that he was animated rather than unconscious; he looked younger than his forty-eight years – more how he remembered him. Knightley held the lighter closer to his face and smiled, eyes shining.

'It's good to see you, Doc,' he said.

'It's good to see *you*,' said Darkus, and lunged towards him, until Knightley thought twice and held up his hand to stop him.

'No – not here. Downstairs.'

'You came back for me. I knew you would . . .'

'No, Doc. I came here for transport.'

'Transport?'

'And clothes. There's not a moment to lose,' Knightley whispered, then closed the cupboard and crossed the landing to the stairs. 'You know, you've grown at least twenty centimetres?'

'Wait. Where are we going?' Darkus asked, following him downstairs.

'We? My dear boy, *we're* not going anywhere. The game is afoot. I'm going to London, and from there, wherever the trail leads me. *You* . . . are staying here. If anyone asks, just say you slept through the whole thing.'

'Why? I mean, what sort of game are you talking about?'

'The *Combination*, Doc. That's what I'm talking about,' said Knightley, nodding to himself gravely. 'I may've been sleeping, but they weren't.'

'Combination . . . ?' Darkus asked. 'What combination?'

'Go back to bed, Doc. This doesn't concern you.'

'If it's your concern, it's my concern,' insisted Darkus.

'Trust me – you don't want to know.'

Darkus followed his father as he strode through the living room, glancing at pictures and memorabilia on the walls. Knightley paused beside a framed photograph of Jackie in her younger days. She was dressed in a flight attendant's uniform. Darkus often imagined the moment they met, when his father was on a flight to Switzerland in bad weather, and his mother was pointing out the emergency exits. She always said their relationship was turbulent from the start.

'How *is* your mother?' Knightley asked, doing his best to sound casual.

'She's OK,' answered Darkus, trying to keep up with him.

Knightley cast an eye over the kitchen, then turned back towards the entrance hall. 'I like what she's done with the place.' He kept moving, as if he was making up for the years of inertia that had held him back.

Darkus rubbed his eyes to make sure he wasn't seeing things. He'd dreamed of this reunion for four years, but this wasn't exactly how he'd imagined it. 'Look, can we just . . . talk for a second?' he said, following his father towards the front door.

'Not now. But soon, I promise.' Knightley quietly opened the door and exited into the darkness outside. Then he turned back for a moment and gave Darkus a short, sharp hug. 'I'm sorry, Doc.'

Knightley approached Clive's Jag, removed a wire coat hanger from the jacket of his shell suit and bent it into a hook shape. He slid the hook between the driver's window and the sill, then started jemmying the lock with a swift up-and-down motion.

'Wait a minute,' said Darkus, standing his ground on the driveway, now wearing his hat and coat. Knightley looked up from his work and raised his finger to shush him.

Darkus continued in a loud whisper. 'I came to visit you every second I could for the last four years. And now you expect me to just go back to bed?'

'It's for your own good, Doc,' Knightley replied sharply.

'I believed in you. I told them you'd come back,' he insisted. 'You can't just leave me here.'

'That's exactly what I propose to do,' said Knightley, returning to the job at hand.

'You realise if that alarm detects the slightest variation in cabin pressure, it'll wake up half the street.'

Knightley smiled, then answered, 'And I'll be long gone.'

'To the end of the driveway maybe. It's got an immobiliser.'

'I suppose you learned that from Clive?'

'Wake up, Dad. You've been asleep too long.'

Knightley dropped the coat hanger and frowned. 'So what do you suggest?'

'Why not try this?' Darkus opened his hand to reveal the Jaguar key fob swinging like a pendulum.

'Attaboy . . .' Knightley extended his arm for Darkus to throw it to him.

Darkus closed his hand again.

'Don't be childish,' Knightley said without a trace of irony.

'On one condition.'

'There's no time for this, Doc.'

'I'm coming with you, at least as far as London. No debates. It's half-term, so it's perfect timing.'

'I can't take you with me. I can't afford any baggage.'

'I'm not baggage. I can help.'

'I wish you could,' said Knightley, shaking his head and walking up the driveway towards him, until Darkus raised his hand, ready to throw the key fob away into the darkness.

'You wouldn't . . .' Knightley pleaded.

'Try me,' said Darkus.


Upstairs, Clive rolled over in bed, hearing something outside: an unmistakable purr, followed by the crunch of tyres on gravel. He leaped out of bed with panther-like speed and ripped open the curtains.

On the driveway below, the Jag was reversing on to the street. Then its headlights came on.

'No-no-no-no . . .' Clive grabbed his tiny silk dressing gown and raced out of the room. Outside, the Jag paused as Knightley put it into gear and put his foot on the accelerator. The car burned rubber, sending smoke billowing out of the wheel arches, then it sprang forward, pressing its two occupants to their seats.

Clive burst out of the front door only to see the rear lights fishtail around the corner at the end of the street. The purr became a roar.

Clive watched speechless for a moment, then let out a primal scream: 'Jackie . . . !!'

# Chapter 6
## THE KNOWLEDGE

Knightley drove silently and intently, his foot pressed to the floor as the car raced through empty streets and joined a long dual carriageway. At this hour, a few eighteen-wheelers were the only other vehicles on the road.

After what seemed like an eternity, Darkus broke the silence. 'Where are we going?'

'The office,' Knightley answered. Darkus raised his eyebrows. He'd never been allowed entry into his father's professional world, let alone his base of operations. 'We might have time for a cup of tea and possibly a jam sandwich,' Knightley continued. 'Triangles not squares, naturally. Then you'll be on the first train home.'

'What is the Combination?' Darkus asked.

'I told you, it doesn't concern you.'

'Is it something to do with a safe?' Darkus went on. 'Or a bank?'

'Only in as much as they rob them . . . among other,

far more sinister criminal activities, which I'm not prepared to discuss.'

'Who's "they"?'

Knightley switched on the stereo to drown out the question. Smooth jazz blasted out of the speakers and he grimaced, pushed a few more buttons to change channels, then gave up and switched it off.

'Who's "they"?' Darkus repeated.

'I don't remember you being this annoying, Doc.'

'You're exactly how I remember you,' Darkus said frankly.

Knightley frowned. 'I may not have been the best father,' he admitted. 'But my work, well, it didn't keep normal hours, and it didn't involve normal people. And if I didn't talk to you about it, it was for your and your mother's protection. I don't expect you to understand that. Your mother certainly didn't. She thought I was losing my mind.'

'That's what Uncle Bill said too.'

'Uncle Bill?' said Knightley, turning his head.

'I told him I didn't believe him,' Darkus explained in a show of unity, but his father didn't seem to notice.

'What did Bill want with *you*?'

'He said you'd probably turn up at the house,' said Darkus. 'It appears he was right.'

Knightley shook his head. 'He never did understand what he was dealing with.'

'Dealing with? What do you mean?'

Knightley began speaking, almost to himself, as if a safety valve had been released and he couldn't control his own mind. 'The Combination,' he muttered, 'is a criminal organisation. It's a multi-headed serpent – a hydra, if you will – with an almost preternatural ability to remain invisible. Some might call it supernatural. You may see *signs*, the effects of their operations, but never the organisation itself . . . They have contacts everywhere, their reach is so vast. What you see on the TV or read in the newspapers is only a fiction – a mask for their carefully planned and meticulously executed acts of criminal infamy.' Knightley paused for breath, then continued. 'And those who manage to unravel the mystery and get to the truth, well, they're called mad. But when *you* know the truth, and everyone *else* believes the lie, who's crazy then? Huh?'

For the first time in the conversation, Darkus was speechless. Whatever the Combination was, it was the reason his dad was awake and alert – and, by default, the reason they'd been reunited. For now at least.

Knightley turned to him. 'I suppose you think I'm crazy as well?'

'I don't have the empirical data to make that determination,' Darkus replied.

'Good answer. Neither do I . . . yet. But I will. Trust

me. And when I do, I'll use it to break the Combination for ever.' Knightley pressed the accelerator even harder, speeding under the rows of highway lights that indicated they were approaching London.

The city was still shrouded in darkness. The orange glow of the neon caught the rain in the air, forming an artificial mist over the skyline. Darkus had the curious sensation that he knew where they were going, even though – to his knowledge – he'd never been there before. But in the far reaches of his mind there was a vague memory of an office. Perhaps he'd only been taken there once as a young child, or it might have been a made-up memory based on hearsay – a memory of an experience he never actually had.

Knightley guided the car through a series of parks and commons in the outlying boroughs of the city. They passed Richmond Park, the largest of the Royal Parks, and – thanks to King Charles I – home to a sizeable herd of red and fallow deer. They continued on through Wimbledon Common, a favourite haunt of Robert Baden-Powell's during the early days of the Boy Scout movement. Darkus knew his father had promised to take him to all these places, but couldn't actually recall if he ever had – or whether this knowledge was compiled entirely from his own research.

They pressed deeper into the solemn and majestic

heart of London, crossing the River Thames, overarched with bridges and overseen by the London Eye, Big Ben and the Houses of Parliament, all of which appeared to mean little to Knightley. As if on autopilot, he steered the Jag towards north London, and Darkus stopped recognising landmarks and felt as if he was being led into a rabbit's warren.

They entered the borough of Islington, once known as a lair of wild beasts, and subsequently a cattle market for the sale of these beasts, before they made way for its current, more upmarket residents. Knightley drove through a maze of back alleys, past forgotten warehouses and railway lines, until they reached a short residential street with a row of terraced houses, signposted Cherwell Place. The street had an almost imperceptible curve to it, as if it was permanently being observed through a magnifying glass. The odd perspective meant it was mundane yet strangely mysterious at the same time.

Knightley parked the Jag on a double yellow line and quickly climbed out, approaching one of the narrow houses. Darkus went to stand in his wake and followed his gaze up to a dim light on the top floor of the house. Whether the memory was genuine or not, in dreams or reality, Darkus felt certain he'd been here before.

Knightley walked towards the blue door with a brass number 27 on it and pressed the intercom. It crackled, then after a long pause a female Polish voice came out of it.

'Knightley Investigations, hello?' the voice said cautiously.

'Bogna, it's Alan,' said Knightley.

'Alan . . . ?! *O mój Boże* . . .' she praised the lord, and the door instantly buzzed open.

As Darkus followed his father into the house he heard the thundering noise of someone coming down the narrow staircase. He correctly deduced that the large, middle-aged Polish lady who appeared on the stairs in a dressing gown was in fact Bogna.

'You are alive!' she shouted, stifling Knightley in an embrace.

'Yes, but don't tell the whole neighbourhood,' he answered.

'I'm sorry, Alan. I just thought . . .'

'I know, everyone did. But I'm perfectly fine,' he assured her.

Bogna spotted Darkus standing behind his father and did a double take. 'This is Doc,' she announced, grabbing Darkus by the shoulders and inspecting his features.

'It is,' said Knightley. 'But he won't be staying long. I have work to do.'

'Nice to meet you,' said Darkus, then turned to find his father already pacing up the stairs and set off behind him.

'The phone keep ringings for over one year,' Bogna explained breathlessly in her broken English, following them upstairs. 'Then it was not ringings so often, and now it doesn't ringings at all. I have keep everything exactly how you left it,' she continued.

They reached the top of the house and Knightley strode across a small landing to a heavy, oak door with his name etched on the outside. He paused a moment, then turned the handle and opened the door. Darkus watched from behind as his father beheld his former office: a large wood-panelled room lined with shelves weighed down with books and periodicals. Sat at the window was a broad, mahogany desk accented with Carpathian elm, with a leather office chair and a globe mounted on a brass spindle. A slightly dated computer faced the empty seat, as if the user was temporarily out of the office. There was not a cobweb or a speck of dust in sight. Knightley approached a closet and opened it to find a row of herring-bone coats and tweed walking hats, neatly arranged. He fell silent, sparing a moment to take it all in.

'Shall I prepare some sandwich?' enquired Bogna.

'That would be most accommodating. Triangles not squares,' said Darkus with a nod.

Bogna did another double take, then nodded and thundered back down the stairs. Knightley didn't respond, lost in thought.

'Dad . . . ?' said Darkus, breaking the silence.

'Yes, Doc?' he answered blankly. He appeared to be somewhere else entirely, his eyes slowly roaming the room, noting familiar objects and mementos.

'Have I been here before?'

'Once, with your mother. A long time ago,' he responded softly.

'Are you going to be working here again now?'

'I only wish I could perform all my tasks from the relative safety of this room. But I fear my enemies will draw me out into the open – where I'm more vulnerable,' he said with a hint of trepidation. 'Which is why I must do my best to locate them first . . .'

Knightley walked to a space between two large bookcases, locating a painting of a pastoral landscape. He carefully unhooked the painting to reveal a small old-fashioned safe recessed into the wall. He spun the dial, clockwise then anti-clockwise several times, listening to a series of clicks, until the lock disengaged and he opened the door.

Inside, the space was empty except for a crumpled packet of cigarettes. Knightley narrowed his eyes. 'That was my emergency pack,' he said, perplexed.

'I didn't know you smoked,' said Darkus.

'Your mother and I both did once,' he admitted. 'It did nothing for my reasoning skills,' he added, then without looking up, called out: 'Bogna?!'

More thuds ascended the stairs, then Bogna entered the room breathless, awaiting instruction.

'There were several personal items in here,' said Knightley. 'What happened to them?'

'Mrs Jackie took them,' said Bogna with a shrug. 'She said it was for, how d'you say, sentimental's reason?'

'Sentimental reasons?' Knightley asked, puzzled.

'That's what she say, yes.'

'I'm looking for one particularly sensitive item, which you may recall,' Knightley told her calmly. 'A device that contains the sum total of all my notes.' Clearly he was trying hard not to alarm her with the importance of his request.

A light bulb went off in her head. 'Ah . . . You mean, the Knowledges?' she said. Her Polish accent made the words hard to distinguish – the meaning even harder.

'Yes, the Knowledge,' said Knightley impatiently. 'What happened to it?'

Bogna shrugged hopelessly and shook her head. 'Two men come looking for it, after you went into your coma state.'

'What sort of men?'

'They said they were policemens. I tell them it's not here, I don't know where it is. They make a lot of mess.'

'Did you tell them anything else?'

'No. I know the rule,' said Bogna obediently. 'Strictly needs to know.'

'Dad?'

'Not now, Doc.'

'What does it *look* like?' Darkus went on. 'This "Knowledge"?'

'It's a hard drive, about yay big, stowed in a small leather case with a strap.' Knightley gestured in the air to aid the description.

'Ah . . .' said Darkus deliberately.

Knightley's eyes lit up. 'You mean you know where it is?'

'I know more than that,' said Darkus enigmatically. 'I know everything . . .'

Knightley looked at his son, mystified for the first time.


Jackie watched as a squad of bumbling police constables marched through the house, scribbling on their notepads. She had been married to a private investigator long enough to know these local officers of the law would have trouble locating their own shoelaces, let alone her son.

Nearby, Clive sat slumped in an armchair, still in his pyjamas, his head in his hands.

A burly man in uniform approached Jackie with his pen poised. 'Chief Inspector Draycott, ma'am,' he announced himself. 'Now, you say you believe the boy's father is the kidnapper,' he said, stroking the thin moustache under his nose.

'I never used the word kidnap,' she responded.

'What about carjack?' Clive piped up from his chair.

'Shut up, Clive,' she said firmly. 'He might not have left if you'd kept your mouth shut.'

Chief Inspector Draycott made another note. Clive grimaced.

'He's not answering his phone,' Jackie said anxiously. 'He always answers his phone.'

'Then exactly what crime would you like to report?' Draycott enquired.

'A missing kid. A missing car. And a man who may have taken leave of his senses,' explained Jackie.

Draycott thought carefully about how to word this last piece of testimony. As he returned to scribbling, Tilly brushed by indifferently. The others cleared a path as she marched up the staircase looking decidedly unimpressed. One officer made a note, but struggled to describe the colour of her hair. The end of his pencil broke and he gave up.

Tilly reached the top of the stairs to find two hard-faced constables who appeared to be conducting their own search of the upper floors, independently of the rest. One of the men was tall and lean, the other short and stocky. She watched, unnoticed, as they exchanged a conspiratorial glance, then slipped into Darkus's bedroom, quietly closing the door behind them. Moments later, one of them poked his head out to check the coast was clear, then they exited on to the landing, only to see Tilly's silhouette watching from the safe distance of her own bedroom doorway. The men stopped dead in their tracks, smiled at her, but remained frozen a moment too long.

'We'll be off now,' said the taller policeman.

Tilly didn't respond, but just examined them suspiciously.

'Take care then,' the stockier policeman announced, then descended the stairs. His partner gave him a pointed look and they rejoined their colleagues as they filed out of the house.

Tilly watched them go without saying a word.

Outside, Chief Inspector Draycott stood at the front door with Jackie and Clive, then turned to address the ranks assembled in the predawn light: 'I have promised Clive and Jackie here that we'll find her son,' he proclaimed, then glanced at Clive, adding, 'and their car.' Clive nodded eagerly. 'I intend to keep that promise,' said Draycott, raising a gloved finger prophetically. 'Ladies and gents, file your reports and begin your inquiries. We have work to do.'

\*

Knightley couldn't take his eyes off his son, finding the preceding twenty minutes almost impossible to comprehend.

Having finally got his father's undivided attention, Darkus fought the temptation to revel in it and soberly continued his account.

'So I found it in the attic, then I connected it to my computer and started reading,' Darkus explained. 'I didn't understand it all at first – some of it took years – but I persisted, and by last summer I'd been through most of the case studies, skimming over the less interesting crimes of course.'

'Of course,' said Knightley, raising his eyebrows.

'And, well, I soon found I had a little knowledge about a lot of things,' said Darkus.

Knightley studied his son as a scientist studies a newly discovered species, not quite believing his eyes.

Darkus carried on, apparently unaware of the effect he was having. 'And to my surprise I found myself detecting things . . .' he added. 'Seeing the world the way you must have done.'

'I don't want you to see the world the way I do,' said Knightley. 'I don't want that at all.'

Darkus felt his throat tighten with emotion at the idea that all his efforts had somehow had the reverse effect; that he'd pushed his dad further away, instead of bringing them closer. He swallowed hard, then went on.

'Reading it helped me understand . . . why you were the way you were.'

'I know the way I was,' his father responded. 'I know I could be hard on you. I was silent, morose, inaccessible. I disappeared upstairs for days at a time.' He paused, losing himself in his own memories for a moment, then added by way of explanation, 'The truth is, I loved you and your mother, but I couldn't allow anything to bias my judgement, to compromise my ability to reason soundly. Emotions have no place in what I do. For better or worse, that was my life. But I never wanted it for you. Never.'

Darkus looked down, sensing his worst fears confirmed: for all his good intentions and long hours of study, he'd merely done something wrong.

Knightley lowered his head into his hands, muttering incoherently and smoothing the hair away from his brows. 'The game is afoot,' he said like a mantra. 'There's no time for this.'

'Dad? Are you OK?'

'I'm fine.'

Darkus watched him rocking in his seat, looking almost as if he was re-entering the state from which he'd so recently emerged. 'Dad,' he ventured, 'I can help.'

'Don't be ridiculous.'

'You don't understand. I really can.'

'If you think this is going to be some kind of Take Your Child To Work Day, well, you're even crazier than I am,' Knightley snipped.

'In the Knowledge you wrote: "Reasoning is to construct at least two theories explaining why an event took place",' stated Darkus, '"until the most logical explanation presents itself."'

'And?'

'I can be your second theory. The other half of your brain.'

'Over my dead body. You're not getting any deeper into this than you already are.' Knightley shook his head. 'It's time to stop this nonsense, retrieve the Knowledge and get you back home where you belong.'

'That might be a little difficult,' said Darkus, spotting something through the office window on the street below. 'They're taking the car.'

Knightley went to the window to see the Jaguar being grab-lifted off the double yellow line by the mechanical arm of a massive tow truck.

'I see law enforcement has at least improved in some areas,' he remarked.

'What are we going to do now?' said Darkus.

'We'll use mine.'

*

Knightley led Darkus out of the front door of number 27 and around the corner on to another terraced street. He had changed into a herringbone coat, corduroy trousers and a tweed hat uncannily resembling Darkus's own outfit. Darkus half expected his dad to take his hand, then remembered he was too old for that now.

Knightley approached a gap in the pavement, where a cobbled path led behind the houses. Darkus followed him down the alley towards a row of narrow, dilapidated garages. Knightley produced a key and unlocked the padlock of a garage door daubed with peeling black paint. He discarded the padlock and yanked up the door to reveal a dark yet familiar shape, covered in cobwebs. It was a classic London black cab: a Fairway, to be exact.

'Did you work as a cabbie?' enquired Darkus.

'Nope. But around twenty thousand other people do. It's the perfect disguise.' Knightley opened the door, flipped down the visor and caught the car keys as they dropped into his palm. He popped the bonnet and walked round the cab to inspect the engine. 'Of course I made a few modifications . . .' He blew a huge cobweb off the engine block, reconnected the battery, returned to the dashboard and keyed the ignition. The Fairway rumbled to life with a sound unlike any Darkus had heard from a black cab before. It sounded more like one of the performance cars that Clive reviewed on his TV programme.

Knightley revved the engine, sending clouds of dust billowing out of the garage door. 'Rover V8,' he said with a smile. 'First time, every time.' The orange *Taxi* light flickered to life. Knightley opened the rear passenger door for Darkus. 'Where to, sir?'

Darkus grinned and got in the back seat. 'Just drive.'

'Home it is,' replied Knightley, putting the cab in reverse and accelerating out of the alley in a halo of dust.

# Chapter 7
# THE DEPARTMENT OF
# THE UNEXPLAINED

Darkus watched London grind to life as his dad navigated the city, blending seamlessly with the other black cabs carrying suits to work. Darkus sat back and took a moment to absorb recent events. He watched the fare increase on the meter over the dashboard and couldn't help thinking that every increment was taking him further away from the new world he'd discovered, and closer back to the old world of Clive and his mum. It was a sinking feeling that he couldn't reason with.

He was roused from his meditation by the blare of a car horn behind them. They were at a set of traffic lights, but although the light was green, the cab hadn't moved.

'Dad, it's green,' said Darkus through the glass divider.

His father didn't answer.

'Dad . . . ?'

Knightley's voice crackled through the cabin's intercom speaker: 'Not now, Darkus. I'm thinking.' His ears seemed to lift and his eyes gazed off into the middle distance.

The driver behind them leaned on the horn again, holding it down until the pitch wavered and complained. Darkus sunk deeper into his seat with embarrassment.

Then he realised what his father was looking at. A line of red London buses extended ahead of them, each displaying its route number on the back in large digits: *14, 49, 70, 74.*

Knightley appeared to be mouthing the numbers to himself, oblivious to the cacophony of horns that was reaching a crescendo behind him. It was as if the numbers meant something but Knightley couldn't decipher what.

'Er, Dad? Maybe we should pull over?'

The traffic lights changed back to red and there was a temporary lull in the horns. Knightley kept looking dead ahead.

'The Combination, Doc . . .' Knightley said through the intercom. 'We're getting closer.'

'What d'you mean?'

'I don't *know* . . .' Knightley replied honestly, his eyes glazed over with moisture, as if the stress was too much for him.

Darkus examined his father's haunted face in the rear-view mirror. 'Talk to me. What are you seeing, Dad?'

'Numbers,' said Knightley.

'What do they mean?' urged Darkus.

'I have no idea!' he shouted impatiently.

Suddenly the lights turned green, and before the cars could sound their horns, Knightley threw the cab into gear and lurched away.

Darkus was thrown back in his seat, watching his father anxiously.

'Don't worry, Doc. I'm OK.'

'Has this got something to do with your . . . episode?'

'Are you trying to say I'm crazy?'

'No, I'm trying to understand,' said Darkus. 'What's the last thing you remember before you lost consciousness?'

'Numbers, Doc. A set of numbers.'

'What kind of numbers?'

'I wish I knew,' admitted Knightley. 'Maybe it's not meant to add up. Maybe it's something I'm not meant to remember . . .' he said, spooked.

'We'll work it out, Dad,' Darkus assured him. 'Together.'

'Whatever happens, don't let them take me back to Shrubwoods. Understand? It's not safe there any more.'

'I promise.'

'And not a word to your mother, all right?'

'OK, Dad.'

The city was soon replaced by the suburbs, which

were in turn replaced by the stretch of dual carriageway and the inevitable exit ramp. By the time the fare read £200.20, Knightley was turning on to Wolseley Close. They parked at the corner, several houses away, and sat with the engine idling. A ray of sunshine lit up the symmetrical lawns and tidy flower beds. Knightley admired the view longingly for a moment, then turned around and slid open the glass divider.

'This is your stop, Doc.'

'Do I have to, Dad?'

'Yes, I'm afraid you do,' he replied. 'I suggest you enter through the back garden unseen. Retrieve the Knowledge and pass it to me over the side wall.'

'Aren't you going to at least say hello to Mum?'

'Not this time,' he answered. 'I've got work to do.'

On hearing those words, Darkus understood there was no point arguing any further. Knightley pressed a button and the doors unlocked with a heavy click.

Darkus stepped on to the street and hesitated, seeing everything with fresh eyes: Wolseley Close was both happy and sad, like a treasured piece of clothing he'd suddenly grown out of. He lowered his head and walked away from the cab, until he noticed something odd: a small black cone with a silver shield on it appeared to be hovering behind a nearby hedge. Darkus's catastrophiser went into overdrive as he detected several more cones hidden in the undergrowth at vantage points along the street.

'Dad!' he shouted.

Knightley stamped on the accelerator and roared into the kind of tight U-turn only a London cab could perform, but his path was instantly blocked by an arriving police car. Officers leaped out of every available door, more of them emerging from the undergrowth. Knightley threw the cab into reverse, only to find another panda car behind him, cutting him off. Knightley rested his hands on the steering wheel in defeat.

A constable grabbed Darkus and hoisted him on to the pavement, as half a dozen officers pulled the cab door open and dragged Knightley out, pinning him to the ground.

'Dad!!!' Darkus yelled.

'It's OK, Doc,' he replied from underneath the writhing mass of uniforms.

Darkus struggled as he was escorted to the house. A burly shape stepped out of a police Vauxhall and approached the throng.

'Hello, Alan,' said Draycott, trying to conceal the smile under his moustache.

'Inspector Draycott,' replied Knightley, glancing up.

'*Chief* Inspector,' he corrected him. 'I thought you were having yourself a well-earned rest?'

'Well, I woke up with this irrepressible urge to get back to work.'

'Not if I've got anything to do with it.' Draycott nodded to his officers, who promptly handcuffed Knightley and hauled him to his feet. 'This is a nice, quiet community of decent, law-abiding people. It's been a haven of peace and tranquillity since you've been away. We don't need you coming round scaring everyone with your . . . ideas.'

'Chief Inspector Draycott,' Knightley began, 'you've never been the brightest spark in the police force, but I believe you've always been a loyal servant of the law. So I'd ask you to let me go and allow me to do my job unmolested.'

'I don't approve of your methods, Knightley, and I don't approve of you. You've already left a trail of terrified seniors at Shrubwoods Hospice. Not to mention Clive and Jackie here. In light of the evidence, I'm going to recommend the doctors put you under observation for a few weeks, maybe a month. Make sure you're not getting up to anything . . . *dodgy*,' said Draycott with relish.

'That would be detrimental to the forces of law and order, an insult to your already limited intelligence and a serious risk to the fate of the case I'm currently working on.'

'And that is . . . ?' Draycott enquired.

Knightley paused, then lowered his voice. 'An organisation I believe to be responsible for almost every unexplained crime, both great and small, in towns and cities across the country, maybe across Europe and possibly even the world.'

'Oh, is that all?' quipped Draycott.

'I didn't expect for one second you'd believe me, but if you'll allow me access to my former home, I'd be glad to show you the evidence.'

Draycott stifled a laugh. 'I think I'd like to see this evidence,' he said sceptically, then turned to his uniformed colleagues. 'Chaps, indulge me.'

The officers fell into line behind him – all except for a taller one and a stockier one, who exchanged a knowing glance and returned to their panda car.

Darkus was already waiting on the driveway, instructing a weary constable, 'I wasn't kidnapped. I volunteered to go. To help.'

'Of course you did.'

'Sweetie!' Jackie cried out, running from the front door and grabbing Darkus in an embrace. 'Don't ever do that again . . . Ever.' She held him tight.

Draycott marched Knightley up the driveway. Darkus disengaged himself and turned to face his father's captor. 'If you use excessive force on this vulnerable man,

75

recently recovered from a serious medical condition, I won't hesitate to see that you're disciplined to the full extent of the law,' he advised him.

Draycott straightened up in surprise. 'Duly noted.'

Knightley looked up, seeing his former wife, and smiled. 'Hello, Jackie.'

Jackie seemed unsure how to react. 'Hello, Alan.' She smoothed an errant hair behind her ear.

'Hello, Alan,' echoed Clive, appearing behind her on the lawn. 'Where's my *car*, Alan?' he demanded.

'Ah . . . yes,' Knightley muttered under his breath. 'Is it . . . OK?'

'It corners impeccably, Clive.'

'Is it *OK*, Alan?' Clive half shouted.

'You'll find it in the capable hands of Transport for London.' Knightley turned to Draycott. 'Shall we proceed?'

Draycott reluctantly waved him on, until Clive blocked the doorway in protest.

'Mr Knightley just wants to show us something before we take him away,' the inspector explained.

'Jackie . . . ?' Clive urged, shaking his head fervently.

'Go ahead, Alan,' she answered.

'Show them the Knowledge, Doc.'

'OK, gentlemen. Follow me . . .'

Darkus led the entire procession through the house,

76

upstairs and across the landing to his bedroom. Knightley followed obediently behind Draycott and his officers.

Darkus paused at his bedroom door and turned to address them all. 'You'll have to excuse the state of my room. I left in something of a hurry.'

'He's a very neat boy,' explained Jackie.

Clive harrumphed in agreement.

Draycott and his officers watched impatiently as Darkus opened the door to his room, then stopped dead, instantly detecting something wrong. He turned to his father, confused. 'Someone's been here.'

'What d'you mean, Doc?'

Darkus walked briskly into the room, mentally recording every object that was out of place. He saw his laptop on the desk with the cable still attached, but lying limp, leading nowhere. The hard drive was gone.

'I must've forgotten to lock it away,' said Darkus, looking up at his father apologetically. 'I always lock it away,' he added, hardly believing his error.

Knightley took a moment to process this, then nodded soberly. 'It's OK, Doc. There are forces at work that are obviously closer at my heels than I thought.'

'How *very* convenient,' said Draycott. 'The one piece of evidence that might substantiate your story and it's mysteriously gone missing.'

'There's nothing mysterious about it,' said Knightley

plainly. 'It's the work of the Combination; you can be sure of that.'

'The what?' Draycott asked, stroking his moustache, curious.

'The organisation I was telling you about. They know I've woken up and they've traced me here. And by their good fortune they've managed to stumble on the single most important piece of evidence I have against them. Clearly they gained access to my son's room in the past twelve hours, probably with the collusion of your own officers.'

'You're accusing *my* men of being involved?' Draycott bristled.

'Unfortunately the heinous fraternity I refer to draws its members from both crime and law enforcement. And that hard drive was our best chance of finding them.'

'And what exactly was on it?' asked Draycott.

'Only a detailed record of every case in my illustrious career, every crime scene, every clue, every lead to the location and membership of the Combination.' Knightley sighed heavily. 'I must conclude that the Knowledge has already been passed up the ladder, or destroyed, and I'm left with nothing but . . .' He trailed off, looking at Darkus with a newfound intensity.

'Nothing but me,' said Darkus, finishing his sentence. He quickly followed his father's logic, without Knightley having to say a word. 'I've got the Knowledge . . . up here.' Darkus pointed to his own head.

'It's impossible, Doc,' Knightley barked, not wishing to accept the truth.

'I'm telling you, it's all here,' Darkus repeated with complete conviction.

'If you think I'd utilise my own son . . .'

'If everything you've said is true,' said Darkus, 'that's exactly what you should do.'

'Damn it, Doc . . .' Knightley rubbed his head, wracked with anxiety.

'OK, show's over, Alan,' Draycott announced. 'You're coming with me.'

Darkus grabbed his father's arm. 'If you don't take me with you, I'll be in more danger here. I'm a sitting duck,' he said gravely.

'This is insanity,' murmured Knightley.

'I couldn't have chosen a better word myself,' said Draycott. 'Now come along. You're under arrest.'

'Wait a second,' Knightley said, examining Darkus closely. 'If you're so sure of yourself . . .' He paused, then launched into a carefully chosen line of questioning: 'What was the prima facie evidence in the investigation of the Man with the Harelip?'

The entire group looked from Knightley to Darkus.

'The bloody paw print,' answered Darkus.

79

Everyone turned back to Knightley, whose eyes lit up wildly. 'Where and when did I first encounter the Jade Dagger?'

Darkus wasn't even aware he'd become the centre of attention – his brain was too busy producing the answer, with the speed of a well-oiled machine.

'December 2001,' he said without hesitation. 'On a train bound for Didcot Parkway. The 15.40.'

'Excellent. Excellent!' Knightley exclaimed, thrilled.

Draycott turned to Jackie, stroking his moustache. 'This sort of rapport is common in kidnap cases. I believe we're witnessing what's known as –'

'Stockholm syndrome,' said Jackie warily.

'Yes, exactly,' Draycott said, clearing his throat.

'Or maybe it's just father–son syndrome,' she said drily.

Fearing he might have been intellectually outmanoeuvred, Draycott got back to what he knew best. 'All right, Alan, come quietly.'

The officers manhandled Knightley back across the landing as he struggled to slow them down, turning to face Jackie. 'Doc's right. He's not safe here,' he said flatly.

Jackie shrugged, helpless. 'What d'you want me to do?!'

Inexplicably, Knightley stopped resisting for a moment and sniffed the air, then answered, 'Nothing.

He'll be protected. It's OK.' He relaxed and let the officers guide him as Jackie watched, mystified.

'What d'you mean it's OK?!' she demanded.

Draycott escorted Knightley down the staircase. 'I hereby arrest you on suspicion of theft of a motor vehicle, child abduction and public disorder –'

'That will *nae* be necessary, Inspector,' a voice interrupted him.

Darkus immediately recognised the voice and matched it with the aroma he'd detected moments after his father did. 'Uncle Bill . . .' he uttered under his breath.

'It's *Chief* Inspector!' Draycott called out, unable to see who he was addressing.

By this time, the wisps of cigar smoke were visibly climbing the stairs, although Bill himself was planted firmly in the entrance hall, his girth apparently too abundant for the crowded staircase.

'And *you* are . . . ?' said Draycott.

'A friend,' Bill replied, then lowered his smouldering stogie and held up a leather ID wallet.

'And not a moment too soon,' said Knightley, offering his cuffed hands to Draycott.

Draycott parted his way through the smoke and examined Bill's ID. 'SO 42 . . . ?' he scoffed. 'Never heard of it.'

'Dinna surprise me. Yer'll find a phone number

there . . .' Bill held it up to Draycott's face. 'I suggest ye call it.'

Draycott snatched the ID wallet out of his hand and drew a mobile phone from his utility belt. He marched into the living room, punching the number into the keypad, then stopped, surprised to receive an immediate answer on the other end.

'Hello? Yes, this is Chief Inspector Draycott. Who is this?'

There was a long pause as the voice on the other end delivered a long and thorough explanation.

'But –' Draycott tried to interject, but the voice continued for a further ten seconds.

The rest of the police officers listened in silence. Knightley took the opportunity to exchange pleasantries with his old friend.

'You've lost some weight, Bill. Approximately a kilogram, I'd say.'

'Aye, thank ye for noticing, Alan.'

Meanwhile, Draycott slowly went a shade paler and lowered the phone, unconsciously clipping it to his belt. Then he went completely quiet for a moment.

'Sir?' a constable asked, concerned.

'Yes . . . ?' Draycott replied, dazed. 'Yes,' he repeated, regaining command of himself. 'Move out, men. We have a . . .' He searched for the right word. 'A jurisdictional issue.'

The assembled officers looked at each other.

'You heard me,' he said, pointing to the door. 'Chop-chop.' Draycott thrust the ID wallet back at Bill and turned to Knightley. 'Until next time, Alan,' he said, unlocking the handcuffs and reattaching them to his belt. 'And there will certainly be a next time,' he warned, then followed his officers out.

Clive and Jackie descended the stairs, unsure of what had just happened.

'Clive, Jackie, would ye give me a moment alone with Alan and young Darkus?' Bill requested.

'Doc, is that OK with you?' Jackie asked.

'Absolutely, yes-yes,' he replied, unable to hide his enthusiasm.

Then a new voice interjected. 'If you're missing something, you might want to talk to me too,' said Tilly, standing above them on the stairs. 'I saw a couple of cops snooping around Darkus's bedroom . . . Only I don't think they were real cops.' She had their attention now. 'They left five minutes ago.'


Darkus listened carefully as Tilly relayed her story to Knightley and Uncle Bill, giving a full description of the two suspects, along with mobile-phone video footage of them leaving the scene in their panda car. Bill instantly relayed the details to the local constabulary, who confirmed that the two officers in question never reported back to the station.

First they'd stolen Knightley's case files, then they'd made sure his progress was obstructed by Draycott. Now the Knowledge, and its thieves, were long gone.

Struggling to keep pace with events, strangely, Darkus found himself wondering about Tilly's hair, and the fact that it had changed colour again since the previous day. He marvelled at how she found time for anything else, let alone to observe the suspicious behaviour of two so-called police officers. He had to admit he was impressed. After Tilly finished her account, Uncle Bill thanked her and asked her to wait next door until he had interviewed Darkus.

'I'm not finished yet,' she protested. 'I've got a few questions of my own.' She turned her attention to Knightley.

'All in good time,' he answered vaguely.

Tilly narrowed her eyes, assessing the situation before letting Uncle Bill usher her out of the living room and close the door behind her.

Bill sat opposite the Knightleys, his homburg hat resting on his generous midsection. 'Nou, Darkus,' he began.

'Call me Doc.'

'Doc. Yer father and meself worked together on many of the cases ye apparently know so well.'

'I never saw your name mentioned,' said Darkus.

'That's because ma name is nae technically Uncle Bill. It's Montague Billoch.'

'You work for Scotland Yard,' said Darkus, remembering the name from the Knowledge.

'Indeed.'

Knightley added, 'That's where he got his nickname from. Uncle Bill – Old Bill. The Bill – it's slang for the police.'

'Logical,' said Darkus with a nod.

'Aye. Only I don't work for any department ye or many other people will've heard of,' Bill went on.

'SO 42,' said Darkus.

'Aye,' said Bill. 'Specialist Operations branch 42. Only among the likes of yer father and meself, it's known as the Department of the Unexplained. It does nae operate in the world of Draycott or the regular police force. It's too secretive for that. It exists outside the regular world, just like the crimes it investigates.'

'And what crimes are they?' asked Darkus.

'Highly organised crime, parapsychology, the occult, the dark arts and well nigh everything in between.'

'In other words . . . the Combination,' said Knightley.

'We'll see about that, Alan,' said Bill, then turned

back to Darkus. 'Yer father and me don't always see eye tae eye. Alan believes there is *one* organisation that is responsible for *all* these unexplained events. The Combination, he claims. I however find it hard tae believe such a web is possible, and am yet tae see the evidence.'

'That's why I assembled all my cases into one file: the Knowledge,' added Knightley. 'For reasons of security, I never referred to our enemy by name.'

'Indeed.' Bill explained to Darkus: 'Yer father was preparing tae hand over the sum total of all his investigations, tae prove or disprove his theory once and for all. But befoor he could do that, he had his wee . . . episode.'

Knightley nodded gravely. 'Now the Knowledge is gone and we're back to square one. And my brain is nothing but a dull blade.'

Uncle Bill shifted uncomfortably in his seat, the chair creaking under his weight.

'Nou, Doc . . . how d'ye feel about everything we've told ye?' he enquired gently.

Knightley waited with bated breath for his son's response.

'I don't have the empirical data to determine whether or not one organisation is responsible for all my father's cases,' said Darkus. 'However, having had the chance to digest the Knowledge, I would agree with him that there

86

are certainly connections: all those clues going missing, forensic evidence being mishandled or ruled inadmissible in court, witnesses changing their stories.'

Knightley cleared his throat and took over. 'My memory's not what it used to be, but Darkus knows the history. Throughout my career, there were clues, traces, that formed a common thread running through every case. Follow the thread and you locate the Combination.'

Darkus watched his father, concerned. It was clear that whether the Combination existed or not, his father wasn't about to let it go. Uncle Bill shrugged, unconvinced, his chair creaking in complaint.

Knightley continued undaunted: 'Clive's daughter observes two police officers abscond with the Knowledge. You think that's coincidence?'

Bill shifted in his seat again, apparently too exhausted to weigh the theories any more. 'I have bigger fish tae fry, Alan,' he wheezed.

'And what, pray tell, are they?' said Knightley.

Bill sighed, uncertain whether involving Knightley would be beneficial or not. He produced a fresh cigar, struck a match to it and resumed puffing smoke. 'I have six unexplained bank robberies, across six different counties, committed by six individuals with nae criminal backgrounds,' he complained.

'It was on the news last night,' added Darkus.

'Piquant,' said Knightley. 'Are there any patterns relating to age, gender or ethnicity?'

'None whatsayever.' Bill blew a smoke ring.

'Any casualties as a result of the robberies?' continued Knightley.

'Nae.'

'Any suspects in custody?'

'Just one. And I'm off tae see him shortly.'

'What about tools or weapons of choice?' Darkus ventured.

'Aye. *One* clue was discovered at the scene of every crime. Only it's nae a weapon exactly,' said Bill, looking perplexed. 'It's a *boook*.'

# Chapter 8
## THE AVID READER

Knightley's ears lifted at Bill's last answer. His nostrils flared and he leaned forward, as if all his features were streamlining themselves, preparing for the hunt.

'A book. That is *most* interesting,' Knightley remarked. 'And the particular book was . . . ?'

'A self-help book. Nae something I go in for meself,' replied Bill, a little too defensively. 'It's called *The Code*, by Ambrose Chambers.'

'Doc? What do you know about it?'

'Only that it's the work of a first-time author whose background is shrouded in mystery,' said Darkus. 'And he's never been photographed. Most believe it's a marketing ploy. Since the book's publication a few months ago, it has been steadily climbing the bestseller lists, combining New Age motivational strategies with ancient mythology and pop psychology. The reviews were mixed. The general consensus is that it's harmless.'

'But clearly it's not,' said Knightley.

'Nou, Alan, there's nae evidence tae suggest the book has anything tae dae with the crimes.'

'There's no evidence to suggest the book *doesn't* have anything to do with them either,' said Darkus.

'Exactly,' said Knightley. 'And this bears all the hall-marks of our usual foe.'

'A'right. Seeing as you've decided tae return tae the land of the living, Alan, why don't ye come wi' us? Prove the existence of the Combination.'

'What about Doc?' he asked.

Darkus looked from one man to the other, sensing his future was hanging in the balance.

'Ye said it yerself, Alan . . . If the Combination's out there and Draycott's men are compromised, he's in more danger here,' reasoned Bill.

'You're suggesting we bring him on the case? He's only a boy.'

'With the mind of an experienced investigator . . . With *yer* mind, Alan.'

Knightley shook his head.

'In yer current state, Alan, we *need* him.'

'Then it's settled,' said Darkus. 'I'm coming.'

Knightley frowned. 'What you've read in the Knowledge is nothing compared to reality, Doc. This is no urban myth. The forces of good date back through the centuries, and I understand their appeal. But the forces of evil are far older . . . and more powerful. And the closer you get to them, the more malevolent they become,' Knightley concluded, visibly anxious.

'If he's going, so am I,' a voice interrupted them.

The three of them turned to find Tilly standing in the doorway.

'Nobody's going anywhere,' Knightley ordered.

'I've still got questions,' she replied.

Knightley gestured impatiently. 'Fire away.'

'About my mum.'

Knightley went quiet. 'Yes . . . I'm terribly sorry, Tilly –'

'Was it an accident? Or was it another one of your unexplained cases?' she demanded, biting her lip nervously.

Darkus realised she'd been eavesdropping on the entire conversation from outside the door.

'Because you know what I think?' she went on. 'I think it had something to do with whatever you were working on, Knightley. And until I find out the truth, I'm holding *you* responsible for her death.'

Knightley swallowed hard, then composed himself. 'Based on the state of the car, the inquiry concluded it was a tragic accident, nothing more,' he replied in measured tones, controlling his emotions. 'Your mother was the finest researcher I ever worked with. And she loved you very, very much. I did everything I could to protect her.'

'You couldn't even protect your own marriage,' she answered back.

Knightley winced. 'It's never easy losing someone you love,' he said, unconsciously glancing through the doorway to where Jackie's voice could be heard from the kitchen. 'And you, Tilly, learned that younger than anyone should ever have to . . . Now, if you'll excuse me, I have work to do.'

With that, Knightley closed his eyes and leaned back in his chair, steepling his fingers and resting them on his brow, as if soliciting guidance from a higher force. His lips pursed and his breathing reduced to a shallow whistle through his nose.

'Dad?' prompted Darkus.

'Alan?'

Darkus drew closer, concerned. 'What's wrong with him?'

'He does this sometimes when he's on a case. He's just thinking. Alan . . . ?'

Bill nudged him; then nudged him again; then gently rolled up Knightley's sleeve and took his pulse; then prised open his eyelids and checked the size of his pupils. He turned back to Darkus, flummoxed. 'Well, I'm afraid he appears tae be in another narcoleptic trance . . . Essentially, asleep.'

'But he only just woke up,' said Tilly.

Darkus felt a sick feeling return to his stomach. 'Is it another . . . "episode"?'

'It's tae early tae say. If it lasts longer than twintie-four hours, we ought tae seek medical attention.'

'He's not going back to Shrubwoods. I promised.'

Bill ignored him and continued to observe Knightley. 'It appears tae be stress-related – a relapse of some kind. Alan, if ye can hear me, gie us some kind of a sign.'

There was no response.

'Dad?' Darkus persisted, tugging his arm.

Bill gestured to Tilly to leave the room, and realising this was perhaps more serious than it first appeared, she obliged.

'Dad?' urged Darkus.

A curious expression glanced across Bill's face, and Darkus caught sight of it: as if his father's mishap was somehow Bill's good fortune.

'Dinna worry, Doc,' he said. 'Leave this tae me . . .' Bill paused a moment, then whispered to Knightley: 'Alan, if ye want Darkus tae help us with the case, gie us some kind of a sign.'

His father provided no response.

'A'right,' said Bill. 'If ye *don't* want him tae help us with the case, gie us some kind of a sign.'

Darkus looked at Bill incredulously. He knew exactly

where this was going. Knightley's face remained as still as the surface of a lake; his body didn't move a muscle.

'I'll take that as a yes,' concluded Bill. 'Yoo're on the case, Darkus.'

'But –'

'That is, if ye think yoo're up tae it.'

'Well, of course I'm up to it,' said Darkus defensively.

'Good.'

Darkus struggled to make sense of the predicament he found himself in. 'But . . . what about Dad?'

'We'll make sure he's well taken care of. There's nae much ye can do for him here. And I'm afraid we dinna have time tae waste.' Bill excavated himself from his chair and ushered Darkus towards the hallway.

Darkus lingered by his father's side. He'd patiently waited four years for him to wake up, and through some cruel twist of fate he'd simply fallen asleep again. But this time Darkus knew he couldn't remain in limbo any more. His father's return – albeit brief – had brought with it a valuable inheritance: a calling. And having honed the necessary skills over a number of years – albeit by accident – Darkus saw no choice but to answer the call.

Next time his father woke up, Darkus would prove himself a worthy partner.

'Sleep tight, Dad.' Darkus carefully laid a tartan

blanket over his father's lap. Then he looked up to see his mother watching from the doorway.

'I'm so sorry, Doc,' she choked, grabbing him in a hug.

Clive loitered in the background. 'Now, now, dear.'

'It's OK, Mum,' Darkus reassured her.

Bill put a massive hand on her shoulder. 'Jackie, yoo're going tae have tae trust me.'

'What do you mean?' she asked.

'Although yoo're his mammy . . .' he went on, 'Darkus is safer with me.'

Darkus nodded slowly, expressing his agreement. Clive made no objection. Jackie turned pale.

'I hope you know what you're doing, Bill,' she said gravely.

'Right nou, you're in nae position tae protect him. We are.'

'What about me?' Tilly chimed in from the hallway, until Clive cut her off.

'You're staying right here, young lady.'

Tilly sat on the stairs sullenly.

'Doc . . . ?' Jackie rested her hands on his shoulders. 'Is this what *you* want?'

'It's the logical solution,' he answered.

Jackie's eyes welled up and she lost the capacity to speak.

'Keep your phone switched on, all right?' she managed.

'Of course,' he replied, knowing that she wanted a bigger display of affection, but he had a job to do, one that required his full and immediate concentration. He straightened his collar and took his Donegal tweed hat from the stand. 'I suggest you call Bogna and ask her to take care of Dad until he wakes up.' He reminded her, and himself, 'All the available evidence indicates that he *will* wake up.'

'OK, sweetie.' She nodded, dazed.

Darkus fixed his hat on his head and followed Bill down the driveway. On cue, the silver Ford saloon car pulled up to collect them. Bill slid himself into the back seat and Darkus squeezed in beside him. Jackie watched anxiously from the front garden, as the driver hit the accelerator and the car pulled away.

On the doorstep, Tilly watched them go, her fists clenched.


Uncle Bill directed the driver on to an A road heading further into the countryside.

'Give me yer phone, Doc,' he said.

Darkus obediently retrieved it from the inside pocket of his jacket and handed it over. Bill slid the back of the phone off, removed the battery and the SIM card, tossed them out of the car window and handed the useless handset back to Darkus.

'What d'you do that for?'

'Ye can be traced with it. We cannae afford that. Yer mother will understand. Alan always said, we cannae let anything distract us when we're on a case.'

Darkus looked at the handset, shrugged and put it back in his pocket. It had just been confirmed that he was now officially on a case. Darkus knew he had to temper any excitement or apprehension with the need to remain acutely calm and observant. Despite his father's absence, a long-cherished dream was finally becoming a reality, and the catastrophiser had to be kept well oiled and in perfect working order. He directed his attention outside and tested himself by memorising the turns and road signs.

Meanwhile, Uncle Bill sat next to him in silence, his eyes closed and his chest heaving. Darkus observed that this wasn't a state of meditation: Bill was in fact asleep. His head lolled back with his mouth ajar. Fortunately, the driver was focused on the road, turning the wheel precisely. They descended through a wooded valley into a large cathedral town, taking a bend that finally roused Bill from his slumber.

He grunted and looked up. 'Nou, Doc, the young man we're going tae meet is Lee Wadsworth. A fifteen-year-old schoolboy with nae previous convictions of any kind. That is, until he read *The Code*. His mam says he bought it ten days ago from a local branch of a chain bookshop. When he first looked at it, he was admitted tae A & E wi' an epileptic fit of some kind. Tae be exact, he was saying insects were coming out of the book and trying tae kill him.'

'Most peculiar,' remarked Darkus.

'Strange thing is, after the fit, he returned tae the same shop and bought the book. In fact, according tae the shop assistant, he bought several copies of it for family and friends.'

'Any history of mental illness? Problems at school?' said Darkus.

'None,' replied Bill.

Darkus mulled it over. 'Proceed.'

'Well, he appeared tae show nae signs of any problem, life returned tae normal, until several days later when he failed tae show up for school,' explained Bill. 'His teachers couldnae find him, nor could his mam, until he was apprehended by local police trying tae rob a bank, armed wi' a claw hammer.'

'Which I assume was stored in the house for domestic use, not purchased expressly for the crime,' said Darkus.

'Correct,' replied Bill. 'The crime was nae well planned or executed at all.'

'Intriguing,' said Darkus. 'Did he give any explanation for his actions?'

'Aye,' said Bill. 'He said the book told him tae dae it.'

*

The police station was a drab mid-century design with whitewashed walls and faded signage. Uncle Bill led the way, displaying his ID to the attending constables, who inspected Darkus with curiosity. Darkus avoided eye contact and followed Bill to a holding cell in the centre of the building.

As they approached the bars Bill concluded his account quietly. 'The six robbery suspects have only one thing in common,' he explained. 'Their apparent fixation wi' the book . . .'

Darkus peered through the bars. Inside the cell, Lee Wadsworth was reclining on a bunk bed still wearing his school uniform; his shoes had no laces and his trousers lacked a belt, both confiscated for his own safety. His hands were gripping a copy of *The Code*. He looked up, attempting a smile through his dental braces, then returned to reading, as if he was in a library rather than a police station.

'Mr Wadsworth,' Bill addressed him. 'We're here tae talk to ye about what happened in town lest week.'

'Can't you see I'm reading?' the young man replied.

'Aye, but we have some questions that need answering,' said Bill. 'Questions it seems only ye can answer.'

'*This* . . .' Lee lisped, holding up the book. 'This has all the answers. Would you like a copy?'

'We hae several copies.'

'Then I suggest you read them.' He buried his head in the book again.

Darkus observed the suspect carefully, feeling his breath speed up and his nostrils flare, drawing extra supplies of oxygen to his pulsing brain. After all, this was his first real case and he didn't want to let the side down.

Bill spoke to Darkus in hushed tones. 'Each of the suspects had a copy of the book on them when they committed the crime. We have nae seen anything like it since *The Catcher in the Rye*,' he said grimly. He turned to address the suspect. 'Lee, I understand your book *spoke* to ye. Perhaps ye can tell us what it said?'

Lee lowered the book and began to talk. 'That we're approaching a new consciousness, a new unity between us and the universe.'

'I see.'

'No, you don't,' Lee challenged him.

'Dae continue.'

'Our destinies are guided by one infinite power, an inner voice, the spiritual transmitter. All you have to do is focus it, and concentrate on what you want,' he said wisely. 'What do *you* want?'

'I want tae know why ye robbed that bank.'

'I only took what was already mine,' said Lee. 'The book told me that good things would come to me . . . and they did. The universe rewarded me.'

'But that money was nae yours,' Bill objected.

'Yes, it was.'

'According tae our records, ye don't even have an account there.'

'I attracted it to me,' he replied.

'Ye broke the law,' Bill reminded him.

'Not the universal law,' said Lee. 'You see, the truth is, anything's possible with the power of the mind.'

Bill looked stumped by this. 'But that does nae bring us any closer tae solving the mystery nou, does it?'

Lee turned his attention to Darkus. 'Perhaps *he* can understand. A young mind is always open.'

Darkus caught Lee's eye, finding a cold abyss where he suspected a perfectly normal teenager once resided. Feeling his piercing stare, Darkus was reminded that he was a long way from the harmless, amateur detective work he'd previously engaged in.

Suddenly the book dropped from Lee's grasp and his hands shot through the bars of the cell, finding Darkus's neck.

'*Read the book!*' Lee shouted. 'All your questions will be answered!'

Darkus recoiled, finding the suspect's fingers tightening around his neck, blushing red against his skin. Before Darkus could respond, Bill wheezed and hurtled to the rescue.

'Let 'im go!' Bill yanked Lee's arms, slamming the suspect's head against the bars. Lee slumped back, stunned. 'Ye OK, Darkus?'

Darkus straightened his collar, and took a moment to compose himself. 'I'm fine,' he replied, steadying his breathing.

Bill exhaled and took a notepad from one of his voluminous overcoat pockets. 'It may interest ye tae know, Lee, that other readers have experienced similar effects. Do ye know or have ye ever consorted wi' Marcus Morris, Sheila Trimball, Brian Pilkington . . .' Bill trailed off as Lee picked up his book, raising it as a shield, and continued reading. Bill turned to Darkus. 'We're quite certain there's nae connection between them.'

Darkus nodded, inwardly examining the available evidence. 'I'm not a believer in the supernatural, but on the surface this bears all the hallmarks of a "grimoire".'

'A grim wha . . . ?' asked Bill.

'Followers of the black arts call it a "necronomicon",' Darkus added.

'Nae helping,' complained Bill.

'A book of magic,' explained Darkus, 'dating back to incantations first discovered on clay tablets in ancient Mesopotamia, then appearing later in the Dead Sea scrolls.'

Bill listened, impressed.

'The books contained charms reputed to bring health, success and fulfilment,' said Darkus slowly. 'Of course, it's all a myth.'

'Perhaps not tae those who *believe*,' Bill suggested.

'Indeed. In early Christianity, the Church feared these books were cursed and capable of manifesting demons . . . bringing madness and eternal damnation upon all those who opened them. The books were burned and the libraries ransacked.'

Bill raised his eyebrows.

'I have one last question for the suspect,' said Darkus. 'Dad always wrote: "Start any investigation with the line of least resistance." So that's what I'm going to do.'

'Be my guest,' Bill replied.

'Mr Wadsworth, if you will,' Darkus began, 'describe the voice that you heard.'

Lee looked up. 'It's the book . . . It speaks on a frequency that is specially tuned to me.'

'I understand, but describe it for me. Was it male or female?'

'Male. It was a male voice.'

'Was it your own voice?'

'No.'

'Was it foreign?'

'No. It was English.'

'Good,' said Darkus. 'Would you characterise it as baritone, tenor or soprano?'

'Mid-range,' said Lee. 'Sometimes . . .' he continued, 'the voice cut out, then came back again.'

'I see,' said Darkus. 'Anything else?'

'That's all I can remember.'

Bill turned to Darkus. 'Where are ye going with this, Doc?'

'It's too early to say.'

'Aye, yoo're a chip off the old block,' remarked Bill.

'That concludes my line of questioning,' said Darkus. 'Thank you, Mr Wadsworth.'

Lee frowned and returned his attention to the book.

Bill guided Darkus away from the cell, past the constables, who were still watching with sceptical curiosity.

'Have ye got any more ideas?' Bill enquired.

'I suggest we interview his mum.'

'Me tae,' replied Bill.

# Chapter 9
## THE LAW OF GUESSWORK

The short drive to the Wadsworth residence was accompanied by heavy rain that obscured the windscreen and did little to erase the sense of doom surrounding the case. Darkus turned the facts over in his mind, but saw no clear solution. Was the book somehow to blame? Or was it merely an innocent bystander, a talisman for the likes of Lee Wadsworth to use for his own misguided entertainment and financial gain? The first rule of detective work was never to succumb to the luxury of coincidence. There had to be a connection. And Darkus hoped that he could work out what it was.

Bill took the opportunity to give Darkus a potted history of the Department of the Unexplained and how its oddball ideas had fallen victim to far-reaching budget cuts. As a result, the department was now little more than a loose-knit collection of bureaucrats, conspiracy theorists and those that the rest of Scotland Yard (the few that even remembered the department's existence) simply regarded as quacks. It was in this climate of pen-pushing and penny-pinching that Bill had approached his Oxford pal Alan Knightley, someone he could rely on to carry out an investigation by any means necessary, even if Bill didn't always approve of – or sometimes even believe – the results.

Now that Knightley Senior was once again out of action, Bill seemed more than happy to rely on Darkus instead.

The driver turned into an estate of neatly arranged newbuild houses, all with identical lawns, dotted with crazy paving. They pulled up and parked outside the Wadsworth residence. Uncle Bill led the way, removing his hat and ringing the doorbell.

An exhausted, slightly overweight woman in jogging trousers answered the door.

'Yes?'

'We're wi' Scotland Yard, ma'am,' said Bill, displaying his ID. She looked him over, then spotted Darkus.

'Both of you?'

'Work experience,' explained Bill, patting Darkus heavily on the shoulder.

Darkus removed his hat courteously.

The woman looked doubtful but opened the door

wider. 'I suppose this is about Lee,' she sighed. 'Well, I'm afraid I won't be any help. He's clearly lost the plot, hasn't he?'

They entered the house to find it in disarray. Clothes hung discarded on chairs and lampshades, papers littered every available surface, teacups sat forgotten on ledges. But, most noticeably, dozens of cardboard boxes blocked the hallway, the stairs and much of the living room. Bill gracefully manoeuvred his girth around the obstacles and followed Mrs Wadsworth into the kitchen.

The kitchen table was also covered in and surrounded by boxes.

'May I?' asked Bill.

Mrs Wadsworth nodded, and Bill lifted one of the lids to find the box filled to the brim with hardback copies of *The Code*.

'There are more in the garage,' she explained. 'Ordered them all on my credit card, didn't he?'

'When did this behaviour begin?' enquired Darkus.

Mrs Wadsworth looked at Bill, uncertain whether to respond. 'Do you want me to answer him? He's only a boy.'

'Certainly ye should answer him,' said Bill.

'Well, it began after he started reading that infernal book.'

'Something in the book clearly appealed to him,' Darkus speculated.

'Do ye believe he may have resorted tae robbery tae fund his habit?' asked Bill.

'I hope that's what he was doing!' Mrs Wadsworth erupted. 'It's cost a fortune.'

Darkus examined a box of identical books, then looked up. 'Have you read the book yourself, madam?'

'Yes, I have. I had to, didn't I?' she continued. 'To see what all the fuss was about.'

'And what did you think of it?'

'I thought it was rubbish,' she replied. 'New Age twaddle.'

'And it didn't have any ill effect on you?' Darkus went on. 'No feelings of discomfort, nausea, dizziness? Anything at all?'

'Nope. Just boredom,' she said, looking to Bill again, as if to ask whether it was really necessary for her to explain herself to a child.

'Intriguing,' said Darkus, nodding.

'What is this?' asked Mrs Wadsworth, losing patience. 'What's going on? Why's my Lee gone bonkers? And why am I being questioned by a twelve-year-old?'

'Thirteen, actually,' Darkus corrected her.

Bill turned to her reassuringly. 'Did yer son say anything else about his experience wi' the book?'

'He said it changed his life. He said it made him feel like he was on television. Watching himself on telly – that's what he said.'

Darkus nodded. 'A common symptom of paranoid schizophrenia. The old Lee seemed to be watching the new Lee as he carried out his criminal act. Similar to the Affair of the Missing Accomplice,' Darkus reminded himself.

'Aye,' said Bill. 'One of yer father's benchmark cases.'

'Meaning?' said Mrs Wadsworth impatiently.

'I'm afraid I don't yet have an answer for you,' admitted Darkus. 'But I do have one more question, if I may?'

Mrs Wadsworth shrugged her consent.

'From the well-dusted condition of your ceilings,' began Darkus, 'in contrast with the otherwise unkempt nature of the living space beneath them, and judging from the effort required to carry out such high dusting, and your apparent aversion to housework, I propose that your son Lee has an unusually powerful fear of *insects*. Particularly crawling ones. Am I right?'

Mrs Wadsworth's jaw dropped in a combination of awe and deep, personal affront.

'I thought so,' concluded Darkus, then turned to Bill. 'That might explain the description of insects coming out of the book.'

'Aye.'

Their conference was rudely interrupted by Mrs Wadsworth physically pushing Uncle Bill towards the front door. 'I've told you everything I know. Now get out!'

Bill artfully negotiated the hallway, apologising as he went. 'Thank ye for yer time, Mrs Wadsworth.'

Darkus gave Bill a wide berth, and swiftly exited the front door before it could be closed on him. Bill, however, turned to face Mrs Wadsworth's wrath one last time.

'A suggestion, Mrs Wadsworth. I advise ye tae get these books oot of yer house immediately. Return them tae the shop or hand them over tae the local police.' Bill thought about it further, then added, 'If necessary, burn them.'

Mrs Wadsworth looked them both over once more. Before another word could be said she slammed the door.

'Well, we can assume two things,' said Darkus, replacing his hat on his head. 'Firstly, the book does *not* affect every reader the same way,' he observed. 'Secondly, if it *does* affect the reader, it draws on their innermost fears.'

'Aye,' concurred Bill.

Darkus turned the matter over in his mind. 'While the idea of a "grimoire" is certainly appealing, it's too easy to simply blame this on the supernatural.'

Bill shrugged. 'Aye.'

'Dad once wrote,' began Darkus, 'that "reasoning is merely guesswork, until one of the guesses leads to a universal rule that applies to the entire problem". And so far, we don't have enough evidence to find that universal rule. We still don't know what the affected readers have in common, or how to explain their extraordinary reaction to the book.' Darkus pondered a moment. 'But we *do* know there must be a rule,' he declared. 'Because, as Dad said, there *always* is.'

'Aye.' Bill nodded, having no idea what this rule might be.

'So far, all we know for certain is that the *book* is the common thread. Ergo the next logical port of call is the author himself,' said Darkus.

Bill took out a fresh cigar and ambled back to the car. 'Unfortunately, Ambrose Chambers is a verra private man, and we don't have reasonable cause tae force his cooperation. But fortunately I've already made arrangements tae speak wi' his literary agent at Beecham Associates in South Ken this afternoon.' He got in and instructed the driver: 'Tae the train station.'

# Chapter 10
## THE AUTHOR'S HAND

After several minutes spent trying to operate the automated ticket machine, Uncle Bill bought one adult's and one child's fare to London Victoria. As they boarded the waiting train, Bill reached into his capacious overcoat and produced an unusual-looking mobile device; he extended a long telescopic antenna from the top of it, and handed it to Darkus.

'It's a secure phone,' Bill explained, out of earshot of the other passengers. 'Can't be traced. It also scans, prints and faxes. Took me close tae three weeks tae learn how tae switch it on.'

Darkus pressed a small button and the device came to life. 'Looks straightforward enough.'

'Aye,' sighed Bill, before a public address system drowned him out, announcing that the train was due to depart in five minutes. 'Nou, I have a wee business call tae take care of. Back in a jiffy.' He waddled off down the platform.

Darkus took a few minutes to familiarise himself with the phone, then looked around to discover there was still no sign of Uncle Bill. A final announcement sounded, and the train doors slid shut.

As the train moved away from the platform, Darkus looked around urgently, catching a glimpse of Bill's unmistakable physique through the window of a public house beside the station. Bill was propped on a bar stool, heavily engaged with a frothy pint of bitter, until he looked up and noticed the train was moving. Bill lurched to his feet for a moment, then realised it was a lost cause and sat back down, hailing the barmaid for another.

Darkus fought the urge to panic, and instead used the phone's web browser to find the South Kensington address of Beecham Associates. He was interrupted by a garbled phone call from Bill, apologising for his unavoidable delay and assuring Darkus that he would be on the next train to London. Knowing that each passing minute was leaving the trail colder, Darkus decided to overlook Bill's shortcomings and press on with the investigation alone. He consulted his notes, which had been briskly committed to paper in a small black book, and spent the remainder of the journey turning the evidence over in his mind, waiting for the universal rule to present itself: the rule that would provide a solution to the facts.

\*

After disembarking at Victoria train station, consuming a sandwich of indifferent quality and travelling two stops by Tube, Darkus arrived outside the modern, glass-fronted offices of Beecham Associates. He entered the revolving doors and was discharged into a marble foyer, where a male receptionist wearing a telephone headset watched over the stark waiting area. Darkus approached the desk and announced himself.

'I have a four o'clock with Bram Beecham.' He removed his hat and offered up his ID. 'The name's Knightley.'

'This is a library card,' the receptionist answered.

'That is correct.'

The receptionist peered over the desk and looked him up and down. 'I have a . . . *Darkus Knightley* at reception?' he asked his headset.

Darkus glanced around for something to look at, but found nothing of note. A few moments later, a set of lift doors opened to reveal a tall blonde assistant. She scanned left and right, looking right past Darkus, then clocked him and gazed down curiously.

'Mr Knightley . . . ?'

Darkus nodded.

'I was expecting someone . . .' She searched for the right word.

'"Master" is the more appropriate prefix.'

'Right,' she responded. 'I'm Chloe. Mr Beecham will see you now.'

'Thank you.'

Chloe led him towards the lift, swivelling her hips in a way that Darkus couldn't recall seeing before, except perhaps in a film.

Inside the lift Darkus felt more distracted than usual and found himself perspiring more than usual. He put it down to first-night nerves and focused on the red numerals illuminating one by one as they made their ascent.

'Step this way.' Chloe led him to a corner office overlooking the city, where Bram Beecham was sitting at a large black desk. He was a well-maintained man in his fifties, with black hair pushed back from his temples, a telephone headset and a black tailored suit designed in Italy. There was no sign of clutter or mess on his desk, nothing that might constitute a clue – only an ornamental tray of pebbles and sand which Darkus recognised as a miniature Japanese Zen garden. Clearly any paperwork was stored elsewhere.

On the wall, Beecham had photos of well-known faces from the worlds of publishing, film and TV. Beside his computer was a framed photograph of a smiling eight-year-old girl, presumably his daughter.

Beecham stood up to inspect his visitor.

'Master Knightley,' Chloe announced.

'Thank you, Chloe,' answered Beecham, appearing puzzled and gesturing towards an uncomfortable-looking modernist chair.

Darkus nodded and took a seat, his shoes just touching the floor.

'There must've been a mix-up. I was expecting Detective Billoch,' said Beecham, attempting a paternal smile. 'Is he a relative, or guardian?'

'Technically neither,' replied Darkus. 'But he's given me permission to speak on his behalf.'

'I see.' Beecham's expression deepened. 'Perhaps I can offer you a soft beverage of some kind?'

'Unfortunately I don't have the luxury of time,' said Darkus frankly. 'I'd like to arrange an interview with Ambrose Chambers.'

Beecham raised his eyebrows and removed his headset to indicate Darkus now had his complete attention. 'As I told Detective Billoch on the phone, I'm afraid that is quite impossible. My client is ultra-private, and besides, he's travelling at the moment. I haven't had contact with him in months.'

'I'd be happy to meet at a place of his choosing,' Darkus went on. 'Exercising complete discretion of course.'

'I'm afraid he categorically does *not* give interviews,' Beecham answered a little more sternly.

'Given the circumstances, I thought he'd be more willing to assist our investigation.'

'*Your* investigation?' asked Beecham.

'His book, after all, has become something of a favourite among the criminal classes.'

Beecham's face stiffened. 'Mr Chambers is a writer, and freely exercises his poetic licence, which is not yet a crime. If a handful of misguided readers choose to interpret his work the wrong way, I'm afraid that is neither his concern nor mine.'

'Technically, you're correct,' replied Darkus. 'However, we're talking about a series of unexplained crimes – extremely serious ones – by readers with no prior record of criminal activity. So I would appreciate any insight you or your client could give me, particularly in regards to the origin of the work and its basis in ancient mythology.'

Beecham loosened his tie and went a shade paler. 'To suggest that anything in the book might be inspiring criminal acts is clearly absurd,' he insisted.

'Is it?' asked Darkus. 'There's a rule in my business, which states that when all other factors have been eliminated, the one that remains must be the truth. However improbable it seems.'

Beecham's eyes widened, then regained their even gaze. 'I can try to pass your request along, but there's no guarantee I'll get a response.'

'Very well,' replied Darkus. 'Thank you for your time, Mr Beecham. And one more thing . . . if it's not too much trouble, may I take you up on your offer of a soft beverage?'

'Of course.' He nodded in the direction of the door. 'There's a kitchen at the end of the corridor. And a variety of snacks if you're hungry.'

'I never eat between meals.'

'I see,' said Beecham.

Darkus got up and walked to the door. Outside, Chloe sat in a cubicle, having listened in on the conversation via an intercom. She smiled efficiently at Darkus, who smiled back and straightened his jacket. 'Don't get lost,' she said pleasantly.

'I'll do my best.'

Darkus took in the basic floor plan and deduced that the files must be stored within easy reach of Beecham's office. He continued along the corridor under a row of dim spotlights, locating the kitchen . . . and an unmarked door.

Darkus reached into his pockets, put on a pair of leather gloves and slowly turned the door handle. He found a narrow room lined with filing cabinets, all neatly ordered and alphabetised. Darkus moved quietly down the aisle until he reached the letter C.

He slid open the cabinet and located a large folder tagged *Chambers, A*. He leafed through the papers, finding several drafts of *The Code*, unbound and littered with notes and underlinings in red pen. He glanced through, finding nothing more than spelling and grammatical errors and the occasional word change. He carefully removed a few pages of manuscript, laid them out on an adjacent cabinet and trained his secure phone on them. The camera quickly captured the images. Then he pocketed the phone and replaced the pages in the folder.

As he did so, a breeze suddenly blew through the room, ruffling the manuscript as it lay in the cabinet. Spooked, Darkus swiftly closed the drawer and looked round to locate the source of the disturbance. There were no windows in the room. Feeling his heart rate rise as the catastrophiser whirred to life, he scanned the room, then chastised himself, seeing an air-conditioning vent discreetly blowing from the corner of the ceiling.

He took a breath and continued to search the folder, finding a typed letter at the back that read:

Dear Mr Beecham,

Please find enclosed the manuscript for my debut book, tentatively entitled 'The Code'. I look forward to your thoughts.

Yours sincerely,
Ambrose Chambers

There was no address, and no signature.

Darkus replaced the letter, closed the drawer and returned to the door. He checked that the coast was clear, then darted into the kitchen, just as Chloe's face appeared from her cubicle to check on him.

'Find everything OK?' she called out.

'Just fine, thanks,' he replied, holding up a Perrier water.


Moments later, Darkus waved goodbye to Chloe as he exited the revolving doors past employees smoking cigarettes on the pavement outside. As he wafted the smoke aside, his attention was drawn to the opposite building, a tall Victorian structure lined with windows.

He felt the catastrophiser hum to life again, and quietly cursed it for haunting him so relentlessly. It had unnerved him for no reason in the file room, and now it was threatening to do an encore. He scanned the rows of windows overlooking him, until something caught his attention: a glint in the sunlight. In fact there were *two* glints, side by side.

He squinted, narrowing his focus, and clearly saw a pair of binoculars watching him from an upper floor. They reflected again, accompanied by a brief flash of colour, then vanished behind the window sill.

Keeping the window in his peripheral vision, Darkus made a brief calculation of the number of floors, found a gap in traffic and crossed the road. Several vehicles screeched to a halt, leaning on their horns as he narrowly made it to the other side.

He pushed through the lobby doors of the Victorian building and found himself in an upmarket gym. A muscle-bound receptionist flexed as he walked towards him, but Darkus darted up a narrow staircase.

'Hey!'

Darkus reached the third floor breathless, overtaking several large men in towelling robes. He looked around, seeing a fire exit at the end of the corridor. On instinct, he walked briskly towards it.

He knelt down, seeing something on the white floor tiles. He picked up what appeared to be an orange strand, then pushed through the fire exit into another stairwell. Darkus looked down to see a flash of orange descending the stairs at a high rate of speed. He instantly began his descent, two stairs at a time, tracking the flash of orange as it circled the stairs, continually one flight below him. As he arrived at the basement, an access door swung shut in front of him.

Darkus pushed through the access door to find a dark garage supported by concrete pillars, crammed with vehicles. He listened closely, hearing footsteps retreating into the foreboding darkness. Good sense told him to wait, but he kept following, until the footsteps came to a halt and an apparition turned to face him – no more than a shape in the darkness.

'Tilly, you don't have to run any more. I know it's you,' Darkus said to the shape.

'You think you're so clever, don't you?' The shape emerged from the darkness to reveal Tilly in her black leather jacket and leggings, her hair an interesting shade of orange. How she had managed to change its colour again and still track him across London was beyond Darkus's powers of comprehension.

'Why are you following me, Tilly?'

'Because your dad wasn't straight with me,' she said defiantly, silhouetted against a flickering strip light.

'About what?'

'About what happened to my mum.'

'It was six years ago,' he contended. 'The inquiry said it was an accident.'

'I'm not interested in what the inquiry said. I'm interested in the *truth*.'

'She was the closest thing Dad had to a partner.'

'That's why they killed her.'

'I don't know what you're talking about. Her car left the road during an ice storm –'

'I'm talking about the Combination.'

'You're not meant to know about that.'

'I know a lot more than you think. I'm going to help you find them.'

'I don't need a partner, Tilly.'

'Fine. Then you won't need this.' She took something from her jacket and walked under the strip light, revealing an almost maniacal smile. She was holding a Manila envelope.

'What is it?' asked Darkus, curiosity getting the better of him.

She tossed the envelope to him. He peered inside and slid out a neatly colour-coded folder containing a series of printouts: web pages, social network profiles, online searches. 'Those two cops who took your dad's precious hard drive,' she explained. 'I tracked them down. They're not local, they're Special Constables – volunteers. I know how to find them.'

'How?' said Darkus.

She shrugged. 'You just have to know where to look.'

'Like you found *me*, I suppose.'

'That was simple. I overheard you talking about *The Code*. Chambers is MIA. The next logical port of call was his literary agent.'

Darkus nodded. She'd followed his train of thought exactly. He leafed through the pages, then stopped. 'There's no address here.'

'That's right,' she replied. 'It's an Internet Protocol address.'

'Of course,' said Darkus. 'An *online* address – a set of numbers leading to a precise geographic location.'

'Top of the class,' said Tilly. 'And you don't get it until you agree to fully cooperate.'

'With what?'

'With *me*. We're after the same thing. The only difference is I don't trust anyone. Not even you. And whoever's responsible for my mum's death – I don't want them brought to justice, I just want them *dead*.'

Darkus couldn't deny he was impressed by her resolve, even though it wasn't exactly conducive to calm, reasoned investigation.

'And why should I trust you?' he asked.

'Because you don't have a choice. One call to social services and I could make a world of trouble for you, and you know it,' she warned. 'Or we can work together. Like your dad and my mum did.'

'By all accounts, your mother was a brilliant woman,' Darkus said, examining her doubtfully.

'I know that,' Tilly said, biting her lip – something Darkus had seen her do before when she was under stress. Her eyes suddenly welled up, but she controlled them. 'Maybe some of it's rubbed off.'

'You're resourceful,' he admitted, 'if lacking in some

of the qualities of a seasoned investigator.'

'Like what?'

'Patience. A firm rein on your emotions.'

'Don't underestimate emotions. You and your dad could use some.'

'Emotions are unpredictable,' Darkus answered. 'We're disciples of reason.'

'Evil can't always be reasoned with.'

Darkus nodded, realising she could be right.

'Look, I've only got a matter of hours before Dad realises I've gone AWOL. If we're done negotiating, can we get out of here? I'm not getting any younger.'

# Chapter 11
## PRELUDE TO A CLUE

Darkus used the secure phone to email Tilly's tip-off to
Uncle Bill, then led her by Tube to his father's office. On
the way, he gave her a brief account of his investigation
into *The Code* and the strange occurrences surrounding
it – much of which she had already pieced together from
her own research. She absorbed the rest of the information with a minimum of expression, aside from the
intermittent readjustment of her hair.

Darkus concluded his account by counselling against
a rush to judgement on the supernatural qualities of the
book. However, Tilly confessed that she was quite open-
minded when it came to paranormal phenomena, and in
fact the five senses would never be enough to account
for every unexplained incident in the world. Darkus
resolved to prove his point with hard evidence, as and
when it presented itself.

As dusk fell, they arrived at 27 Cherwell Place, and

Darkus rang on the narrow blue door. On cue, Bogna's voice came through the intercom.

'Knightley Investigations, hello?'

'It's Doc,' he replied, and the door buzzed open.

Having thought she'd seen enough ghosts for one week, Bogna beheld Tilly and did another double take. 'Mój Boże, it is . . .'

'Tilly.' She extended her hand. 'Nice to meet you again.'

'Mój Boże . . .' Bogna repeated, shaking her head in amazement. She fastened the strings of her apron and asked Darkus, 'I make extra round of sandwich, yes?'

Darkus nodded. 'How's Dad?'

'They bring him in his taxi-car. He upstair now. He hasn't made a peeps. Not even when I give him bed bath.'

'I'd like to see him.'

Bogna led Darkus upstairs to his father's office, where Knightley's unconscious form was laid out on the sofa, still wrapped in the tartan blanket. His motionless face was raised to the heavens, his jaw proud and composed, his chest heaving and falling at regular intervals. His brow was furrowed, as if the inner workings of his mind were engaged in a conundrum that required every last reserve of his power – even having stolen the use of his body.

Darkus felt the familiar sick feeling in his stomach and went to rest his hand on Knightley's shoulder. His dad felt warm, but inert – just as he had for those four long years.

Tilly watched quietly from a distance, unsure how to react.

Bogna stomped in carrying a large TV, which she set up on a chair by the sofa.

'I make it as homely as possibles.' She plugged it in, then slapped her hand against her forehead, remembering something. 'The book you ask for – I have.' She exited the room, returning moments later with a Waterstones bag.

'Is that what I think it is?' asked Tilly.

Darkus reached inside and took out a fresh copy of *The Code*. 'I had to purchase it at random,' he explained, 'in order to validate the test.'

'What test?' said Tilly.

'Well, first I'm going to read it. And then so are you,' he said calmly. 'At the first sign of madness, the sensible party must restrain the insensible one until the police arrive.'

Tilly looked at him, incredulous. 'You're serious?'

Darkus nodded. 'Obviously if we both suffer symptoms, it'll be up to you, Bogna.'

'*Mój Boże* . . .' She crossed herself and descended the stairs again.

'Good.' Darkus took a seat at his father's desk and angled a reading lamp.

Tilly's phone started vibrating and the word *Dad!* filled the screen. She clicked to reject the call. 'Have I got time to freshen up?'

'The bathroom's across the landing,' said Darkus. 'I'll read slowly.'

A thundering on the stairs heralded Bogna's arrival with a tray of mixed sandwiches cut into triangles. 'The brown bread is dinner and the white is dessert,' she announced.

'I don't eat wheat,' said Tilly.

Bogna cocked her head, while Darkus ignored the comment. 'Thank you, Bogna. It's going to be a long night.'

He opened the book at page one, and began to read, impatient to find out what was inside. The first line began:

*Change your life now.*

It was an effective opening. Intrigued, he continued.

*You hold the key to unlocking your future, your power, your potential. 'The Code' has been handed down over thousands of years*

*in order to find its way into your hands
right now . . .*

He skimmed to the next page.

*The wise always listen to their inner voice,
because it's the sound of the universe speaking
to you. And it never lies. The voice is telling you that whatever you want can be yours,
if you want it enough . . .*

Darkus wanted to find the answer to this book; he
knew that much.

*Make what you want the only thought in
your mind. Imagine your brain is a transmitter,
transmitting only positive messages.*

Darkus felt lulled by the monotony of the book's unre-
lenting message. It was a selfish message, thinly disguised
as New Age philosophy and rammed home with the
persistence of a jackhammer.

But it was having no sinister effect on him. There was
nothing inherently evil about this book.

Fifteen minutes later, Tilly returned to the room as a brunette and was mildly peeved that Darkus didn't appear to notice her transformation. His gaze remained focused on the book, his eyes steadily flicking left to right.

She examined him once more, just to be sure he wasn't undergoing any transformations himself. Satisfied, she curled up in an armchair with her phone, while Darkus speed-read late into the night.

Bogna returned several hours later to find the investigators asleep. She examined them carefully for any unusual symptoms, then reached in her apron and quietly applied cling film to the tray of sandwiches.

'Sleep tights,' she whispered, and closed the door behind her.

Darkus and Tilly were woken in the early hours with a start by the Armageddon-like ring of the secure phone. Bogna appeared through the door in a flash. Knightley was in the exact same position as before; Tilly pulled a pillow over her head, while Darkus fumbled and answered the call.

'Hello?'

'Aye, good morning tae ye,' Uncle Bill's voice blurted.

Darkus rubbed his eyes and tried to focus. 'Based on the information ye supplied,' Bill went on, 'we nou have an address under roond-the-clock surveillance. We believe one suspect's in the hoose, and the other's in the vicinity. There's still a chance they have the Knowledge on them. There's a car waiting outside for ye.'

The suspects' address was an anonymous suburban house off a busy ring road on the edge of the city. A nondescript Ford saloon pulled up at the end of the street, then Darkus and Tilly got out of the back and walked towards a white Transit van parked on the corner. The van had a ladder strapped to the roof and a builder behind the wheel with his feet on the dashboard, reading a tabloid newspaper. The builder glanced over his paper and discreetly nodded to Darkus, who opened the rear door for Tilly, then climbed in behind her.

The back of the van was lined with TV monitors and surveillance equipment. Uncle Bill was compressed into a wheelie chair beside a lanky male technician at a computer keyboard.

Bill attempted to swivel his chair. 'A'right, Doc. I'd offer ye a seat, but . . .' He trailed off, gesturing to the cramped confines.

'Proceed,' said Darkus.

Bill craned to look at Tilly. 'Aye, yer Internet Proty-col address led us here, to a safe hoose of some kind. Yoo're looking at the first suspect, Bogey One . . .'

The main monitor displayed an image of the house, but painted in blues, oranges and reds, as seen through the lens of a thermal imaging camera. Heat rose in pink waves from a radiator, and a glowing male figure, Bogey One, sat on a sofa, watching an orange square: his TV.

Bill pointed an unlit cigar at the screen. 'What yoo're seeing is the individual heat signature of the suspect —'

'I know,' said Tilly. 'I've got an app like that on my phone.'

'Aye,' said Bill, slightly deflated. 'Bogey Tway is being tailed on the high street tway kilometres from us.' He pointed to another monitor, which showed a surveillance image of the taller suspect, Bogey Two, walking past a row of shops carrying a large sports bag.

'It's them all right,' Tilly confirmed. 'What are we waiting for? Let's make the grab.'

'We're keeping a safe distance,' Bill explained, 'till we know what's in the bag.'

'Sounds logical,' said Darkus.

'In the meantime, Doc, I suggest ye tway approach the safe hoose and attempt a swatch.'

Darkus and Tilly looked at each other, unsure of exactly what Bill had said.

133

'You want *us* to go in?' said Tilly.

'Nae one suspects a kid.'

'He's right,' agreed Darkus.


Back at the office, Knightley's chest heaved and fell at long intervals. Bogna sighed mournfully from an armchair, then slotted a videotape into the machine at the base of the TV, which was set up at the end of the sofa. A dated-looking title sequence appeared on the screen, and she sat up in her seat a little.

A large clock dial filled the frame, surrounded by a jumble of letters and numbers. A punchy theme tune accompanied the ticking clock, then ended with a flourish as the letters came together to form the title. The presenter smiled at the camera. 'Hello, and welcome to *Countdown*.'

Bogna produced a notepad and pen and prepared to join in.

The presenter continued: '. . . the game where the right *combination* of letters or numbers will put one of our contestants in the champion's chair . . .'

Bogna hovered over the notepad with her pen poised.

Knightley's eyelids fluttered with an eddy of recognition. His right hand tensed up into a silent gesture.

On the screen, a male contestant said, 'Can I have a consonant, please?'

From the sofa, Knightley's lips began to curl into a malformed word. 'Coh . . .' He repeated: 'Coh . . . mmm . . . !'

Bogna started: '*Matka!*'

'Coh . . . mmmmmm . . . ! The Combination!' Knightley sat bolt upright, causing Bogna to scream.

'Alan!!'

'What am I doing here? Where's Darkus?' Knightley threw off the tartan blanket and looked around.


Darkus and Tilly stepped out of the back of Bill's white van and walked across the road towards the target address. Tilly went up the garden path first and rang the doorbell. Footsteps could be heard approaching the front door. A few moments later it opened.

'Can I help you?' the stocky suspect demanded, wearing a string vest and permanent-crease trousers.

'We've lost our football,' Tilly announced innocently. 'It went in your back garden.'

The suspect examined them closely, and Tilly tensed up, fearing he might have recognised her. But instead he just looked up and down the street to see if anyone was watching them. 'Well, you'd better come inside and get it.'

'Thanks,' said Tilly, and Darkus hesitantly followed her inside. The door slammed behind them.

In the van, Bill shifted in his wheelie chair, watching their heat signatures on the monitor – which made for uncomfortable viewing. A bagpipe melody announced itself from somewhere on his person, and he started patting himself down until he located his mobile phone and took the call: 'Alan . . . ?!'

Inside the safe house, Darkus instantly detected the acrid smell of body odour, which strangely complemented the familiar metallic taste in his mouth, the slight weakening of his bladder and the constant whirring of the catastrophiser – all signs that indicated only one thing: fear.

'The garden's that way,' said the suspect, pointing to a grubby kitchen.

Black smoke drifted past the back door, from a bonfire of some kind. Darkus and Tilly exchanged a glance. Then Tilly walked through the kitchen to the back garden, while Darkus waited in the living room.

The suspect kept an eye on him, as the news played on the TV in the background. All the curtains were drawn. The rooms and hallways were piled high with cardboard boxes. Darkus decided he would need a better look around.

'Excuse me, sir?' he asked. 'May I use your facilities?'

'Facilities?'

'Your toilet . . . If it's not too much trouble.'

The suspect grimaced. 'Up the stairs, on the right.'

'Much obliged,' said Darkus, and moved towards the hallway.

'Hold on.' The suspect looked down at Darkus's shoes, then back to his face. 'What are you *really* doing here?'

Darkus paused. 'Retrieving a football, just as she said.'

'You play football in *those* shoes?'

Darkus looked down at his flawlessly polished brogues and realised the game was up.

Tilly returned from the back garden empty-handed. 'We must have the wrong house,' she said, until the suspect grabbed her, gagging her with his massive forearm.

'Who sent you?' he demanded, forcibly restraining her.

Darkus answered calmly, 'You can cooperate, or we can make life difficult for you. Your decision.'

'*You?* Make life difficult?'

Darkus turned towards the wall of the living room and waved at it. The suspect watched, baffled.

In the van, Bill saw the brightly coloured shape waving on the monitor and instantly barked into his earpiece, 'Gae, gae, gae!'

In the living room, Darkus turned to see the suspect manhandling Tilly forward, in order to ensnare them

137

both. The catastrophiser was already flicking through potential self-defence scenarios. He remembered the diagram of the fist and the upturned hand from the Knowledge, but now, in the heat of the moment, the surge of adrenalin had left his limbs feeling leaden. Before he could settle on a solution, the front door burst open and the builder from the white van walked straight into the living room. Darkus stood back as the builder took a device from his construction belt and aimed it at the suspect. Tilly stamped her boot down on the suspect's foot, dislodging his grip, and stepped to one side. The builder fired, and a pair of Taser wires shot across the room, attaching to the suspect's string vest, and hitting him with several thousand volts of electricity. The suspect fell with a static, clattering sound.

Outside, a black Fairway cab swung round the corner and skidded to a halt. Knightley jumped out of the driver's seat and ran inside, breathless, to find Darkus and Tilly standing over the suspect. He took a moment to examine them.

'You OK?' he gasped.

They nodded.

Darkus took a moment to process his father's features again, hardly believing his eyes. 'You're back.' A child-like smile crossed Darkus's face. But his father appeared more interested in processing the crime scene. Darkus reminded himself that they had a job to do, and both he and his father had to remain professional.

'It would appear a good deal has happened in my absence,' Knightley began.

Uncle Bill appeared behind him, filling the doorway.

Knightley turned to face him. 'Bill, you've got some explaining to do.'

Bill shrugged repentantly. 'Aye, Alan, I know.'

Knightley pointed at Darkus. 'What's he doing here?'

Bill pouted and shifted on his feet.

'He's *thirteen*,' said Knightley.

'He's already building a case,' replied Bill.

'Is that right?' Knightley demanded.

'It's too early to say,' said Darkus. 'But I'm confident I'll find an explanation for the facts.'

Knightley examined his son again, finding him hard to argue with.

'Aye, he's a chip off the old block, Alan.'

'And what's she doing here?' He pointed to Tilly.

'Helping you find your precious hard drive,' she answered. 'This is one of the cops who took it.' She nudged the suspect in the ribs with her boot. The suspect grunted. 'In return, I want the Combination, on a plate,' she continued. 'Served cold.'

'I've got enough on my plate without you, Tilly. Go home. This doesn't concern you.'

'Not until I find the truth.'

'I don't negotiate with teenagers,' said Knightley.

'She's useful, Dad . . .'

Knightley looked from one to the other, possibly wishing he'd stayed asleep. His brows furrowed deeply, doing battle with each other, then he winced and swallowed, coming to a decision.

'OK. I'll agree to this coalition of the willing,' he announced, 'on a trial basis only. And on one condition . . .' He addressed Tilly directly: 'The moment you adversely affect this investigation, in any way, is the moment you cease to be involved in it. Are we clear?'

Tilly nodded. 'Crystal.'

The suspect began to stir, finding the Taser wires still attached.

Knightley knelt beside him. 'Where's the Knowledge?!' The suspect twitched but didn't answer. 'The hard drive – what have you done with it?' The suspect kept his mouth shut. Knightley moved back and grimly nodded to the builder, who prepared to use the Taser again.

'Wait!' shouted the suspect. 'It's in the garden.' He gestured towards the smoke drifting past the back door.

Knightley followed the trail outside to a makeshift bonfire, which was by now only a collection of dimly glowing embers. Darkus arrived behind him and immediately recognised the leather carrying case discarded nearby. In the centre of the funeral pyre were the cremated remains of the hard drive, its circular disk melted beyond repair, its contents rising into the sky along with the last wisps of smoke.

'No . . .' whispered Knightley, defeated. He turned back to the house, his eyes glittering.

Darkus returned to the living room and stood over the suspect. 'Who told you to do it?' he asked. 'Who are you working for?'

'The *book* . . .' muttered the suspect. 'The book told me to do it.'

Knightley cocked his head and leaned in next to his son. '*What* book?'

'*The Code* . . .'

Darkus went over to one of the cardboard boxes and lifted the lid, taking out a brand-new copy of the book from the top of the pile. Tilly opened another box, finding another batch of copies.

'We found the same thing at the bank robber's house,' Darkus explained.

'Aye,' confirmed Bill.

'I read it myself, last night,' said Darkus. His father's eyes went wide. 'Don't worry, it had no effect.'

'Singular,' said Knightley and stared off into the middle distance, entering his customary state of complete absorption.

'Is he all right?' Tilly asked Darkus. 'He's not going to sleep again, is he?'

Knightley raised a finger to shush her.

'Strange forces are at work . . . And only one organisation comes to mind: the Combination. At first it was only supposition. Now it's probability.' Knightley looked down at the suspect prone on the floor. 'Did the book talk to your partner as well?'

'No,' replied the suspect. 'He never read it. He said he only takes orders from the top.'

Darkus and his father exchanged a look. Darkus turned to Bill. 'Where is Bogey Two now?'


Less than a minute later, the white van arrived at the edge of an urban park, and the Knightleys quietly exited the rear of the vehicle with Tilly in tow.

They approached the centre of the park and found the second suspect in plain view, standing by a tarmacked recreation area. Knightley raised his hand to signal a halt and they took cover under an elm tree. He then reached into his pocket and took out a small pair of binoculars, focusing them on the scene. Darkus reached in his own pocket, took out his own pair and did the same. Tilly looked at the two of them, identically posed, their faces pressed against the eyecups.

'What can you see?' she asked.

Through the binoculars, Bogey Two approached a group of half a dozen teenagers in hooded tops loitering by the wire fence. The group exchanged words with him, obviously warning him off, but instead of leaving he unslung his sports bag and knelt down.

'He's opening the bag,' observed Darkus.

Bogey Two unzipped the bag and reached inside. Darkus and his father both tensed up behind their lenses as the suspect's gloved hand took out a copy of *The Code*.

'It's the book again,' said Darkus.

The suspect took out another half-dozen copies and began distributing them to the teenagers, who turned them over in their hands uncertainly. Before the teens could react, they were interrupted by a piercing, high-pitched whistle. Knightley's binoculars panned wildly to locate the source. Darkus's lenses zeroed in on a nine-year-old boy standing lookout on a park bench, who was now stabbing an accusing finger in their direction.

'We've been spotted,' said Darkus.

The hooded tops looked in the direction of the Knightleys, then scattered. Meanwhile, Bogey Two zipped up his sports bag, slung it over his shoulder and sprinted away across the park.

'Come on!' shouted Knightley, and took off after the suspect, but almost instantly lagged behind, clutching a

143

stitch. Darkus and Tilly quickly overtook him. 'Wait!' he shouted after them.

Bogey Two approached a children's playground, hurdled a see-saw and continued towards the main road. Darkus and Tilly deviated around the playground and moved to cut him off, with Knightley loping after them hopelessly.

Bogey Two turned back to see them in pursuit, tripped, nearly lost his footing, then pressed on and swung himself over the fence on to the pavement by the main road.

He looked left and right, weighing his options.

The white van accelerated out of an intersection, taking up position at one end of the street, marking its territory. The Ford saloon pulled up at the other end, blocking the way.

Darkus and Tilly reached the fence, unsure what to do next.

'Wait!' wheezed Knightley, catching up with them.

Bogey Two looked right, looked left, looked right again, then ran straight across the road – not seeing a large London bus that was barrelling down its own lane, in the blind side behind the van. Bogey Two felt a gust of wind, heard an almighty screech of brakes and a horn blast; he looked up at the red double-decker, then glanced down at the brown tarmac

– which meant he was in a bus lane – then looked up again for the last time.

Knightley instinctively held out his hands to cover Darkus and Tilly's eyes as a dull *whump* accompanied the suspect's disappearance under the vehicle.

The bus barely registered the obstacle and lumbered to a halt at the side of the road. Darkus and Tilly parted Knightley's fingers and peered out at the scene.

Bogey Two had been reduced to little more than a crumpled suit, blessedly face down in the road. The body was intact, and there was a remarkable lack of blood visible, but there was no doubt he was dead. His sports bag was almost a hundred metres away, its contents discarded on the pavement, the book pages ruffling in the wind.

Darkus felt a rush of fear again. It was a definite, physical response: a prickling sensation across the back of his neck, accompanied by an increased pulse in his chest and ears. He controlled himself, remembering that although this was the first dead body he'd been unfortunate enough to encounter, he had spent a good part of the last four years in the presence of his father, who, to all intents and purposes, had been dead too.

'Stay here,' ordered Knightley.

Tilly looked nauseous, finding herself unexpectedly jarred. Passengers started spilling out of the bus to see what had happened.

'We mustn't let them corrupt the scene,' said Darkus.

'What about *it* corrupting *you*?'

Darkus ignored his father and walked towards the body through the growing crowd of bystanders.

'Doc!' Knightley went after him, while Tilly waited on the sidelines.

Bogey Two's pockets had been emptied by the force of the impact, spewing keys, cash and bits of paper across the street, as if his whole person had been turned inside out and scattered for all to see.

Darkus knelt by the body, completely focused on the job at hand. He didn't want to admit it, but the feeling of fear wasn't altogether unpleasant.

'Don't touch,' said Knightley.

'I won't,' replied Darkus, taking out a pair of tweezers and carefully combing through the detritus that had formed a circle around the body.

'Careful.'

'It's OK, Dad.' Darkus kept following the trail of paper with his tweezers, finding supermarket receipts, wadded-up money, confectionery wrappers, until he paused, locating a rolled-up piece of paper with something scrawled on it. He gently unrolled it to reveal a note that said:

*Star lot, Regency. 7.30 p.m.*

# Chapter 12
## GONE TO THE MAN
## IN BLACK

As clues go, this one needed little unravelling. The world-famous Regency Auction House, located in South Kensington, was holding a special event at seven thirty that evening. The event was a charity gala auction to raise money for a London children's hospital. Only hours earlier, the surprise 'star lot' of the evening had been unveiled: a signed first edition of the bestselling book *The Code* by Ambrose Chambers – the only known signed copy in existence. Regrettably, Ambrose Chambers himself was unavailable to attend due to travel and work commitments. All proceeds from the event would go towards paediatric research into the most virulent of childhood afflictions, a cause whose merit few could deny.

Knightley drove Darkus and Tilly to the venue in his cab, occasionally observing Tilly suspiciously in the rear-view mirror. The fare on the meter had now ticked up to £500.40. Darkus took the opportunity to brief his father on every relevant detail of the case so far. Knightley digested the facts and found no fault with his reasoning.

'First rate, Doc.'

'Thanks, Dad.'

Knightley then described the unusual circumstances of his latest wake-up call, and the fact that his only recollections of the recent trance were two things.

'The number 2. And the letter D,' said Knightley, mystified.

Even for Darkus, these two characters were too obscure to decipher, but he reassured his dad that whatever the meaning, they would work it out. Together.

Darkus observed that the last time they'd travelled in the cab, his father had kept the glass divider closed, keeping a safe distance between them: a clear partition between their two worlds. But now it was different – the glass divider was open. They were more than father and son. They were partners.

The plan was for the Knightleys to pose as prospective bidders. Bill would be confined to the van, monitoring the surveillance systems. *The Code* was sure to attract a good deal of attention, especially among those who viewed it with an almost religious fervour. These were the very people the Knightleys were seeking to investigate.

In private, Knightley explained to Darkus that if Bogey Two had been ordered to attend the auction, there was little doubt that the Combination had an interest in it, and other enemy agents would almost certainly be in place. However, they were still nowhere near a credible theory to explain *The Code*, the Combination, or the crimes. Knightley reminded him that the possibility of supernatural forces could not be dismissed.

Also in private, Bill explained to Darkus that his father's obsession with the mysterious organisation was still a belief based on conjecture, not fact; there was no evidence at all of supernatural involvement; and Knightley's faculties were still impaired, and could not be relied upon.

For his part, Darkus decided to focus on the facts alone and forgo interpretation until a logical solution presented itself.

While Knightley went to examine the auction room, Darkus walked through the corridors and galleries to find Tilly sitting in the foyer surrounded by other bidders – all (including her) were reading *The Code*.

'Any symptoms?' he asked her.

'Actually I quite like it,' she said, without looking up from the book. Darkus's brows furrowed. 'I'm just messing with you,' she admitted with a smile. 'It's everything that's wrong with the world.' Her phone started vibrating again, and the word *Dad!* flashed up on screen. She quickly rejected the call.

'How many times has he called?' said Darkus.

'Sixty-three so far.'

'At least he cares.'

'He said if I ran away again he'd send me back to Cranston permanently. Looks like it's "go to jail" time.'

'Freedom's a state of mind,' said Darkus.

'Where's that from?'

'Krishnamurti. He's an Indian spiritual thinker.'

She looked him up and down. 'You've got even more hidden in that brain than I thought.'

'Thanks,' said Darkus, unsure whether it was a compliment.

'I guess you can't judge a book by its cover,' she concluded.

'It would seem not.'

'I thought I could handle anything. I mean, have you seen what people post on YouTube? But that dead guy. That was something else.'

'I suppose I'm just a bit more familiar with that sort of thing.'

'How?' she asked, puzzled.

'From the Knowledge.' He shrugged. 'I guess you could say I know a bit about a lot of things. Or, conversely . . .

not much about anything.' He looked unhappy at his own deduction.

'Relax. Most people don't know anything about anything.'

'Very true,' said Darkus.

'You know, this is easily the longest conversation we've ever had?'

'It's also the longest you've gone between hair colours. The brunette does suit you though.'

'You noticed.'

'It's my business to notice.'

They stood opposite each other, and anyone who had known Knightley and his former assistant Carol could have been forgiven for seeing an uncanny resemblance in Darkus and Tilly.

'Well, we'd better take a seat,' said Darkus. 'The auction's about to begin.'

'You go ahead. I'm going to finish this chapter.'

Darkus nodded and started making his way through the crowd towards the main gallery, until a hand stopped his arm.

'Darkus?' A male voice interrupted him. 'Darkus Knightley?'

Darkus turned to see a medium-sized, middle-aged man standing before him, wearing a dark suit and trench coat. He had short-clipped, dark hair and bottle-top glasses that enlarged his eyes unnaturally in proportion to the rest of his face. The result was that his features were almost impossible to describe, and Darkus would later have trouble remembering the exact details of his face – which was most unlike him. The stranger was virtually motionless, which lent the effect that his clothes hung off him like a scarecrow's, and gave very little impression as to what, if anything, lay beneath.

The crowd moved around the two of them as if they weren't there.

'Do I know you?' asked Darkus.

'I'm a f-friend of the family,' said the man, with a slight stutter. 'You probably don't remember me.'

'What's your name?'

'Names aren't important. What is important is the Knowledge.' The man studied Darkus's expression for any reaction.

'I don't know what you're talking about.'

'You're a very clever boy,' the man continued, 'but I've been watching you. In fact, I was watching you at Shrubwoods Hospice. I *know* that you know about the Knowledge.' The man's features spread into a broad grin that made his face resemble an excavated skull.

'The Knowledge has been destroyed,' said Darkus.

'Not entirely. It still exists inside your head,' the man countered, examining Darkus like a lab specimen.

'Which is why I must warn you that any f-further inter-ference by you in this matter will jeopardise both your life and your f-father's.'

Darkus felt a familiar chill down his spine, accompanied by the prickling sensation at the back of his neck. 'Why don't you come and talk to my father? I'm sure he'd be happy to discuss it with you.'

'No, that won't be necessary. If you end this investiga-tion now, I won't need to interfere in your life again. However, if you persist, I guarantee you will lose your f-father all over again – at best, to another coma; at worst, to a more . . . permanent state of unconsciousness.'

'Who are you . . . ?' demanded Darkus.

'Do as I say, and spare yourself and your f-father a world of trouble,' he warned him. 'Enjoy your evening . . .' He turned away and rejoined the flow of people. Darkus tried to follow, but within seconds the stranger had been completely absorbed by the crowd.

A moment later, Darkus was already struggling to recall the details of his face.

What he was left with, however, was a sizeable dilemma . . .

If he told his father about this stark warning, the investigation would be aborted and Darkus's relation-ship with his dad would return to the everyday, becoming a faint shadow of its current incarnation. The case would remain unsolved, and all the possibilities of their working partnership would be banished to the realms of 'what if'. However, if Darkus concealed the warning long enough to gather the necessary evidence, he could buy himself enough time to solve the case *and* cement the partnership with his father for good. This second option was too tempting to pass up, and Darkus was confident that he would find a solution before the stranger's threat became a reality.

Besides, a 'world of trouble' was still more appealing than a return to the domestic monotony of Wolseley Close.

Darkus walked into the auction room with the secret weighing heavily on him. He sat beside his father at the back as the audience shifted in their seats and shuffled their catalogues. Bidding on the lesser items was already under way, proceeding swiftly and efficiently under the direction of a portly auctioneer in a three-piece suit. Above the podium a large screen displayed a picture of each item, from weekend getaways to collectible memorabilia. A security guard stood in the shadows backstage with his arms crossed.

Knightley's nostrils flared as he scanned the faces of the prospective bidders, who all appeared to be extremely wealthy. He noted every minor tic, as they raised their hands, competing to outbid each other. Knightley's fierce expression was punctuated only by the report of the auctioneer's gavel on the block, which caused a minute twitch with each hit.

Meanwhile, Darkus scanned the room for the man who had delivered the stark warning, but failed to find him. Tilly snuck in and sat beside him.

'Anything to report?' Darkus whispered.

She shook her head. '*Nada.*'

'Remember, tonight is for the children,' the auctioneer announced. 'Do I hear fifteen to benefit the children? Fifteen.' He pointed to a bidder in the centre of the crowd. 'I have fifteen. Do I hear seventeen?'

A bidder in the front row raised his hand.

'Seventeen from the front row. Seventeen? Any more bids?' He paused another few moments, then slammed the gavel on the block. 'Seventeen.'

The auctioneer did a pirouette, eliciting careless applause from the crowd.

'As you know, tonight is a very special night,' he went on, 'and one particular lot I know is of great interest to many of you . . . I refer, of course, to the signed first edition of *The Code* by Ambrose Chambers.' The crowd cooed and rumbled. 'As I'm sure you know, Mr Chambers is a very private – let's be honest, a *completely* private man. But fortunately for us, his literary agent Bram Beecham was generous enough to contact Mr Chambers to procure us this very sought-after and unique item.' Darkus and his father exchanged a glance. 'And I might add,' the auctioneer continued, 'that tonight's cause is one that is especially close to Mr Beecham's heart as he lost his own beloved daughter Samantha to leukaemia two years ago. So let's pay a special tribute to her and say a heartfelt thank-you to Mr Bram Beecham.' The auctioneer pointed off towards the back of the crowd. 'Bram?'

Sitting at the end of a row, finding himself almost launched to his feet by the crowd, Beecham reluctantly took a bow, looking as if he would rather be anywhere else on earth.

'Thank you, Bram,' said the auctioneer, as Beecham quickly sat down again. 'So, let's take a look at what we've all been waiting for . . .'

An auction assistant walked on to the stage carrying a small black leather case. Simultaneously a photograph appeared on the screen overhead, showing the title page, clearly signed:

*Know The Code.*
*Ambrose Chambers. 19th October 2015.*

The auctioneer made a show of opening the case. 'Without further ado, may I present *The Code* by Ambrose Chambers. A motivational – nay, inspirational

– book, based on ancient mystical wisdom drawn from across the globe. A phenomenon that is currently topping the bestseller lists. I have here a signed first edition. The only one in existence.'

The auctioneer held up the book, opened it to the signature page and displayed it to the audience, which in turn descended into reverent silence, underlaid by the faint hum of bidders fanning themselves with catalogues.

'Dad,' whispered Darkus.

'Yes.'

'Beecham told me he hadn't had any contact with Chambers for months. But the signature's dated three days ago,' said Darkus, indicating the image on the screen.

'Then it would appear Beecham was being economical with the truth.'

The auctioneer solemnly closed the book and replaced it in the black leather case.

'The bidding opens at ten thousand pounds. Do I hear ten?' A hand went up in the aisle. 'Ten.' Now a catalogue was raised. 'Fifteen . . .' Another hand leaped up. 'Twenty. I have twenty. I have twenty-five.'

A sea of hands began darting up across the room, so fast that Darkus couldn't keep track of them. Each bidder appeared to be outfitted in either a dark suit or a black dress; each appeared equally sinister or equally innocent, depending on how one chose to view them.

'Thirty. Thirty-five!' called the auctioneer.

As the bids arrived in rapid succession, Knightley fell into a state of extreme concentration – or extreme confusion; it was hard to tell which. The slew of numbers being shouted and hands fanning catalogues seemed to have lulled him into a trance.

Darkus and Tilly both noticed it, turning to him.

'Knightley?' said Tilly.

'Dad . . . ?'

'Fifty!' announced the auctioneer, pointing to a woman on the front row.

'Dad,' Darkus repeated. 'Say something . . .'

Knightley stared through the sea of hands, beyond the podium and the auctioneer, right to the very back of the stage.

'Presto,' he said mysteriously.

'*What?*' Darkus and Tilly said in unison.

'Presto,' he repeated.

'What's he going on about?' asked Tilly. 'Is he having one of his –?'

'I don't know –'

'I'm perfectly fine,' responded Knightley, staying focused on the back of the stage. 'I've just spotted the Combination, that's all,' he said calmly.

'Fifty! I have fifty thousand,' the auctioneer repeated exultantly, pointing to the woman on the front row.

'Where?!' Darkus whispered to his father.

'Mr Presto. He's extremely tall, with shoulder-length hair and a goatee beard, and he's standing on that stage right now.'

'I don't see him,' said Tilly.

Darkus mentally flicked through the contents of the Knowledge until he reached the letter P. 'Presto . . . the illusionist . . . from the Disappearance of the Chancellor's Briefcase.'

'Can someone *please* tell me what we're talking about?' demanded Tilly.

'Presto is number two at the Combination,' explained Knightley, turning to her impatiently.

'If he's number two, who's number one?' she asked.

'I don't know. That's the thing about the Combination, it's always changing,' snapped Knightley. 'What I *do* know is that Presto's taken the place of that security guard.' He pointed to the back of the stage.

'What security guard?' said Darkus.

Knightley looked up to find the guard had vanished. 'Ye gods . . .'

'Fifty thousand,' the auctioneer repeated. 'Going. Going . . .' He slammed the gavel on the block. 'Go–'

The auctioneer stopped dead in his tracks and looked down at the podium.

'It's *gone!*'

The black leather case containing the book was no longer in front of him. The audience burst into fits of laughter and applause, thinking it was a joke.

'No. It really is gone!' the auctioneer shouted, looking about wildly, then calling frantically for the guards positioned around the room. 'Security!'

Darkus stood up to get a better view. The audience looked at each other as the applause quickly petered out and was replaced by a piercing burglar alarm.

'Hurry,' said Knightley, and started wading through the tide of bewildered bidders who were now flooding the exits.

Darkus and Tilly made their way through the melee of tailored suits and dresses. A woman in pearls shoved Tilly out of the way, and Tilly shoved her back, shouting, 'Hey, watch it, lady!'

Over the well-coiffed heads, Knightley spotted an unusually tall man in a security guard's outfit, walking in the opposite direction to everyone else, heading backstage. The trio set off after him, pushing through a set of double doors into a long corridor hung with fine art. Presto was already at the other end of it, his bony limbs running in long, measured strides, the leather briefcase in his hand.

'We've got you surrounded!' called out Knightley.

Presto let out a laugh and burst through another set of double doors, going deeper into the building.

'Why do they have to run . . . ?' moaned Knightley as they kept after him. Presto led them down another passageway, past a row of sculptures, around a corner; then Knightley stopped dead, grabbing Darkus and Tilly by the scruff of the neck, as Presto faced them at the end of the corridor, his shoulder-length hair half concealed, sticking out from under the security guard's hat.

'Stop chasing, Alan,' warned Presto. 'For your own good.'

'What are you talking about?' shouted Knightley, breathless.

Presto smiled and turned away, parting a pair of heavy velvet curtains and slipping through them.

The trio raced after him, beating back the curtains to find a narrow walkway and a black door. Darkus reached out and yanked the handle, but the door opened straight on to a brick wall. There was no doorway.

'Where'd he go?' demanded Tilly.

'His escape route was planned,' Knightley replied, testing the strength of the bricks, then pressing his foot against the linoleum floor. 'He could be anywhere by now.' He examined the ceiling, then ran his hand over the wall, finding nothing.

'People don't just disappear,' Tilly protested.

Darkus answered for his father: 'Presto does.'

\*

Bill met them at the security office located at the back of the auction house.

'We cannae see him on the cameras.'

'That's no great surprise,' said Knightley. 'What about Beecham?'

'Ah dinna know he was a suspect.'

'Everyone's a suspect,' Knightley reminded him. 'Put a unit outside his address.'

Meanwhile, Darkus was lost in thought; his eyes narrowed, his nostrils flared. 'When Beecham put that first edition up for auction, he set a cat among the pigeons. Someone wanted it taken off the market . . . The question is why.' He assembled his thoughts, then turned to the auction house's Head of Security, who was holding his head in his hands. 'I need that photograph of the title page with Chambers's signature on it.'

'Of course. If it would be of any use,' the man replied remorsefully.

'I believe it might,' said Darkus, as the man left to fetch the evidence.

'What are you thinking, Doc?' enquired Knightley.

'It's not about what I *think*, it's about what I can *prove*.'

'Sound familiar?' Bill asked Knightley with a wink.

'All too familiar,' replied Knightley, his pride shaded by the faintest tinge of professional jealousy.

'He's his father's son; ye can be sure of that.'

Tilly looked at her phone nervously, then turned to Darkus. 'I'm running out of time.'

'I'm afraid you are,' said Knightley, and nodded privately to Bill.

Bill frowned and opened the door to reveal Clive, looking exasperated in a crimson shell suit.

Tilly froze, momentarily disorientated. 'Dad . . . ?' Then she spun to face Knightley. 'You told him where I am! You sold me out –'

'I told you,' he replied firmly, 'that the moment you adversely affected this investigation, you would cease to be involved in it.'

'Investigation?' said Clive.

'What did I do?' Tilly demanded.

'You were clearly uncomfortable at the crime scene,' said Knightley.

'Crime scene?!' protested Clive.

'We had a deal!' Tilly shouted.

'That is as it may be,' said Knightley. 'But although Darkus has performed adequately in your presence, the fact is that without distraction he may perform even better. I can't have his judgement biased.' Knightley shrugged by way of apology. 'I'm afraid I can't afford the responsibility, Tilly.'

Tilly flushed with anger, and Clive moved towards her diplomatically, using her given name. 'Now come on,

Matilda,' he suggested, 'let's be grown up about this. There's no need to get all . . . wobbly.'

Tilly ignored him and looked to Darkus, who shook his head to indicate he had no prior knowledge of the betrayal. Then she looked back to Knightley, finding her resolve.

'Well, when you need help – and you will – you'll know where to find me,' she said, and brushed past Clive. 'Don't worry, I'll come quietly.' She surrendered, flashing the briefest of smiles at Darkus as she marched out.

'Now look here, Alan,' began Clive. 'This won't get past Jackie. She wants Darkus home in one piece. You can't be involving kids in your . . . weird stuff. We'll be having words, you and me –'

'I dare say we will, but until then, you're interfering with my investigation. Bill, please show them out.'

'Aye, Alan,' said Bill, and manoeuvred his bulk into the doorway, prompting Clive to retreat.

'Now to business,' said Knightley, nodding to Darkus as Bill closed the door, leaving the two of them in private.

'She was useful, Dad,' said Darkus, finding it impossible to look him in the eye.

'She was distracting, Doc. As female counterparts frequently are. Now, we have a case to solve.'

In the blizzard of preceding events, Darkus had forgotten just how cold his father could be when it came to work. Despite all the changes that the last four years had wrought on Darkus, and the unique set of skills he'd acquired, he had somehow overlooked the simple fact that his dad was exactly the same as he had ever been. And Darkus was still the unappreciated son. He was only useful as a sort of reference manual; as a reminder of his father's career, rather than his family. He was baggage.

The avalanche of thoughts tumbled together to form one logical conclusion: that the only way Darkus could truly prove himself to his father was to break the case on his own.

As if Knightley had divined what his son was thinking, he glanced at him across the room. 'A penny for your thoughts, Doc.'

Darkus decided that if all his dad cared about was work, then that was all they would discuss. 'Clearly Beecham is protecting Chambers. Now we must determine if Chambers is somehow responsible for the criminal behaviour of his readers.'

'And how the Combination is involved,' added Knightley.

'I'm yet to see definitive evidence of a larger organisation behind *The Code*,' said Darkus.

Of course, Darkus knew full well there was evidence of a larger organisation, based on the stranger's warning in the foyer. But childish as it might have seemed, he wanted to punish his father for banishing Tilly, in the only way he knew how.

'The evidence is clear,' said Knightley. 'The Special Constables who destroyed the Knowledge were instructed to do so by *The Code*. Now Presto has stolen the only signed copy. *Quod erat demonstrandum*,' he concluded in Latin.

'*Quod* non *erat demonstrandum*,' Darkus argued. 'It is *not* fully proved. The evidence is circumstantial. At this point it could be coincidence.'

Darkus knew that without the complete picture, his father would be unable to contradict him.

'You're letting your emotions get in the way of your reasoning, Doc,' Knightley reprimanded.

'No, Dad, you are. You always said the facts must infer the theory . . . not the other way around. You believe in the Combination; therefore you believe it is responsible for everything that's happened.'

Darkus was painfully aware of the fact that by ignoring the stranger's warning his emotions *had* got the better of him, but on this occasion he couldn't allow his father to win.

'I do believe the Combination is involved,' Knightley said frankly. 'I wish I was wrong.'

'You said it yourself.' Darkus quoted from the Knowledge: '"The vast majority of cases point to the *lack* of criminal organisation in the world; the lack of higher reasoning and the predominance of chance."' He paused, constructing his argument for maximum impact. 'You may have seen Presto, but no one else can identify him. If it was Presto, he may have been here for the purposes of petty theft, nothing more. Either way, there is still no evidence of a larger organisation – certainly not one with supernatural powers.'

Knightley sighed, losing patience. 'There are monsters, Doc, just like the ones they talk about in bedtime stories, only these ones are real. As real as you and me, and they're organised; they move in packs. You might not believe me – most people don't, because they won't allow themselves to.' He paused. 'The greatest mercy bestowed on mankind is that their minds aren't open enough to see what's around them. But those with an open mind – children, for example – they can see them. And adults, if they look long and hard enough, they can see them too.'

'I suppose seeing is believing,' said Darkus.

The door opened and Uncle Bill rejoined them. 'Tilly's safely on her way tae Cranston School, and there's a unit staking oot Beecham's penthoose.'

Darkus spoke up. 'Tell them we plan to pay Beecham another visit.'

'There's nae sign of him yet,' replied Bill.

'Then we'll wait until there is,' said Darkus, putting on his hat.

# Chapter 13
## AN INTERESTED PARTY

En route, Uncle Bill furnished the Knightleys with some further background on Bram Beecham.

Beecham had worked as a literary agent for over fifteen years and discovered several bestselling authors during that time, launching him to the top of his profession. However, his meteoric rise was interrupted by the tragic death of his daughter Samantha from leukaemia and the subsequent breakdown of his marriage.

It was around this time that Beecham was contacted by a new writer named Ambrose Chambers, who refused to divulge his identity but was believed to be American and evidently had an exceptional gift for motivational writing and an extraordinary array of contacts in the fields of mythology and spirituality. It was from this array of contacts, from far-flung corners of the globe, that Chambers drew together the various threads that would eventually become the literary phenomenon that was *The*

*Code*. For his part, Beecham personally credited Chambers with keeping him on the rails during his tragic trials of fate, and he vowed to bring Chambers's inspirational writings to a wider audience, which he duly did.

The road to publication, however, was not without obstacles. The editor of *The Code*, Lester Norris, died in a car accident one month before the book's release. Other members of the publishing team resigned amid rumours of a curse surrounding the book – rumours that were never substantiated, Uncle Bill was quick to point out.

Chambers himself continued to shy away from any kind of public attention, insisting on being paid through a network of front companies and offshore bank accounts. *The Code*, meanwhile, ascended the bestseller lists, driving Chambers deeper into hiding and leaving Beecham with the unusual dilemma of representing an author who didn't wish to be represented.

The latest turn of events would only have served to heighten Beecham's predicament: how could he defend his author from accusations of inciting criminal acts when his author refused to comment or appear in public? Beecham couldn't betray the man who was not only his most prized client but also the person to whom he felt he owed his own life.

Beecham's penthouse was located in an elegant portered apartment block in Marylebone. Knightley parked the cab on the opposite corner while Darkus and Bill sat in the back seat, observing the scene.

The Transit van was positioned outside the foyer, with two of Bill's officers in the front seats. A dim lampshade was the only sign of life from Beecham's window, which overlooked a modest roof garden and the unobstructed London skyline, lit up in the night.

Meanwhile, Knightley switched on a reading light over the dashboard and opened a copy of *The Code*. Darkus caught a glimpse of his father's eyes moving left to right in the rear-view mirror. Knightley scanned through the first chapter of the book, making disgruntled noises and flicking the pages dismissively. 'Amazing what people choose to read these days,' he complained.

Satisfied that the book was having no ill effects, Darkus trained his binoculars on the apartment block and the surrounding area, employing his catastrophiser to detect anything that might be worthy of note.

His lenses focused on a second black cab pulling up at the kerb outside Beecham's building. A long pair of legs stepped out.

'Dad?' said Darkus.

'Yes?' he answered, without looking up from the book.

'Someone's going inside.'

Bill craned his neck to look out of the window. 'Aye, he's right,' he said with a twinkle in his eye.

The new arrival was dressed in a short business skirt under a raincoat, her stilettos clicking as she paid the cabbie and entered the building.

'Her name's Chloe. She works for Beecham,' Darkus explained, as they watched her cross the foyer and enter the lift.

A moment later, a light flicked on at the summit of the building. Chloe emerged on to the roof garden and posed with one stiletto heel resting on a flowerpot, using a watering can to tend the plants.

Knightley and Uncle Bill both reached for their binoculars and angled them up towards the roof.

'Anything of interest?' Darkus asked, curious.

'No,' both men responded in unison.

Darkus kept his binoculars at street level and noticed a silver minivan with tinted windows. Fumes were rising from the exhaust, but its lights were off.

'Uncle Bill?' he asked.

'Aye?'

Darkus pointed to the silver minivan. 'Is that one of yours?'

Bill adjusted his focus. 'Nae.'

'Then whose is it?' Just visible through the untinted front windscreen, Darkus could detect two middle-aged men also training binoculars on the roof garden.

'Alan,' said Bill, reaching through the glass divider to prod him. 'We've got company.'

Bill and the Knightleys stepped out of the cab and approached the silver minivan.

Bill went first, shielding Darkus with his bulk. He pulled a massive torch from his coat and directed the beam on to the driver and passenger, momentarily blinding them.

'Ho ye. Police. Open up,' he demanded.

Knightley rapped on the back window and the rear doors opened to reveal four middle-aged men, a woman and a young boy, all dressed in matching black hooded robes. None of the occupants seemed alarmed; they merely squinted into the torch beam as it illuminated their faces one by one.

Darkus noticed a line of Latin text embroidered on the arm of the robes. '*Ordo Novi Diluculi*,' he recited, then translated it: 'The Order of the New Dawn.'

'That's right,' said Knightley. 'They're a secret society. Devoted to the study of the occult.'

'In this case, a study of evil forces,' interjected one of the passengers – a gaunt man with greying hair and whiskers, evidently their elder statesman. 'You may remember me, Mr Knightley. My name is Brother Allwyn.'

'I'm afraid I took a rather long sabbatical and my memory's not what it used to be.'

From behind his father, Darkus whispered, 'The Case of the Missing Pharaoh.'

'Ah yes, Brother Allwyn, of course,' said Knightley, feigning recollection. 'How is . . . the pharaoh?'

'*Still* missing,' Allywn said accusingly.

'Ah.'

'It seems we're both here in the same capacity. To locate Ambrose Chambers, and to protect the world from the book.'

'I assume you're referring to *The Code?*' said Knightley. 'I'm reading it right now and find it to be quite harmless.' Darkus realised his father was fishing for a response.

'It is not called *The Code*,' answered Allwyn. 'Chambers has borrowed from a far older text and harnessed its power, moulded it to fit his purpose,' he went on. 'The text has no name, but it has been ubiquitous throughout history. It has been handed down through the generations, by both leaders and despots, guarded by some and coveted by others.'

The youngest member of the group, a boy no older than Darkus, took up the story: 'The original came into the Order's hands several years ago. The Order undertook to guard it, to act as custodian of its secrets and if necessary to destroy it, should it fall into the wrong hands, but in the face of more powerful forces than ours, we failed,' he concluded grimly.

'What kind of forces?' Darkus asked.

The boy hesitated, looking to the elder for permission before responding. 'We don't know. Several unrelated events conspired to deny us possession of the text. It was supposedly lost by a museum in Rome, then incinerated by a fire in a library in Cairo during the Arab Spring. In the absence of any physical evidence, there was no way of confirming whether it survived or not. That is, until certain passages of the text appeared in the manuscript of Ambrose Chambers's book.'

Allwyn twitched his whiskers cryptically. 'As my grandson here says, these were unrelated events, but I for one detect an organisation behind them, a greater, more malevolent force. It's the only explanation.'

Knightley and Darkus looked at each other. Uncle Bill raised an eyebrow. It was clear they were all pondering the spectre of the Combination.

Allwyn glanced about nervously, as if detecting a paranormal presence, then added, 'Whoever is behind this latest incarnation must know that wherever the text goes, it brings only damnation and destruction.'

The words hung in the air like bodies on a gallows.

'I assure you we have only the best intentions,' said Knightley.

Allwyn shook his head. 'Your intentions are of no consequence, Mr Knightley. We've learned that the book

174

has already been linked to several criminal acts, and we believe this is only the beginning. If the text spreads, the inevitable result will be chaos – Armageddon.'

'To what do you attribute these powers?' Darkus demanded. 'Why does the text have this effect? And why not on every reader?'

Allwyn paused before answering. 'I don't know. A curator in Rome was analysing the text when it was stolen. We're convinced it survived the fire in Cairo, and is still out there.'

'And if Chambers didn't write it . . . then who did?' asked Darkus.

'Once again, I don't have that answer for you,' the elder replied.

'Seems like ye don't have much tae go on at all,' observed Bill.

Knightley took a moment to summarise: 'A self-help book for leaders and despots that has been passed around the world for centuries and somehow landed up on the bestseller lists. Sounds a little implausible, even to me.'

Allwyn's grandson mounted a defence: 'Every leader throughout history has harboured their own personal source of inspiration, to feed their thirst for power,' he lectured them. 'For some it was religion, for others it was communing with the supernatural.'

Darkus shrugged. 'Yet every despot, however powerful, has ultimately proved mortal and been defeated by ordinary, often mundane, methods.'

'I assure you there is nothing ordinary about this text,' Allwyn responded. 'It contains magic and necromancy that have baffled some of the greatest minds that ever lived. And in some cases it has infected, consumed and destroyed them.' The elder punctuated the sentence with a grim nod. 'We will not rest until every copy of *The Code* is incinerated, along with the original – if it cannot be adequately protected.'

The Order members in the front seats turned their binoculars to the roof garden, ignoring the detectives. Uncle Bill bristled at this, then a bagpipe ringtone announced itself from somewhere on his person. He began patting himself down, locating his phone in a commodious inside pocket.

'Aye,' he said, answering the call. 'Aye,' he repeated, his eyebrows rising. He stepped away from the minivan privately. 'Aye,' he said conclusively, and ended the call, beckoning the Knightleys to follow him out of earshot.

'What is it?' asked Knightley.

Bill's eyes lit up. 'Bram Beecham. He's contacted Scotland Yard. He wants tae cooperate.'

'Excellent,' said Knightley.

'He's agreed tae meet us here in twintie minutes.'

176

'What if it's a trap?' said Darkus.

'We have protection,' said Bill, nodding to his officers.

'Right now Beecham's the only lead we've got,' argued Knightley.

Bill shone the torch beam at the driver of the minivan and informed the occupants, 'A'right, party's over, muckers. Move along. There's nothing tae see.' He waved them off.

The driver begrudgingly switched on his headlights. As the minivan pulled away from the kerb, Brother Allwyn powered down his window and addressed the detectives: 'I say again – don't be fooled. You are not dealing with an ordinary author, or an ordinary book.' The window rolled up and the minivan accelerated away into the night.

Knightley visibly winced at the warning, then shrugged at Darkus as if to downplay it. 'Kooks . . .' he muttered, in an attempt at reassurance. They both checked their watches in unison, looked up and down the street, then returned to their vantage point.

Uncle Bill issued a request then a few minutes later a Metropolitan Police van took up position outside the apartment building and a uniformed officer delivered three hot cups of tea and a packet of chocolate diges-tives to the back of the cab. Although it was approaching midnight, Darkus's mind felt sharper than ever – or at least he hoped it was, for he knew that the next twelve hours would prove crucial to the investigation.

After approximately twenty minutes, another black cab arrived outside the apartment building, and Bram Beecham stepped out. When he reached the pavement, four uniformed officers quickly hustled him into the foyer. Beecham made no attempt to resist, and was carefully patted down and declared safe. Satisfied, Bill led the Knightleys inside and the throng of officers entered the lift with Beecham in their charge.

Resigned to being treated as a suspect, Beecham said little other than to unlock the door to his penthouse apartment and invite them in. Bill ordered two officers to stand guard, then followed the Knightleys inside.

The penthouse was even sleeker and colder than Beecham's office. The furniture was uniformly black and uniformly leather, with the occasional cashmere scatter cushion. The floor itself also appeared to be leather or some synthetic equivalent, and the overall impression was of being inside the carcass of an exotic black animal of some kind.

Chloe closed the glass doors to the roof garden and greeted Beecham in a surprised but professional tone. 'Bram. I didn't know you were expecting guests. I would have done the watering another time.'

'That's quite all right.' Beecham's voice betrayed a

hint of anxiety – possibly even fear, Darkus thought. 'Chloe, you remember Darkus Knightley,' he went on, ushering his guests into the living room. 'This is his father.' Knightley bowed enthusiastically in Chloe's direction. Beecham gestured uncertainly to Uncle Bill. 'And this is . . .'

'Montague Billoch,' said Bill, using his birth name, 'but ye can call me Monty,' he added, with a smile that seemed to inflate his cheeks close to bursting. 'Verra canty.' Neither Darkus nor his father made any attempt to comprehend this last comment.

'I'll see you in the morning then,' said Chloe hesitantly.

'Thank you, Chloe.' Beecham closed the door behind her. Then he removed his coat, went to a marble-topped bar and poured himself a large neat whisky, using a monogrammed napkin to dab his shining forehead. 'Can I offer you anything?' he asked Knightley and Bill, who looked at each other and shrugged.

'Not on the job,' Darkus responded for them. Knightley and Bill nodded in agreement, as if the thought had never crossed their minds.

'Fair enough,' said Beecham, taking a seat and gesturing for his guests to do the same. He pressed a remote control and a set of electric blinds descended silently over the windows, blocking out the roof terrace.

Knightley and Bill watched, impressed, while Darkus examined the imposing bookcase that took up one entire wall of the living area.

'I understand you've decided to cooperate,' began Knightley.

'I've come to realise my options are fewer than I thought,' said Beecham, sipping deeply from his whisky tumbler. 'Like my client, I am now the subject of rumour and innuendo. I am a target for those who seek to use *The Code* for their own purposes, which are beyond my control,' he went on, his voice wavering more noticeably.

'Would you care to elaborate?' said Darkus, continuing his survey of the room.

'In short . . .' Beecham replied, 'I believe my life is in danger.'

# Chapter 14
# HIDDEN CHAMBERS

'Proceed,' said Darkus.

Beecham looked from Knightley to Bill, then began talking. 'I'm aware that certain fringe groups hold my client responsible for events that could not have been foreseen. I also believe another, larger organisation has manipulated the book's release for their own personal agenda – an agenda that I cannot fathom, nor do I wish to.'

'What kind of organisation?' asked Darkus.

'I don't know. But I believe Lester's death was no accident.'

'The editor?' said Darkus.

'That's right.' Beecham drained his glass.

'And do you have any idea who might be orchestrating this?' said Knightley.

'No,' said Beecham, looking down and to the left. Darkus knew enough about body language to know this was a 'tell': a sure sign that Beecham was lying. It hadn't escaped Knightley either.

'And you expect us to believe this story of a shadowy organisation?' said Knightley. 'With no tangible evidence? Only wild hypotheses?'

'It is not my job to investigate crimes,' answered Beecham. 'It's yours.'

'I gave you the chance to deliver your client to us, and you refused,' said Darkus. 'You obstructed our investigation.'

Beecham went white, then turned to Knightley. 'I'll give you Chambers's location. I'll tell you everything I know. But first I want guaranteed round-the-clock protection, and immunity from prosecution. In writing from a high court judge.'

Knightley looked to Bill for approval. Meanwhile Darkus completed his assessment of the room, then calmly turned to face Beecham.

'Before we grant your request, Mr Beecham, I believe there are some more immediate issues that need to be addressed,' he said. 'Starting with this bookcase . . .' Darkus approached the heavily lacquered bookcase, running his hand over the shelves, where a variety of Far Eastern trinkets were lined up for ornamental effect.

'Careful, Doc,' said Knightley, the anxious parent in him coming out.

'Is your son always this poorly behaved?' said Beecham curtly.

'Not without good reason.' Knightley watched with nervous interest. 'Don't break anything, Doc, for God's sake,' he whispered.

'Don't worry, I won't.' Darkus inspected the edge of the bookcase and the adjoining wall, then turned to face the others. 'It's clear from the layout of this room that there is significantly more space behind this bookcase than meets the eye.'

'I don't know what you mean,' protested Beecham.

'I think you do,' said Darkus, moving aside some of the Far Eastern trinkets on the shelves overhead.

'Gently –' beseeched Knightley.

'Don't worry, Dad.' Darkus took what appeared to be a small make-up compact from his inside pocket. He opened it and removed a miniature blusher brush, dipped it in a small amount of white powder, tapped it once, then ran it along the shelves, over the spines of the books, leaving a white residue.

'What's he doing?' demanded Beecham.

'My line of reasoning began with the notes I discovered in the file room at your office,' said Darkus, blowing away the white powder to reveal a cluster of fingerprints centred on a large hardback book entitled *Secrets of the Ancients*.

'What were you doing snooping around my office?' raged Beecham.

Darkus continued undeterred. 'The handwriting was a perfect match for the signature on the title page of *The Code* that you donated to the auction. A foolish move on your part, but driven by good intentions no doubt. They were what betrayed you.' Darkus reached for the hardback book.

'Don't touch that!' barked Beecham.

Darkus ignored him and removed the book from the shelf, which resulted in an audible click. Darkus looked to his father for permission. Knightley nodded encouragingly, a look of stunned pride spreading broadly across his face.

'My theory was confirmed rather simply by your monogrammed napkin, which contains the letters B.R.B. Which I assume stand for Bram . . . Ross . . . Beecham,' declared Darkus, then pulled on the bookcase, which swung open on hidden hinges to reveal a secret room with a desk, a chair and a laptop computer stationed inside. 'Or – if you rearrange the letters – should I say . . . Ambrose Chambers.'

'Excellent!' exclaimed Knightley.

'*He* is Chambers . . . ?' said Bill, pointing at Beecham. 'How?'

'A monogram that led to an anagram,' said Knightley, nodding proudly.

'I rest my case,' said Darkus, looking at Beecham, or, as his pen name would have it, Ambrose Chambers.

'A'right, lads, we've got our man,' Bill said into his walkie-talkie.

The apartment doors opened and uniformed officers surrounded Beecham, who looked at Darkus with something approaching admiration – but not quite.

'You're very good, son, but I'm afraid your reasoning is only half sound,' Beecham announced. 'You see, there really is no Ambrose Chambers. I didn't write a word of it. I only transcribed it from an existing text, for someone, or some*thing* else.'

'Who?' demanded Darkus.

'I've already made you my offer,' said Beecham, turning to the assembled members of law enforcement. 'Grant me immunity, and I'll tell you everything I know. Refuse it, and Chambers won't say another word.'

'Save it for the station,' said Bill, and nodded to the officers, who took hold of Beecham's arms and raised him to his feet.

'You're making a big mistake,' he called out, struggling with the officers as they guided him out of the apartment towards the lift. 'You don't know who you're dealing with –' Beecham shouted as the lift doors closed behind him.

Darkus calmly closed the compact and returned it to

his inside pocket. He looked up at his father, who was now studying him more closely than ever.

'Impressive,' said Knightley.

Darkus shrugged. 'It was the only explanation that would support the facts.'

Knightley nodded, suddenly feeling very old.

'Shall we continue Beecham's interrogation at the station?' said Darkus.

'In the morning,' said Knightley. 'First, I think it's time you got some kip,' he added tenderly.

'As you wish.'


The gentle rhythm of the cab's progress through London soon lulled Darkus to sleep in the back seat. Traffic lights and Belisha beacons blurred past the window as Knightley guided the Fairway towards Cherwell Place. Somewhere a clock struck one, and the stars were just visible above the neon shroud.

Knightley reflected that London was never calmer or more innocent than in the dead of night – and yet no time of day was more apt to be used for ill gain. In the years since he'd unwillingly gone to sleep, the city had changed and evolved, adding corporate insignias and chain outlets, without ever managing to lose its prehistoric skeleton of nonsensical but somehow interconnecting parts. It was a sort of ordered disorder, much like the inner workings of a brain: a brain that could be used for good, or for bad; for dreaming or for nightmares.

Knightley glanced in the rear-view mirror and saw Darkus slumped with his head resting against the window, his breath steaming up the glass. Knightley smiled privately to himself, then turned the wheel, pulling up outside number 27. He quietly got out of the driver's seat, slowly opened the rear passenger door and scooped up Darkus in his arms without waking him. He hadn't done this for longer than he could remember, and it probably wasn't advisable in his current state, but sometimes reason and common sense were irrelevant. Knightley crept across the pavement to the house, keeping his balance, inserted the key into the lock and opened the front door.

He heard the rumbling, bronchial snores of Bogna emanating from the first-floor bedroom. Knightley carefully ascended the stairs, carrying his burden, trying to minimise the creaking sounds that were either coming from the staircase or his knee joints; he wasn't sure which. He reached the top floor and crept into his office, lowering Darkus on to the chaise longue. He drew up, panting and holding his chest until his breathing slowed down.

'Are you OK, Dad?' Darkus whispered, looking up at him. 'How long have you been awake?'

'Just the last flight of stairs or so.'

'You could've told me.'

'I thought you were having . . . a moment.'

'I'm having a heart attack is what I'm having,' said Knightley, getting his breath back.

'Mum's right,' said Darkus matter-of-factly. 'For a detective you can be pretty oblivious.'

He shook his head. 'There's a distinction between "oblivious" and "focused", Doc. Your mother never understood that. I require close to one hundred per cent of my brain when I'm conducting an investigation.'

'I know,' replied Darkus. 'And female counterparts are a distraction.' He quoted his father's words back to him.

'I thought maybe *you* would understand that, seeing as you've become an investigator in your own right. And a very good one,' Knightley said proudly, then frowned again. 'Perhaps I wasn't the most attentive father. But I never expected anything of you, I never tried to push you in any particular direction, to be a suit, or a desk jockey, not like most parents.'

'That's because you never took the time to get to know me,' said Darkus. 'You never bothered to deduce what direction I might want to go in.'

Knightley took a moment to digest this. 'I wanted you to be able to stand on your own two feet. And look how right I was,' he said, cheerfully unaware of the effect he was having. 'Judging by your performance with Beecham – or should I say Chambers – I must have done something right.'

'On the contrary,' said Darkus. 'In the absence of guidance, I took the only course that presented itself. I followed you.'

A wave of guilt crashed over Knightley. He took a deep breath and waited for it to pass. 'If I left you in the dark, it was because I wanted to spare you the *real* darkness. The kind that you need more than a night light to protect you from.' He took a blanket from a cupboard and unfolded it over Darkus on the chaise longue. 'I see no point in revisiting past history. We have a case on the boil, and we need our minds in tip-top shape. Get some rest, and that's an order.'

'OK, Dad,' Darkus answered sombrely.

As his son closed his weary eyes, Knightley retired to the armchair opposite, but found himself out of sorts. He steadied his breathing and watched Darkus for several minutes. Knightley's face was an indecipherable mask, caught between emotion and reason. His son was the one case he would never crack, a case that would go on long after his own demise. Perhaps someone would solve it: someone more deserving; someone better than him.

Knightley closed his eyes, hoping to sleep, but knowing he wouldn't manage a wink – he had already slept enough for a lifetime.

# Chapter 15
## UNFORESEEN
## CIRCUMSTANCES

Clive rolled over in bed, having a bad dream. In his nightmare, Knightley had stolen his car again and was driving it through a Norwegian fjord. Clive was swimming after it in vain, only to find he had left all his clothing behind on shore.

Clive let out a whimper and sat bolt upright, realising where he was. Jackie was fast asleep beside him. Tilly was safely locked away at Cranston School, under the supervision of her housemistress, just as he had threatened.

He crept out of bed in his pyjamas and went to the window to check the Jag was still in the driveway, which it was. He then padded into the bathroom and squinted as he switched on the light. He looked in the mirror and his face was bleary and tired. He released a heavy sigh and angled the mirrored cabinet door to observe his greying thatch of hair.

Clive had been having an increasing number of bad hair days, and even the Jag didn't seem to get him noticed lately. But hopefully all that was about to change, thanks to something he'd overheard his colleagues and co-presenters talking about – something that had changed their lives; something that would help him build a new improved Clive, Clive 2.0, the Clive GT, more successful in every way. He took his e-book reader from the top shelf of the bathroom cabinet and switched it on. The title page flashed up on the screen, along with a striking symbol: *The Code*. Clive examined it, giddy with pleasure at his little secret.

He sat on the toilet seat and began to read.


When it came to babysitting Bram Beecham (or 'Ambrose Chambers', depending on how you wanted to look at it), Uncle Bill decided to take no chances. He rested his prodigious weight on an office chair in a corridor directly outside the row of holding cells at Marylebone Police Station, one of the more high-tech stations in London.

The cells currently contained two vocal drunks, a sleeping vagrant, a sullen youth held on assault charges and one bestselling author who was now the prime suspect in a far-reaching criminal investigation. Aside from an occasional yell or belch – the latter of which admittedly came from Bill himself sometimes – the corridor was mostly quiet.

Behind a specially reinforced window, Beecham sat quietly on his bunk as if engaged in some form of meditation. For his own safety he had been deprived of his belt, his shoelaces and anything else that could have posed a threat to himself or others.

Bill took it upon himself to rise from his seat and amble down the length of the corridor to check on Beecham once every fifteen minutes. He completed the circuit by rewarding himself with a biscuit or two from a rapidly diminishing packet of chocolate digestives positioned on a nearby desk. It was during the ninth or tenth repetition of this routine – Bill didn't remember which, but he vaguely remembered thinking that he would soon require another packet of biscuits – that a figure dressed in black appeared at the end of the corridor.

Having achieved access to the inner sanctum of the police station with a set of carefully forged documents and the assistance of several intercepted phone calls – which the duty officer believed were from his superiors at Scotland Yard – the figure now calmly approached the row of cells. Of course that age-old weapon, charm, had a lot to do with making the operation a success.

And charm was something that the figure had to burn, so to speak.

Hearing footsteps, Uncle Bill turned away from the biscuits, recognising the unexpected visitor.

'Chloy?' he said, butchering her name.

'Why yes,' answered Chloe, flashing him a smile, still dressed in business attire but looking, according to witnesses, in their defence, like a catwalk model.

'We-e-ell,' Bill stuttered, overwhelmed with more questions than his brain could efficiently handle all at once. Why was she here? How did she get in? Would a girl like her ever look at an old runkle like him? Bill's brain momentarily short-circuited. 'What can I do ye for?' he managed.

'I'm here to see Mr Beecham,' she replied calmly.

Bill began to wrestle back control of his senses. 'Ahm afraid that's completely impossible,' he said apologetically.

'Oh, I wouldn't say that,' she said, and took something resembling a lipstick tube from her handbag, then pointed it directly at his face.

'Ho ye!' exclaimed Bill, and moved with surprising speed to block whatever it was – but he was too late.

A pressurised burst of nerve gas exploded out of the end of the lipstick into Bill's face. Chloe quickly reacted by pulling a gas mask from her handbag and fastening it over her face.

'Aye yer maw!' Bill shouted out, clawing at his eyes, which were stinging, while the other elements in the gas were working to relieve him of consciousness. He stumbled backward, pirouetted down the corridor past the cells, then, as if controlled by an invisible tractor beam, collided directly with the desk, lost control of his legs and fell, head-butting the rest of the chocolate digestives and the tabletop on the way down. He was already unconscious before he hit the ground, with a thud that detainees later described as resembling a king-size mattress dropped from a great height.

As the detainees fell asleep in their bunks one by one, Chloe approached the inert mound of Uncle Bill, knelt down and systematically checked his pockets. Not relishing the job, she quickly located a digital key card in his rear trouser pocket. She then took a large stride over him, stepping out of the threat radius, and continued on towards Beecham's cell, removing her gas mask.

Fully woken from his meditation, Beecham already had his face pressed against the glass to investigate the commotion.

'Chloe?' he said with a start, as her face appeared at the window.

She swiped the key card and opened the cell door. Bram quickly retrieved his jacket from the bunk.

'Thank God you're here,' he said. 'Does this mean I'm being released?'

'In a manner of speaking, yes,' she replied, and pulled something else out of her handbag. The object flicked open, casting a sharp reflection across his face.

'Wait . . . What?' Beecham looked down at it, confused.

'You made a mistake, Bram. They don't tolerate mistakes.'

'Who?'

'You *know* who.'

'You're one of *them* . . .' Beecham backed off, a look of pure horror in his eyes.

Chloe paused a moment, then went after him.


Darkus stirred from an unusually deep sleep to find his father shaking him by the shoulders.

'Wake up, Doc.'

'Wh-what's wrong?' Darkus leaned up.

'Uncle Bill's had an accident –'

'What kind of an accident?'

'He's in one piece, just about. But Beecham, well, Beecham's *dead*.'

Darkus raised himself from the chaise longue. 'Incontrovertibly?'

'Categorically.'

\*

Knightley drove with the glass divider open, so they could advance theories en route. Clearly Beecham wasn't working alone, and whoever had created the character of Ambrose Chambers obviously wasn't happy with the way Beecham had played it. This was evidenced by the theft of the signed copy of *The Code* and confirmed by its author's untimely demise. Beecham had not only used his Chambers alias to transcribe the contents of the book, but also to raise money as a tribute to his daughter's memory. His good intentions had indeed got the better of him. When he signed the first edition for the auction, he also signed his own death warrant. Whoever was holding Beecham's puppet strings had not counted on the basic family loyalty that resides in the most amoral of criminal hearts. Beecham had paid the ultimate price, and perhaps he'd always known he would, in order to spend the rest of eternity in the company of his daughter – if his soul was fortunate enough to find the same resting place.

Privately, it didn't escape Darkus's thought process that the stranger who had threatened him at the auction might be responsible for Beecham's death; and sooner or later Darkus would have to inform his father of the threat, and face the consequences – if only to avoid them risking a similar fate.

The sun began to rise over the city, cauterising the

skyline and turning the mist blood red. Knightley drove past King's Cross station, using the taxi lane to bypass commuter traffic, and they soon found themselves outside the towering glass structure of University College Hospital.

A Scotland Yard liaison led them through the green tinted foyer and into a lift to the thirteenth floor. The corridors were blue and deceptively cheery. The liaison took them to a large private room, where Uncle Bill was holding court surrounded by a bevy of young nurses taking notes and feeding him sips of water – which was essential as Bill was entombed in plaster and attached to several cables that suspended his right arm and left leg in full traction.

'Had a bit of a spill,' he wheezed with a weak smile. 'Beecham's assistant Chloy caught me by surprise.'

'So I see,' said Knightley, shaking his head.

'Aye,' said Bill sheepishly. 'I might be laid up fer a while.' His voice trailed off as a nurse attended to him.

'Evidently,' said Knightley.

'Where is Beecham now?' enquired Darkus.

Bill gestured down with his eyes. 'In the basement doon there. I wanted tae keep him close.'

'You don't think he's planning to get up and walk away?' said Knightley.

'At this point, I dinna know what tae believe, Alan.

But I do know it's up to ye tway tae find oot.' Bill let out a long sigh.

A nurse interjected, 'He needs his rest.'

'And some digestives, Alan,' he piped up, before sinking back exhausted. 'Chocolate ones.'

'We'll make sure you get everything you need,' said Knightley.

'Get well soon, Uncle Bill,' added Darkus, as they respectfully exited the room.

The lift moved at the creeping pace of a funeral march, carrying Darkus and his father deep into the bowels of the hospital. They finally stepped out into a basement and followed signs to the morgue.

'Are you sure you're ready for this?' Knightley asked.

'I'd like to see him with my own eyes. To be sure.'

The pathologist was standing in the corridor, assembling his tools on a trolley.

'Mr Knightley?' he asked, then saw Darkus and looked disapproving.

'It's OK,' Knightley assured him, and patted his son on the shoulder, then quietly informed the pathologist, 'he just wants to say goodbye.'

The man frowned and continued arranging his forceps, chisels and saws.

Bram Beecham was waiting for them in a refrigerated

room, laid out on a steel bench and concealed by a black body bag.

Darkus took a pair of latex gloves from a dispenser, snapped them on and slowly unzipped the body bag to reveal the gaping wound in Beecham's torso. Knightley examined it from the other side of the counter.

'Knife trauma,' whispered Darkus.

'I concur,' said Knightley. 'Probably a stiletto blade. Something that could be easily concealed. Major arteries severed. She knew what she was doing.'

Darkus noticed the index finger on Beecham's right hand: it was daubed in dried blood, while Beecham's other fingers were uniformly clean. Darkus quickly deduced an explanation: 'I think Chambers might have left one last message for us.'

# Chapter 16
## AN OLD FRIEND

The Knightleys arrived at Marylebone Police Station fifteen minutes later, hoping to process the murder scene before it could be contaminated. Darkus was getting used to the perplexed and disapproving stares he received when dealing with adults, especially police officers, but he didn't let it break his concentration. The catastrophiser was gyrating and thrumming too insistently for anything to distract him.

On Bill's orders – which were triple-verified this time, to avoid a further breach – the duty officer led the Knightleys to the cell where the murder was committed. The rest of the detainees had been moved to alternative accommodation, still drowsy from the nerve agent.

Darkus examined the floor, noting the sharp imprint of Chloe's stiletto heels in the linoleum, but finding less blood on the floor than he expected. He deduced that Beecham had fallen backward on to the bunk during the attack, resulting in the white shape his body had left on the bedding, which was otherwise soaked in red. If there was a message, it had to be within arm's reach of the bunk where Beecham had expired. Darkus knelt down to get a better look, and sure enough, on the underside of the mattress of the upper bunk, two words were written in blood:

'Under what wood?' Darkus speculated.

'No,' said Knightley, taking a pencil from his top pocket and pointing up at the bloody scrawl. 'There's a flourish joining the R and the W. It's one word.'

Darkus realised he was correct. 'Underwood . . .'

Knightley suddenly looked spooked. 'Yes . . . Underwood.'

'I still don't see how that helps us.'

'It doesn't,' Knightley murmured. 'It doesn't help us at all.' He got that faraway look in his eyes; his nostrils flared and his ears pricked up. But this time there was a pallor beneath his skin; a look of exhaustion, and death. Whatever it was, Darkus didn't like it.

'What does it mean, Dad?'

'I don't know – yet. But I did once know a Doctor Morton Underwood. A long time ago.' Knightley went quiet.

'Who is he?'

'We became friends at Oxford.'

'So Bill knows him too?'

'Different colleges, but yes, they knew each other.' Knightley seemed to pull himself back from the honey trap of memory, debating whether to go on. It seemed there was no option. 'He was your godfather, Doc.'

Darkus took a moment to process this. Perhaps he had heard the name Morton before, but nothing stood out in his memory. For the past four years he had been more preoccupied with the absence of his father than the possible existence of a godfather.

'You said "was"?' asked Darkus.

Knightley went a shade paler. 'Mort was a child psychologist, a famous one.' He seemed to lose himself in a maze of his own thoughts, then found the thread again. 'He took on a patient – a boy from a powerful family. The boy was withdrawn; he wouldn't go to school, wouldn't interact with other people. Much of the time he wouldn't even speak at all. Except to Morton.'

'What was his diagnosis?'

'It never reached that stage.' Knightley paused. 'Mort

worked with the boy for several weeks, employing radical therapy, hypnosis, that sort of thing. He believed he was making progress. Then something happened . . .' Knightley trailed off, reluctant to remember any more.

'What happened?' said Darkus.

'The boy died. He fell from Morton's fifth-floor office window.'

'How?'

'Nobody knows for sure. There were signs of a struggle. The office had been turned upside down. When the police arrived, Morton was unconscious. He claimed the boy tried to kill him, then jumped to his death. But the family didn't believe him, and Morton was named as a "person of interest".' Knightley paused again. 'He hired me to prove his innocence. But all the evidence pointed to one person: him. There was nothing I could do.'

'You never wrote about this in the Knowledge.'

'I was too ashamed.'

'If he was guilty, you have nothing to be ashamed of,' said Darkus.

'No one ever found out if he was guilty or not . . . Morton disappeared from surveillance cameras near the Millennium Bridge, by the Thames. They found his coat and wallet. The police believed he'd drowned. But his body was never recovered.'

'What do you believe happened to him?' said Darkus.

'I don't know. I searched long and hard . . . and turned up nothing.' Knightley examined the name written in blood. 'But in light of the current evidence,' he added reluctantly, piecing together his thoughts, 'I have to conclude that Morton might have joined the Combination.'

Darkus frowned, digesting this latest piece of information and adding it to the catastrophiser.

'What did Morton Underwood look like?' he asked.

Knightley paused, searching for the best description. 'Medium height, medium build . . . He'd be forty-eight by now. Due to his failing eyesight he wore these glasses . . .'

'And he has a stutter,' Darkus interjected.

'Yes,' Knightley replied, incredulous. 'But how could you possibly know that?'

'I have a confession to make . . .' Darkus admitted.

'What have you been hiding from me?' Knightley demanded, eyes shining.

Reluctantly, Darkus gave him a detailed description of his encounter with the stranger at the auction house – who was, without a shadow of a doubt, Morton Underwood. Any anger on Knightley's part was quickly defused by concern for his son's welfare, and the dawning realisation of the danger they were now in.

Darkus explained his reasoning: 'I knew that if I told you, you'd never let me crack the case.'

'And you decided it was worth risking your life over?' his father protested. 'Possibly both our lives, by the sound of it.'

'I'm sorry, Dad.' Darkus frowned. 'It seemed like the right course of action at the time. If it's cost us the case, I only have myself to blame.'

Knightley shook his head sadly. 'For the record, our relationship is more important than any case. And I'm perfectly capable of spending time with my son in a non-professional capacity. It'll just take a bit of practice, that's all. But I fear, for the purposes of *this* case, and for your own personal safety, we'll need to keep our detectives' hats on.'

'If Underwood is behind all this, where do you suggest we find him?' said Darkus.

'Unfortunately I think we'll have to wait for *him* to find *us*,' replied Knightley. 'He made his first approach at the auction. I fear the second will be more forceful. We must return to Cherwell Place and prepare ourselves.'

'So you'll still be requiring my assistance?' asked Darkus.

'I've come to depend upon it,' said his father.

# Chapter 17
## THE CENTRE LINE

Every successful investigation has a centre line: a logical train of cause and effect that accounts for the vital components of a case and results in its conclusion. The centre line is the strongest part of the case, and also the weakest. It is the key to solving the crime, but it is also the most vulnerable to attack by those seeking to pervert the course of justice.

In much the same way, the human body also has a centre line: quite literally, a line that divides the body and accounts for its most vital components. The eyes, the nose, the throat, the solar plexus, the groin – all fall along the centre line. They are the key to successful functioning, and by the same token are the most vulnerable to attack.

Later that morning, as Darkus and his father finished one of Bogna's legendary cooked breakfasts – fried egg, fried bread, fried potatoes, fried Kielbasa sausage

Knightley explained the principles of centre-line theory according to his preferred martial art: Wing Chun. Their investigation was leading them closer to both the truth and to those who would protect it with aggression if necessary, so it was only prudent to give Darkus some tools of his own.

To Knightley's surprise, he discovered that Darkus had already studied this particular martial art from the sketches and notes laid out in the Knowledge. Wing Chun was developed over three hundred years ago in feudal China by a female Shaolin monk named Ng Mui. It was designed to rely not on strength but on balance and fluid movement, absorbing the attacker's power and using it against them. Yim Wing Chun was a fifteen-year-old girl who was being forced into marriage to a local bandit against her will. The bandit agreed to withdraw his marriage proposal on one condition: that she could beat him in a martial arts contest. Yim Wing Chun approached Ng Mui, one of the last survivors of the famed Shaolin temple, and requested her help. Ng Mui taught her about the centre line and the effectiveness of the straight punch, and assured Yim Wing Chun that although she was smaller in build, if her balance was correct and her centre line protected, the bandit would be unable to beat her. Sure enough, Yim Wing Chun defeated the bandit and married her true love, Leung Bok Chau, who also learned and then taught the technique, and subsequently named it after her.

Darkus already had a basic understanding of centreline theory: using the strong blades of his forearms to protect the vital organs; stepping to one side to deflect an attack, and thereby opening up the opponent's centre line to a straight punch.

But by his own admission, he had never had anyone to practise on.

Once Bogna's breakfast had been digested – which threatened to take a good portion of the day – Knightley led Darkus upstairs and moved all of the office furniture to one side. Then Knightley stood opposite Darkus and checked his stance. Darkus's feet were shoulder width apart, his knees slightly bent; his guard was up, the left hand leading with the palm raised, the right hand held back as a second line of defence.

'Now punch,' said Knightley.

Darkus released his left hand and followed with a straight punch from his right, hitting Knightley's outstretched palm.

'Good,' said Knightley, smarting a little. 'Now relax, and use your feet a bit. Turn into the punch.'

Darkus swivelled his feet and repeated the attack, making a loud smacking sound against his father's hand.

'Good,' said Knightley, wincing. 'Now show me your block.'

Knightley rushed forward as if to grab him, but Darkus knocked his arm to one side, throwing him off balance, then kicked him in the shin.

'Ow!' shouted Knightley.

'Sorry, Dad . . . Reflex.'

'No, no,' said Knightley, shifting his weight on to his good leg. 'My fault. You only deflected as much power as I gave you – which in this case was possibly a tad too much. Well, that's enough sparring for now,' he said, looking a bit dispirited. 'Let's have a look at your form.'

The 'form' was a slow, ceremonial display that demonstrated the full range of punches, blocks and kicks. They performed it in unison, and Darkus found his father to be reasonably well informed about the moves, but painfully lacking in their application. At one point, while demonstrating a front push-kick, Knightley misfired and put his foot straight through the side of his desk, which resulted in Bogna bursting through the door to make sure no one had been hurt.

'We're fine,' said Knightley, yanking his foot out of the woodwork and waving her away. He slumped into the armchair. 'My instincts aren't what they used to be.'

'It's just like riding a bike, right?' said Darkus diplomatically.

'I'm not sure I even remember that,' he replied, looking disheartened.

Not wishing to dwell on his father's shortcomings, Darkus hoped to trigger his memory by drawing him on to familiar ground. 'Tell me more about Underwood.'

But Knightley's expression grew heavy again, as he gave Darkus a brief outline of his one-time pal. Knightley took Morton Underwood under his wing during their first year at Oxford, and in return Morton had been the best friend anyone could ask for. He was generous, supportive, steady, a good listener. And yet Knightley admitted that, for all of those unparalleled qualities, there was an empty space beneath them, like the dusty, locked-up cellar beneath a happy family home. A profound unknowability. Perhaps that was the reason why Knightley was drawn to him in the first place. His friend was, at his core, a mystery. For that very reason, Jackie had never liked him; not that there was anything specific not to like – it was just an instinct. She pointed to the fact that he had never married, had barely even been in a relationship, and that he had no other friends beyond Knightley and one or two university peers. Of course, Knightley told her she was being irrational, that Morton was just hard to get to know; and she had no evidence against him. His subterranean emptiness was masked so gracefully by their routine of lunches, drinks and chess matches – which always possessed just the right mixture of companionship, humour and bonhomie – that a monument of great friendship had perhaps been built on unstable, precipitous land.

And so it was that when the boy was found dead, five floors down, Knightley could not say, hand on heart, that Morton hadn't done it. However unlikely, it wasn't outside the realm of possibility. Somewhere, deep down, Knightley suspected Underwood could not have been entirely innocent. Who knew what radical therapies he had employed, and to what end? Who could see behind closed doors? Who could presume to judge what causes 'evil' or gives rise to 'evil deeds'?

Darkus digested this history with a neutral, balanced mind. All he knew was, every living thing, however enigmatic, left a trail of clues in its wake, even Morton Underwood – and Darkus would be waiting to collect them.

Knightley showed no signs of rousing from his melancholy. 'You see, Doc, why I never wanted this life for you. There are no certainties. Only degrees of truth.'

'That's exactly what you gave me and Mum,' Darkus pointed out. 'Degrees of truth. You left us in the dark. The logical chain of events was that she'd leave you.'

Knightley's face was a mask of contrition. 'Even if I could be the man she wanted me to be – which is a big "if" – life has moved on . . . and she's found someone she's more compatible with.'

'Hmm,' said Darkus doubtfully.

'We don't have to like him, Darkus. Only she does. Clive's not such a bad person really.' Knightley shrugged sadly. 'He's more reliable than I was. More attentive than I was. He has a nicer car than I have.'

Darkus knew this wasn't the time for marriage guidance counselling, but he had stumbled on to a line of investigation that was very close to his heart. 'Do you think you . . . and Mum . . . might ever . . . ?'

Knightley looked wistful for a second, then regained his composure. 'No. It's a little late for that.'

'Maybe if you just put some thought into it?' urged Darkus.

'I'm told, for a detective, I can be quite oblivious,' said Knightley, with a smile that turned down at the edges instead of up. His eyes glittered with moisture for a split second before returning to their steady gaze. Knightley collected himself. 'Now, I have work to do,' he said, picking up his copy of *The Code*.

Darkus frowned, hearing those familiar words – 'work to do' – and knowing his father would probably never change, regardless of circumstance.

Knightley put his feet up and announced with a mixture of relish and disgust: 'I still have twenty pages of this infernal opus to go . . .'

*

The day began unremarkably for Tilly, in her dormitory bedroom at Cranston School. All the other bunk-desks were empty, as all her peers were spending half-term with their families, while she was now caged up like a delinquent – which, quite frankly, she wore as a badge of honour.

Wanting to finish the book as soon as possible, she read the final chapter of *The Code* and tossed it aside in disgust. Not only was it morally shallow, it held no secrets whatsoever. Much to her annoyance, it had no effect on her at all.

She walked down to the canteen and had breakfast on her own while some of the staff ate together on the opposite side of the room. Pupils and teachers alike treated her with grudging respect, for no one else at Cranston succeeded in flouting the rules as effortlessly as she did. Few pupils dared to get too close to her, for they knew they would score no points with their parents if they invited her over for a meal, or, God forbid, to stay for the weekend. That being said, their fathers did enjoy her father's TV programme, and that might go a little way. But Tilly was unpredictable, in friendship and enmity. Everyone knew it was down to her losing her mother. But that tragic fact had only gone a little way too.

The fact was, Tilly was a wild card – secretly admired by

the girls, secretly fancied by the boys, and secretly feared by the teachers who were charged with her supervision.

The housemistress who was her appointed prison warden watched her suspiciously from across the room. Tilly pushed her food from one side of the plate to the other, then drained her cup of coffee and walked out without acknowledging her.

Tilly roamed the wood-panelled corridors, past libraries and subject rooms, her shoes squeaking on the waxed parquet floors. She hadn't completed any of her homework assignments, but she usually managed to track down her test results online, and sometimes, for amusement, hacked her way to a higher grade. However, she did feel genuine remorse over Miss Khan's science project: a tedious affair involving ticker tape and the velocity of a moving object, which had been due over two weeks ago. Miss Khan was one of the more sympathetic teachers at Cranston, and Tilly felt obliged to explain herself privately, rather than in front of the whole class, where it might be seen as an act of defiance or popular revolution. Miss Khan deserved better than that.

Tilly walked towards the postmodern-looking science department, crossed the atrium and located Miss Khan's classroom – where Tilly had observed the teacher spent most of her free time as well. Tilly peered through the window, but nobody was home. The whiteboard was blank, the chairs all arranged. Then she noticed the door to the lab annex slightly ajar. She knocked gently, nudging it open.

Miss Khan looked up from a lab table, wearing her customary white coat, square plastic specs, and a mane of jet-black hair neatly tied back; her light brown skin was younger than her twenty-nine years. If she let her hair down and adjusted her make-up choices, Tilly was convinced she was capable of being a stone-cold fox, although she doubted Miss Khan would ever submit to such a makeover.

'Oh, hello, Tilly,' she said, removing her specs and setting down an electric soldering iron.

'Morning, Miss Khan.'

'I hope you're having a pleasant half-term?' she enquired gently.

'It's fine.'

'If you'd like to have a chat, please take a seat. I was just finishing up a pet project of mine.' Miss Khan pushed aside a small device held together with clamps. It looked, at first glance, like an asthma inhaler of some kind.

Tilly focused on the task at hand. 'Sorry about the velocity assignment, Miss Khan. It sort of . . .' she looked for the right words, 'got away from me.'

Miss Khan nodded, trying to hide her disappointment. Tilly was one of her most gifted pupils – along with another student, Darkus Knightley. Both were unusual children, to say the least, yet they seemed to share an affinity for science, while being polar opposites in every other way. If Tilly would only apply herself. But the tragedy the poor girl had experienced, losing her mother at such a young age, and left with only that *murkh* of a father . . . Miss Khan silently chastised herself for judging Tilly at all.

'Well, never mind. If you're here over half-term perhaps you could work on it now,' she suggested, glancing down at her own project, as if to remind herself that her talents weren't entirely wasted.

Tilly followed her glance and noticed that one half of the asthma inhaler was open and contained a miniature circuit board of some kind. It was like no inhaler she had ever seen before.

'What *is* that, Miss Khan?'

'Oh, it's just a little gizmo I've been working on,' she said modestly. She picked it up and turned it round in the light, inspecting her handiwork. 'It's a self-defence tool. Very simple really,' she went on. 'Instead of salbutamol or fluticasone propionate, this canister contains pepper spray foam, stored in a highly pressurised state. On contact with an attacker it expands and sticks, blinding for up to half an hour. I had to modify the delivery system, of course.'

'To increase its effective range?'

'Exactly right,' she replied. 'It is effective to over five metres.'

'Nice.'

'Yes, it is.' Miss Khan nodded humbly, then felt obliged to explain. 'My father was an armourer in the British army. I was an only child, so as you can imagine I spent most of my free time in his workshop . . .' She realised she was, in modern parlance, 'oversharing'.

'What else have you got?' asked Tilly.

'Like this?'

'Anything really.'

'Well, I've developed some night-vision goggles that Mr Burke is using to monitor the playing fields.'

'Ah,' said Tilly, realising any future escape attempts would be significantly hampered.

'Other than that,' said Miss Khan, thinking to herself, 'nothing that's near to completion.'

'Well, keep up the good work,' said Tilly, raising her hand in almost a salute. She quickly lowered it again.

'Thank you, Tilly,' the teacher replied, genuinely touched. They exchanged a smile, both realising the conversation had gone off-road and taken an unexpected turn. Miss Khan brought them back on track. 'I look forward to marking your velocity assignment, when it's ready,' she said sincerely. 'I have high hopes for you.'

'I'll get right on to it,' Tilly replied, feeling even guiltier than she did when she walked in. She headed for the door, then turned back. 'And by the way . . . that gadget? Very cool.' She nodded once more, and left the room.

The silence of the office was broken as Knightley looked up from *The Code*, exhaled heavily and slammed it shut.

'I find nothing of substance. Nothing out of the ordinary. Nothing of any interest at all,' he said, discarding it on his desk. 'Perhaps it *is* circumstantial. Or even a coincidence.'

'You always said coincidence is the last refuge of the weak-minded,' Darkus reminded him.

'Indeed I did,' he replied, with a troubled expression. 'But I fear we may be approaching that last refuge rapidly. And we have to accept that there may be an alternative theory that covers the facts more accurately than our own.' He sighed and removed his feet from the desk. 'Let's lay out the facts as we know them. We can be certain of the following: Ambrose Chambers was the pseudonym of literary agent Bram Beecham. Presto sought to cover up this fact by stealing the signed first edition from the auction. QED.' Knightley tapped on his desk conclusively. 'We know Bram Beecham was responsible for writing *The Code*, but he claims he was transcribing from an older text. That argument is supported by the Order of the New Dawn, who contend that the original text harnessed supernatural powers of some kind. But neither Beecham nor the Order can be considered reliable witnesses.' Knightley rapped his knuckles on the desk impatiently. 'Beecham was murdered by his assistant Chloe, for what reason we cannot be sure, but most likely to stop him from talking. So it's likely that she and Presto are connected, possibly through the Combination.' Knightley paused. 'Our only remaining clue is the name "Underwood" written in blood. I strongly believe this is a sign of Morton's involvement, possibly proof of his membership of the Combination. But this last part is conjecture, I'll admit.'

'Which means we *still* only have one solid lead,' said Darkus, rendering his father quiet for a moment. 'The book.'

'Be my guest . . .' He handed it to Darkus, then slumped back in his chair and closed his eyes in meditation.

Darkus opened the cover and, once again, began to read – slowly, so as not to miss anything. The first line began:

*Change your life now.*

He read on . . .

# Chapter 18
## BETWEEN THE LINES

*The wise always listen to their inner voice, because it's the sound of the universe speaking to you. And it never lies. The voice is telling you that whatever you want can be yours, if you want it enough . . .*

Darkus continued reading, looking and listening for any clue.

*Make what you want the only thought in your mind. Imagine your brain is a transmitter, transmitting only positive messages.*

Darkus felt his brain was being bombarded – not by positive but by negative messages. Still he read on.

*As the thought runs through your head you feel the force of its presence, reminding you that the universal laws will grant your every wish.*

Darkus understood his father's frustration with the book: its shallow pursuit of a superficial world; its reliance on expectation and luck instead of the hard-earned achievement of the individual, which was what good detective work depended on. Agitated, he read on.

*Use it properly and it will become a powerful weapon. A magnet to attract everything you want: wealth, prosperity, a new job, a new car . . .*

Darkus stopped. Something about the last passage caught his attention. He went back and read it again, slowly, letting the peaks and troughs of the letters burn themselves into his visual cortex.

There was more to the text than first appeared.

'Dad?'

Knightley opened one eye, to determine if it was worth interrupting his rest. 'What is it, Doc?'

'Can I use your microscope?'

Curious, Knightley prised himself from his chair and walked to the shelf that held his forensic microscope: a white metal apparatus with two eye-cups, a slide and a rotating head with multiple lenses. He plugged it into a small TV monitor. The monitor flickered to life, then snowstormed. Knightley smacked it sharply and the snowstorm switched to a display menu.

'Proceed,' said Knightley.

Darkus held up *The Code* and quickly tore out the page he'd been reading. Knightley winced. He'd seen many dead bodies, and witnessed many brutal crimes, but there was still something violent about ripping a book.

'Allow me to offer up a theory,' said Darkus.

'Continue.'

Darkus held up *The Code*. 'If the book isn't inherently "evil",' he began, 'and its message – while morally questionable – isn't specifically telling the reader to commit a crime . . . then the answer must lie within the text itself.'

'Wrong,' said Knightley with conviction. 'If that was true, the text would affect every reader the same way. Instead it only affects a select few.'

'Let's have a closer look.' Darkus placed the torn page under the lens. A blurred image appeared on the monitor.

'Try this.' Knightley rotated the lens head to a different magnification.

The printed words appeared on the monitor in black and white. Darkus positioned the page to capture the line that had caught his attention.

'There,' said Darkus.

Knightley's eyes narrowed; his nostrils flared. Then his face unwound again.

'Just a printing error. The typeface is corrupted.'

'Exactly.'

'There's no method to it. No logic.'

'Look again,' said Darkus.

Knightley peered into the image on the monitor, genuinely puzzled. Then he moved even closer, the tip of his nose almost touching the screen as his eye picked out the odd letters, which now stood out boldly to him:

*Use pro an wi be c e a p erful weapon. A magnet to attract everything you want: wealth, prosperity, a new job, a new car . . .*

Knightley's eyes lit up. 'Certain letters are printed in a slightly modified typeface, but not every time,' he

223

noted. 'Only when it spells r-a-e-f. You're saying there's a *code* in *The Code?*'

Darkus nodded. 'The same letters are repeated in the same typeface, in the same order, every second paragraph.'

Knightley snatched the page from under the microscope and stared into it like he was staring into a void. The letters R, A, E, F stood out like the optical illusion of a face hidden in an abstract picture, or the haunted face of Jesus appearing on a household object. One moment it was ordinary, the next it was the vessel for a private secret.

Knightley's eyes widened. Suddenly he wasn't looking at a page of text, but a swirling vortex with the same four letters repeated over and over.

'R-a-e-f,' said Knightley. 'If there's a meaning, it's lost on me.'

'You're reading left to right,' said Darkus. 'Try reading right to left.'

Knightley blinked, astonished. '*Fear,*' he said under his breath.

'Precisely.'

'But no one reads right to left,' argued Knightley. 'Not in the Western world.'

'Not true. A boy in my class was diagnosed with Attention Deficit Disorder. He had trouble focusing on words and reading basic sentences. He said it was just the way his brain worked.'

'Involuntary saccadic eye movements,' said Knightley, quoting the medical term. 'Some people can't read consistently left to right. Their eyes have a tendency to run ahead or lag behind instead of travelling smoothly. In theory, that would make them susceptible to the hidden message.'

'The theory's sound,' said Darkus. 'The message only affects readers whose brain chemistry prohibits them from giving the book their full attention.'

'Once again, Doc, you've out-reasoned me.'

'I like to believe there's always a rational explanation rather than a supernatural one,' said Darkus.

Knightley felt his brain racing to catch up with the steel-trap mind of his son. It was a sobering but fascinating pursuit.

'Then tell me this . . .' said Knightley. 'What makes the reader commit the crime?'

Darkus stared into space a moment, turning the problem over in his mind, like a sphere spinning suspended in an electromagnetic field; he observed it from every angle. 'The continual repetition of the word "fear" would create feelings of anxiety and paranoia in the reader, without them ever consciously knowing why. For Lee Wadsworth it manifested as his worst phobia: the fear of insects. For every reader it would be different.'

'That still doesn't explain why Wadsworth would

want to target a bank. Or what he intended to do with the proceeds.'

Darkus turned the problem over in his mind again, divining the answer from the soup of possibilities, negatives and positives, zeros and ones.

'You're right,' Darkus agreed. 'He had to have received an instruction.' A thought struck him like a bolt of lightning.

'What is it?' asked his father.

'Underwood has a stutter.'

'Yes.'

'Lee Wadsworth said the voice that told him to rob the bank cut in and out. And you said Underwood practised hypnosis.'

Knightley realised where he was heading. 'Underwood delivered the instruction.'

Darkus nodded. 'What if "fear" is a keyword? Underwood uses it to place the subject in some kind of hypnotic state, then gives his instruction. In theory, the instruction could be anything,' Darkus went on. 'The Combination could assemble an army of thieves, assassins . . . whatever they require.'

'But how would Underwood contact them? And how would he know which readers to recruit?'

Darkus quickly leafed through the book until he reached the back cover. At the bottom of it, a tag line read:

*Discover more! If you're having trouble understanding 'The Code', dial 0845 111111.*

'The readers contact *him*.' Darkus reached for his phone and dialled the number.

They both listened as an automated female voice said: 'Your call is being transferred. Please hold.' The line continued ringing for another thirty seconds.

'They're bouncing the call, redirecting it so it's impossible to trace,' said Knightley. 'They're covering their tracks.'

Then an automated male voice announced: 'Please leave a message with your name and telephone number after the tone.'

Darkus ended the call. 'That's how Underwood locates them,' he said. 'The readers are perfect criminals. They have no knowledge of each other . . . or of who gave them the orders.' He realised, not without irony, 'They would think the book told them to do it.'

He looked to his father for congratulation, but Knightley's face had suddenly clouded over, appearing more troubled than ever. Darkus opened his mouth to speak as Knightley held up a finger and urgently pointed to the doorway.

A single white dove had entered the room, strutting

across the carpet, blinking at them impassively. It looked like some kind of sentinel, or sign.

'Dad . . . ? What's it doing here?' whispered Darkus, lacking a suitable explanation for what was in front of him.

'Bogna!!' Knightley cried out. For once, there was no response. 'Stay back, Doc. It's a message.'

Knightley knelt down and picked up the bird, finding a small paper scroll attached to its neck. The dove flapped its wings as he gently removed the scroll and unfurled it. The message read simply:

*Let's have no unpleasantness. Regards, Presto.*

'Doc,' said Knightley, feeling his heart thudding in his chest. 'I want you to go and find the best hiding place you can.'

# Chapter 19
## CUTTING THE CORD

Darkus couldn't disguise the panic in his voice. 'But, Dad –'

'Don't argue with me. The Combination is here, and I can't guarantee a satisfactory outcome.'

Knightley walked to the open window and released the dove. He looked down to see a long black saloon car with tinted windows parked outside. It resembled a hearse.

Darkus stood frozen.

'Do as I say,' Knightley ordered. 'Whatever happens, I want you to stay hidden and don't come out.'

'What about you?'

Knightley grabbed Darkus by the shoulders. 'Let me worry about me.'

A creaking noise came from the lower staircase. Knightley silently gestured to Darkus to scram, then went to a wood-panelled cupboard and took out a short baton. He pressed a switch and the baton telescoped out to a length of sixty centimetres. He pressed the switch again and a low electric hum emanated from the tip.

Darkus didn't have time to ask what it was. He looked around, as if playing a bizarre game of hide-and-seek, only this time the stakes were exponentially higher. He crossed the landing to the bathroom.

Behind him, Knightley descended the stairs softly, the baton trained in front of him.

Darkus looked around the bathroom, scanning for options, but found none. He looked back at the office, but it was too obvious, surely. The catastrophiser began ticking and vibrating, generating a variety of possible outcomes, none of them good. He felt the familiar sensation of fear, draining his adrenal glands, quickening his pulse, leaving a dry, sour taste in his mouth. He looked around the room again for a hiding place.

Two floors below, Knightley reached the bottom of the staircase and moved across the hallway, the baton aimed ahead of him, lightly humming. Through the kitchen doorway he saw Bogna's feet laid out on the floor, pointing upward, still wearing her Crocs. Now fear took hold of Knightley too. She couldn't be dead. She had the constitution of an ox. He put his feelings in a locked box and tried to keep his wits about him. He was too old for this, too ill prepared. He crept quickly across the carpeted living area, circling with the baton to cover every angle. He crossed on to the linoleum and knelt by Bogna's body, which was spread-eagled on the floor. He found a strong pulse in her wrist, then she let out a long, bronchial snore. Knightley exhaled with relief and got to his feet, moving back into the living room, then he stopped.

The heavy curtains over the front windows appeared to move. Knightley aimed the baton ahead of him and used it to part them. The tip of the shaft crackled loudly with a rhythmic ticking sound, sparking off the curtain fabric. With a quick movement he tore them open, letting sunlight flood into the room. He shielded his eyes as

Presto appeared from behind a sofa unseen, directly behind him, wearing a Spanish gaucho hat pulled low over his face.

Knightley sensed something, and spun around to find Presto approaching across the carpet. Knightley instantly swung the baton, too wide. Presto ducked and seemed to reappear on the other side of the room, out of range. The stun baton connected with an overhead lamp in a shower of sparks. Blue wisps of high-voltage electricity ran up and down the length of the weapon as Knightley turned to face his opponent again.

'Got any other tricks, Alan?' said Presto, his mouth leering under the brim of the hat.

'What do you want?'

'I warned you not to proceed with this investigation . . . You chose to proceed.'

'Old habits die hard,' said Knightley, slipping his hand through the wrist strap for security.

'You've lost the old magic, Alan – playing second fiddle to the boy.'

'Leave him out of it,' warned Knightley.

'Not my fault you made it a family affair.'

Knightley lunged towards him but Presto dodged the baton again, trapped Knightley's arm, pivoted and threw him over his shoulder.

Knightley gripped the stun baton, which crackled and sparked off everything it touched on the way down. He smashed through a coffee table and awkwardly staggered back to his feet.

Presto spun and kicked his opponent's arm, sending the baton ricocheting against Knightley's chest, giving him the full brunt of the charge. Knightley's eyes rolled back, then the baton made a deafening *pop* and jerked out of his hands, skittering to the floor. Knightley flinched, recoiling on to the sofa in a heap.

'The Coh–' Knightley stuttered. 'The Cohm–'

'What's the matter? Cat got your tongue?' Presto swaggered towards him as if performing for an invisible audience.

Knightley rolled himself off the sofa and crawled towards a bureau desk. 'The Combination . . .' he said, sounding strangely surprised.

'That's right, fella. Alive and well.'

Knightley dragged himself across the carpet, seeing only optical white noise, the remnants of electricity running pell-mell around his head. Then a row of numbers and letters appeared on his visual cortex, burnished like exploding stars, beginning with the characters 2 and D. It was what he'd been looking for all this time, on street signs and on the back of buses. The shock treatment had apparently dredged them up from the depths of his subconscious. His brows knitted as he tried to read them in his mind. He didn't even know what they meant; he only knew they were important.

'Yes-yes . . .' he muttered, crawling on all fours through the jungle of carpet fibres towards where he knew the desk was.

'Where are you going, Alan?' Presto bent down and picked up the stun baton, then held it over Knightley's scuttling body. 'It's sleepy time.'

Presto touched the baton to Knightley's back, sending voltage coursing through him. Knightley cackled hilariously as the current ran through him, causing his limbs to dance crazily, then he rolled over and continued in a sort of backstroke across the floor. Presto laughed too. A forced, bellowing laugh that resounded through the whole house.

While Presto's head was back, roaring, Knightley raised his leg and delivered a spasmodic kick to the groin. Presto's laugh reached a maniacal high-pitched crescendo as he doubled over in pain.

While Presto was distracted, Knightley hauled himself up against the bureau desk. The numbers and letters in his head were now clear as day. His fingers groped blindly across the desktop, quickly locating the notepad and Parker pen that were always kept there. He grasped the pad and pen, pulling them to the floor, then removed the pen top with his teeth and frantically began to scribble, before balling up the note and throwing it under a chair.

Presto came to stand over him, grabbing Knightley's lapels and hauling him to his feet. 'Game's over. Someone wants to see you.' Presto swung his right hand, knocking Knightley unconscious.

Darkus heard a thud from downstairs, but was unable to move due to the confines of his hiding place or to see anything other than a very faint ray of light through the tunnel of darkness that extended some three metres above his head. Darkus stopped believing in Father Christmas many years before the rest of his peers. He considered it his first criminal case. After conducting a cursory examination of the logistics involved, Darkus deduced that children the world over were labouring under an illusion. Now, finding himself wedged inside a chimney, he found the idea even more laughable. He shuffled further up the narrow tunnel, keeping his shoes pressed against the inner walls for stability, not sure if he would make it to the top, but certain he needed to get as far up as possible.

He now heard another noise: a heavy car door being slammed on the street outside.

The catastrophiser told him that his father had already been taken. But, fortunately, if the villains had wanted his father dead, they wouldn't have issued a warning. Darkus had to conclude that his dad was now in the hands of the enemy, and he was on his own.

Whether or not they wanted *him* was another matter.

He pressed down with his feet, keeping himself wedged into the chimney to stop from falling. His clothes would be covered in soot and he imagined himself a Dickensian character stuck in a plot that was far more sinister than anything he had ever read about. He wondered if any other children had followed these same tracks in years gone by, climbing through the darkness, and hopefully emerging intact at the other end.

He heard a different noise now. It was the creak of the office door opening. Someone was still in the house, on the top floor, only a matter of two metres below him. He froze, listening for any noises that were funnelled up to him. He heard a floorboard give slightly, the whisper of a foot brushing the carpet. Then he looked down, seeing a tall, slim shadow fall over the fireplace.

'Come down, Darkus. I know you're up there.' Presto's disconnected voice echoed up the chimney.

Darkus began shuffling higher, dislodging large bits of carbon from the walls. He accidentally inhaled soot and choked, trying to fight back coughs. His throat tightened, his stomach cramped, his lungs burned and contracted until he coughed heavily, unable to stop himself.

The voice appeared again. 'Do you like magic tricks? All kids like magic tricks. Come down and I'll show you one.'

'Leave me alone!' Darkus called down the shaft, feeling the blood pound through his head. He looked down, seeing the shadow over the fireplace grow and expand to cover the whole grate.

Then an arm leaped up the chimney after him. A gloved hand grabbed at his feet. Darkus stumbled and tried to move further up, but lost his footing and dropped straight down half a metre. He cried out in terror as he wedged his back and feet into the inner walls, tearing his jacket but stopping his fall. The hand groped again, getting hold of his ankle and sharply yanking downward. Darkus's teeth chattered, his mouth unable to form words, even to scream. He wedged himself deeper into the narrow space, then kicked down, dispensing with the hand, which crumpled and recoiled.

A muffled curse came from below him in response. Then a series of sounds were funnelled up to him in quick succession. A wailing alarm pierced the walls, blaring out across the whole street. Then a thundering stampede arrived on the stairs, ascending to the top floor, created not by a group, but by a single person. A torrent of Polish swear words accompanied the wild clanging of a frying pan.

Whatever happened was over quickly. A tussle resulted in the shattering of a windowpane, and the shadow vanished from the fireplace. A car door slammed on the street below, an engine revved up and the car screeched away, leaving just the blare of the alarm, which did little to calm the nerves.

'Doc? You are OK?' Bogna's face appeared at the bottom of the chimney like a vision of the Virgin Mary.

'Yes-yes,' Darkus answered nervously, then began his descent into the office.

'Your clothings!' said Bogna, looking appalled.

'Dad,' he stammered. 'They've taken Dad.'

\*

After Bogna disabled the alarm, Darkus explained why they could not contact the police until he had conducted a superficial examination of the scene. Bogna reluctantly agreed, and suspected that this was exactly what Knightley Senior would have done in the circumstances.

Darkus retraced his father's steps, moving across the front room, noting the roughly drawn curtains, the displaced cushion, the collapsed coffee table. He then got to his knees and crawled across the carpet, observing the subtle changes in the direction of the nap. His father had left a trail of sorts, like the path of a large snake, meandering from the sofa towards the bureau desk.

Darkus found the Parker pen without its top. The nib was dripping black ink into the rug. Bogna's eyes went wide and she quickly descended on the stain with a damp cloth until Darkus stopped her. A pen without a top meant his father had to have left him a message.

Lying flat on the floor, he peered under the furniture, swivelling around on his front to check every corner. Discarded under a bookshelf he found what he was looking for. The balled-up piece of paper. He reached for it, his fingers rolling it arduously into his grasp. Then he got to his feet and uncrumpled it, spreading it out on the bureau desk. The paper was creased in all directions, the handwriting was jagged and out of control, but the message was clear enough:

THE COMBINATION IS 2D75#10.

The meaning, however, was anyone's guess.

# Chapter 20
## LOOSE THREADS

Bogna, still clutching the frying pan in a defensive stance, watched Darkus stare at the piece of paper and waited patiently for instruction.

Darkus looked up, mystified, and gently removed the pan from her vice-like grip, then advised her to apply a cold compress to her head, to ease the concussion she'd clearly received. Bogna slipped out, then reappeared wearing a turban made from dish towels and bags of frozen peas.

'You think Alan is OK?' she asked. 'You think they will feed him?'

'I don't know,' said Darkus, then reached in his pocket, pulled out his phone and dialled Bill's number. It rang and rang with no response.

Fearing the worst, he looked up the number for University College Hospital and dialled it. The receptionist put him through to a nurse on the ward; Darkus said he was calling to check on his uncle – using Bill's birth name, Montague Billoch. She put him on hold, and Darkus became convinced that Bill had either been abducted, or worse.

The nurse returned to the line. 'Mr Billoch is currently in surgery, for his leg. It'll be several hours before he comes round from the anaesthetic.'

Darkus breathed a sigh of relief. 'Thank you.' But he didn't have several hours. 'When he wakes up, please tell him Darkus called, and it's urgent.'

He put down the phone, his mind racing. With his father and the Knowledge both gone, he was left with nothing but his own memory, and his own instincts.

Bogna vanished upstairs, then returned with fresh towels and a tall pile of clothes wrapped in tissue paper. 'Alan instruct me to go to Jermyn Street. He gave me your size. I hope it fit . . .'

Taken aback, Darkus received the pile of clothes in his arms; it was so tall it obscured his face. He took a few steps backward and lowered it on to the sofa, admiring it as if it was the best Christmas present he'd ever received, which in a way it was. He slowly unwrapped the tissue paper to find socks, undergarments, collared shirts and a Donegal tweed jacket and trousers. Darkus stared in wonderment. He carefully removed his own soiled jacket and set it aside, then picked up the new one, admiring the cut, feeling the soft yarn of the cloth.

He slowly tried it on. It fit perfectly, and it felt like a dagger to the heart. He had misjudged his father – the one person he had ever really had anything in common with – and now he was gone; worse still, he was in grave jeopardy.

Darkus found his eyes full of tears, unable to reason with them, unable to contain them any longer.

'There, there . . .' said Bogna, and smothered him, patting him gently on the back. 'I know Alan. Alan can take care of himself.' Unseen, Bogna shook her head, looking far less convinced of this.

Darkus wiped his eyes and turned back to the pile of clothes with a mixture of sadness and determination.

'I'll go and get changed,' he said. 'Can you be ready to leave in five minutes?'

'Leave? Leave where?' asked Bogna.

'I'll explain on the way. I'm afraid you're driving.'

'In Alan's taxi-car?' She looked bewildered. 'I haven't drive since I am a teenager in *Kłopoty-Bańki*.'

'Then we'll just have to stay in the bus lane,' said Darkus.

# Chapter 21
## A BAD TRIP

Clive slid into the Jag, put on his seat belt and pressed the *Start* button, waiting for the engine to warm up. He liked his car; he felt safe in it, even though he had to admit it felt slightly less perfect since Knightley had hijacked it. It had been misused, ridden roughshod and generally mistreated. The brakes felt a tad softer, the ride less agreeable. There were some squeaks and rattles that Clive could have sworn weren't there before the incident. What other torments Knightley might have subjected it to during its abduction didn't bear thinking about – particularly the grab-lift, the time spent in the impound yard, in the company of unfamiliars, old Ford Fiestas and who knew what; not to mention the sweaty men in oil-stained boiler suits – hardly the seasoned Jaguar technicians Clive usually entrusted her to. And then of course there was the scratch on the rear quarter panel of the gorgeous midnight-blue paintwork. Darkus had blamed it on the anorak, but secretly Clive was still convinced it was the work of his next-door neighbour.

Clive realised, with reluctance, that he was falling out of love with his car, and deep down he knew he would have to replace it.

As luck would have it, today was a road-test day, easily the best perk of the job. The production offices of *Wheel Spin*, his widely watched (but poorly reviewed) cable TV programme, had brought over a rare Italian supercar for him to review. The detailers would be waxing it to a showroom shine; the cockpit-cam would be set up to record his every impression and off-the-cuff remark as he put the car through its paces on the track. Clive didn't have the ludicrous budget of certain other car review programmes, but he had an intimate knowledge of motor vehicles, and the bubbly personality to back it up – which never ceased to win him compliments at the petrol station or the local pub.

Clive idled on the driveway for another moment, and his thoughts turned to *The Code*, bringing on a warm tingle of positivity. He turned his heated seat down a notch, then accelerated away from the house in buoyant spirits. He hadn't told Jackie about the book – she wouldn't understand. But she'd notice the change in him soon enough; everyone would. He'd only read a few pages but he could already feel the difference. Today was going to be a good day. His 'thought transmitter' was fired up and ready to go. He was going to 'be the change'.

Clive reached the production offices in record time, despite being held up by an infuriating old lady in a compact car, whom he dispatched with a stamp on the accelerator and a horn blast for good measure. Just because she was old, didn't mean she shouldn't be expected to understand the rules of the road. Speed kills, but so do senior drivers.

After a coffee and a Danish pastry in his trailer, Clive took an admiring walk around the multi-vented, cherry-red supercar that was waiting by the track. If anything could ease the pain of losing the Jag, this would.

Finding a moment to himself, Clive took his e-book reader from his anorak pocket and opened it up.

'Camera ready, Clive!' the director called over to him from the camera truck.

'Roger,' said Clive, and got into the supercar, pressing a button to lower the door into place.

The cockpit came to life with gauges and readouts, and Clive set aside the e-reader, tucking it in the glove compartment. He pulled on his driving gloves, checked his hair in the rear-view mirror, glanced at the video camera mounted in the passenger seat and the second camera on the truck behind him.

'Showtime,' he said, and gunned the Italian horses to life. The engine roared and Clive's eyes lit up, glowing with the reds and greens of the dashboard lights.

The director's voice crackled out of the walkie-talkie attached to Clive's belt. 'OK, Clive. We're rolling.'

A red light blinked on the cockpit-cam in the passenger seat, indicating it was recording.

Clive eased the supercar out of the car park and coaxed it down a slip road towards the deserted race-track where the review would be conducted. He turned the wheel, guiding the beast past another camera crew located on a grassy verge alongside the main straight. The crew gave him an enthusiastic thumbs up. Clive returned the signal vigorously with both hands.

The track extended in either direction. A few carefully placed piles of tyres were the only objects on the wide, endless horizon. Clive took up position, pointing straight down the centre. The camera truck idled beside him, focused on the side of the car.

The director's voice came through Clive's walkie-talkie. 'All right, Clive. Give it some welly.'

Clive grinned, pressing various buttons like a fighter pilot preparing for take-off. He revved the engine, checked his hair one final time, then flicked the flappy paddle behind the steering wheel, shifting into gear, ready to launch himself and the vehicle down the track, as one perfect machine. He turned to the passenger seat with an arched eyebrow. 'What we have here . . .' he said to the camera mysteriously, 'is something abso-lutely stu-pendous –'

The walkie-talkie erupted: 'Wait!! Cut! Hold on, Clive – problem on camera two.'

'Oh, bum!' Clive blurted out, and took his foot off the accelerator. The revs descended and the engine sputtered unhappily. He pressed the walkie-talkie on his belt.

'How long, Derek?' he snapped.

'Take five, guv.'

'I was all ready to go,' complained Clive.

'Sorry, guv.'

Clive dropped his hands on the wheel in disappointment. Then he looked up again, as if hearing something in his head. He recited to himself: 'Come on, Clive, positive thoughts, positive thoughts.' He forced a smile that looked like it might split him in half.

He glanced out of the window at the crew busily attending to the camera truck, then glanced at the cockpit-cam in the passenger seat. The light was off: it wasn't recording.

Clive quietly leaned over and opened the glove compartment. The e-reader flopped into his hand, its display showing *The Code*. He looked around again, then propped it in his lap and began to read.

*Make what you want the only thought in your mind. Imagine your brain is a transmitter, transmitting only positive messages.*

Clive nodded eagerly, repeating to himself, 'Only positive messages. No problem.' He suddenly thought about how annoyed he was with Knightley; how he'd have to sell the Jag, probably for a lot less than what he bought it for. Damn that man and his oddball son. If he didn't love Jackie as much as he did, he'd be rid of both of them. Clive forced his attention back to the book and read on.

*As the thought runs through your head you feel the force of its presence, reminding you that the universal laws will grant your every wish.*

Clive paused. That was weird. He actually *felt* the thought run through his head. How very strange. This book really was the most unusual thing he'd ever laid eyes on. He shrugged and kept reading.

'OK, Clive. Ready in two,' the director instructed him through the walkie-talkie. 'Clive? Clive . . . ?'

But Clive was staring into the rear-view mirror, deaf to the world. His eyes were wide, his brows arched in stark terror.

'Clive? Do you read me?' the director asked. 'Clive?'

But Clive didn't hear a word. He was staring at a large black supercar that was idling on the track right behind him. It was multi-vented with matt black bodywork, accented with carbon and even more aggressively styled than his. Steam appeared to be rising from its roof and fins.

The black car's engine revved sharply. Clive's eyes widened, his brows arching higher. It revved again. It was howling like something possessed.

Clive's knuckles turned white, tightening around the steering wheel, then he furiously started pressing buttons, beginning the launch sequence. Both supercars sat poised, ready to pounce; both engines roaring, perfectly matched.

Clive stared into the rear-view mirror, terrified and defiant. 'Showtime!'

At the side of the track, one of the crew heard Clive gunning the engine, and called to the director: 'Derek? Are we meant to be rolling?'

The director turned around, confused. 'I haven't said we're rolling.' He walked towards the red supercar, which was sitting completely alone on the track, revving wildly. He lifted the walkie-talkie to his mouth. 'Clive? I said two minutes. Clive?' He went to tap on the window when –

The ultra-wide tyres spun to life, burning rubber, billowing smoke out of the wheel arches, and projected Clive and the car down the track.

The director threw himself out of the way, rolling to the ground, barking uncontrollably, 'Clive?! What's he doing?'

The crew quickly took up their positions. The director got to his feet, jumped into the passenger seat of the camera truck and shouted, 'Go after him!'

The camera truck revved up and peeled away, following the lone supercar down the track.

Inside the cockpit, Clive gripped the wheel, alternately glancing at the fast approaching bend, and checking the rear-view mirror, which contained the black supercar lunging, hot on his tail – like some kind of satanic beast, engulfed in steam, tongues of flame leaping out of the vents.

'You wanna play?' Clive shouted at the mirror, then turned the wheel, hurling his car into the bend, laughing maniacally.

In the camera truck, the director watched the monitor in confusion. The cockpit-cam was rolling, providing live feed of Clive giggling and shouting hysterically. The director and his driver looked at each other, raising their eyebrows.

Clive wrenched the steering wheel, taking the next bend in a power-slide. 'Ooh . . . bit of understeer,' he commented out of habit. A whitish saliva was forming at the corners of his mouth. He looked in the rear-view mirror.

The black car was still behind him; he hadn't even shaken it by an inch. It lunged at him again, somehow tapping into an even greater reserve of power than his. What kind of engine was under that bonnet? Who – or *what* – was behind the wheel?

Clive rubbed his eyes quickly and rechecked his mirrors. It was *still* there.

'What are you?!! Huh??' Clive rocked the wheel, weaving expertly through a series of tight opposing bends. The black car stayed locked on, right behind him. 'You just messed with the wrong driver!' he shouted triumphantly.

The director stayed glued to the live feed. 'What's the prat doing now?'

Clive let out a yodel and stamped on the brakes. The supercar rapidly decelerated and Clive's whole face appeared to remain at its previous speed, being sucked towards the windscreen, his cheeks and jowls quivering from the g-forces, his eyebrows almost completely covering his eyeballs. He peered up through the folds of skin and could just about make out the black car in the rear-view mirror, performing the exact same manoeuvre.

'Damn you –' Clive spun the car around in a circle, his head lolling from one side to the other, knocking against the window. Then he took off straight for the perimeter fence.

The director realised with horror, shouting at his driver, 'He's heading for the dual carriageway! Stop him!' The driver turned the wheel, steering the heavy camera truck off-road, over a series of grassy bumps, to try to cut him off.

On the cockpit-cam, Clive shouted, 'Across the line!'

Clive's supercar tore through a leafy verge and took down the fence.

On the other side, cars pootled along the dual carriageway, until Clive exploded through a set of bushes, nearly colliding with a caravan. Other drivers swerved to avoid him.

Inside the cockpit, Clive's face was streaked with saliva, his eyes huge, flicking between the windscreen and the mirrors, the beast still bearing down on him. He slalomed through traffic, missing other motorists by inches. A light rain descended over the road, making the conditions even more treacherous. And still the beast bore down on him, dodging and lunging behind him.

'Think you can take me . . . ?!' he screamed, then tore his eyes away from the rear-view mirror and saw a busy roundabout coming straight for him. 'Uh-oh –'

Clive swore and slammed both loafers on the brake pedal, sending the supercar into a barely controlled skid. An array of red lights lit up the back of the car. Smoke and vapour poured from under the wheels, accompanied by a screaming, grinding noise, like sandpaper on gravel.

The red supercar slid nauseatingly to a halt, less than an inch from the busy roundabout.

'B-loody hell!' Clive exclaimed with relief, until he saw the black supercar change lanes and pull up right next to him.

Clive cranked his head to stare at the black tinted windows beside him; unable to see who was driving, unwilling to even consider what could be in there. More steam rose from the vents and fins.

'What d'you want from me?!!' Clive screamed at it through his closed window.

Slowly, the tinted window of the black car descended to reveal the driver: it was Clive. It was himself. Only this Clive was laughing insanely, and the entire cockpit was on fire, flames licking at his clothes, smoke pouring from the dashboard.

'No-no-no-no!' Clive screamed at himself in unholy terror.

Suddenly he was distracted by a loud tapping on the window. A black leather-gloved finger caught his attention, bringing his eyes into shallow focus – and when he glanced back at the black car, it was *gone*.

Clive quickly wiped the drool from his chin and powered down his electric window to find a motorcycle policeman sitting right beside him. The black car was nowhere in sight.

'Do you have any idea how fast you were going, sir?!' the policeman said, leaning over his handlebars, leathers creaking.

'I-I-' Clive stuttered uncontrollably.

The policeman paused, then did a double take: the camera in the passenger seat . . . That face . . . The pieces fell into place. 'Hold on a tick,' he said. 'Aren't you Clive Palmer?' It took a moment for the full significance to hit him. Then his face brightened into a wide smile. 'Am I on telly or something?'

'Not unless you want to be,' said Clive, instantly recovering his charm.

Behind them, the camera truck arrived with its hazard lights flashing, the director gesturing wildly from the passenger seat.

The policeman blushed and adjusted his helmet. 'I must say, I'm a big fan of your programme.'

'Very glad to hear it. Think I just experienced a bit of

unintended acceleration,' said Clive, tapping the dashboard judiciously. 'Italian cars, eh?'

'Made for Italian drivers,' joked the policeman, and got out his notepad and pen. Clive's expression dropped. 'Mind if I get your autograph?' said the policeman. 'It's Sergeant Jayes.'

'Ab-solutely,' said Clive, beaming, as he scribbled on the notepad, then signed with a flourish.

'Just wait till the boys at the station get a load of this.'

'Fan-tastic. Keep up the good work,' said Clive.

The policeman revved his motorbike and pulled away. Clive quietly tucked the e-reader back in the glove compartment, checked his hair in the mirror, then waved at the camera truck as if nothing had happened.

# Chapter 22
## EXEAT

Tilly sat at her all-in-one bunk-desk, putting the finishing touches to her science homework. She had spent the entire day counting ticker tape and measuring the velocity of a toy car, but Miss Khan would be satisfied; she was sure of that. Plus the dulling pleasure of routine distracted her from the perils of her overactive mind.

There weren't many people who held Tilly's interest for any length of time. In fact, the only other person who had crossed her mind that day – in a platonic way, obviously – was Darkus. This revelation was even more peculiar, seeing as he had been residing quite literally under her nose for so many years.

Outside the dormitory window, the sun had dipped below the trees that encircled the Cranston School compound. The other bunk units were empty, except for a few strewn celeb magazines: the remnants of the other girls' extra-curricular reading. Tilly closed her science folder and pushed it to the back of the cocoon-like desk, slumping in her chair, disconsolate. She gazed out into the dark woods beyond the playing fields and let her mind wander. A whole world lay just beyond her reach; a world that promised both good and bad, and all the mysteries that came with it. For now, her only contact with it was a computer screen and an internet connection. The treeline blurred with the falling dusk, until all that was left was –

A pinpoint of light flashed at her.

She blinked, believing it was a reflection in the windowpane. Then the light winked at her again, from deep in the woods, and repeated a series of long and short flashes. She had no idea what it meant, but instantly recognised it as Morse code.

She quickly opened her laptop and typed 'morse code translator' into the search engine. She clicked on the top link and a web page loaded up with two boxes: one for inputting the code, one to display the translation.

She looked back out of the window and saw the light flicker once, then die out. She watched for a long ten seconds. It seemed to have gone altogether, evaporated into the ether. Maybe it was her imagination playing tricks on her.

Then the light came back, more persistent than ever, flashing in long and short bursts. Tilly used the '.' and '–' symbols on her keyboard to imitate the rhythm of the

Morse code. She kept her eyes trained on the woods as her fingers struck the keys like a concert pianist.

The light died out, reaching the end of its sequence.

Tilly turned to the computer screen and saw the message that was displayed in the translation window. It read:

SOS. *Come asap. Darkus.* SOS. *Come asap. Darkus.*

Tilly furrowed her brow, then broke into a smile. It was as if she'd conjured him out of thin air. She debated for a split second whether to go, and instantly decided that if it was important enough for him to be lurking in the woods, then it was important enough to justify another escape attempt. She quickly packed her backpack, pulled on a black anorak and knit cap and exited the dorm.

In the corridor outside, she slipped off her shoes, tucked them in her bag, then jogged quietly over the parquet floors, her stockinged feet barely touching the ground. She rounded the gallery and spotted the house-mistress patrolling the building. Tilly slid to the floor behind a pillar and waited for her to pass. Then she checked her phone was on silent and set the countdown timer, knowing the house mistress would raise the alarm in approximately three minutes.

Seconds later, Tilly descended a set of marble stairs, seeing a male teacher crossing the mezzanine carrying a stack of folders. She paused in full view of him, but he didn't look up from his workload and ambled through an opposite doorway. Hearing more footsteps approaching, Tilly sat on the curving banister, slid down the last flight of stairs and vanished through a fire exit.

By the time the countdown had finished, she'd reached the woods, but the flashing torchlight had stopped sending its beacon and she could only go on her instincts. She picked her way through the forest, taking pains to avoid stepping on twigs or making any rookie mistakes. She could just see the curving concrete shape of the Greek theatre, hidden among the trees – she had never graced its stage, not caring much for amateur dramatics. She moved along the outer wall, looking for any sign of Darkus, then stopped in her tracks, seeing a figure ahead of her.

It was Mr Burke, sitting on a tree stump, wearing a complicated piece of black headgear that obscured his entire face except for his signature handlebar moustache. Instead of eyes, he had a pair of telescopic lenses with a tiny red light at the centre of each barrel. Tilly recognised the work of Miss Khan, which was evidently being put to good use.

Mr Burke adjusted the night-vision goggles to peer deeper into the forest. If Darkus was out there, he wouldn't stand a chance against Burke, whose position as PE teacher was only the epilogue to a long career in the Territorial Army, where he was rumoured to have seen action in Gibraltar. Now his nights were spent surveilling the grounds for intruders and escapees, and tonight he clearly had the scent. Tilly had never been apprehended by Burke, and she didn't intend for this to be the first time.

She examined him from about forty metres to the rear. At least Darkus had had the good sense to extinguish his torch. Or maybe he'd already been caught and confessed all, and she was walking into a trap. Before her mind could follow that train of thought any further, a hand gently tapped her on the shoulder. She flinched and spun around, finding Darkus, dressed in a herringbone coat and a Donegal tweed hat, crouched in the undergrowth. She stopped her mouth, but the surly repositioning of her stance created a loud rustle.

Burke turned, refocusing his goggles in their direction.

'Get down!' whispered Darkus.

'Duh,' she responded sharply.

They ducked behind a felled tree. Burke kept toggling his headgear. Tilly pointed at Darkus then closed her fist to indicate 'freeze', then lowered her palm to indicate 'crouch', then tapped her head to indicate 'follow me' and pointed towards an outcrop of trees to their right. Finally, she pumped her fist to indicate 'hurry up'. Darkus confirmed with a thumbs up.

They crawled through the undergrowth out of sight.

'What are you *doing* here?!' she whispered once they'd reached a safe distance.

'It would help if you answered your phone.'

'Well, I'm all ears.'

'They've got Dad.'

'Who have?'

'The Combination,' said Darkus.

'And how is that my problem?'

'It's not, I suppose, but you're the only one who can help.'

'Help do what?'

'Get him back, of course.'

'What's he ever done for me? Apart from help put me back here.'

'If you won't do it for him, then do it for me,' said Darkus. 'And for Carol.' Darkus knew that bringing up the subject of her mother was playing with fire, but he was in no mood to negotiate. The fact was they had history. A shared history. And whatever Tilly's feelings were towards his father, she would have to put them aside for now.

'What exactly do you want from me?' she asked.

'I've got a problem – a cipher problem.'

'How many characters?'

'Seven.'

'And you can't crack it yourself?'

'No,' he admitted.

'OK. I'll see what I can do, but I can't promise anything.' She glanced at Burke, who was still adjusting his goggles but was now meandering towards them through the darkness. She turned back to Darkus and whispered, 'Have you got an exit strategy for this great escape of yours?'

'I've got a car, about two klicks that way . . .' he said, pointing into the woods. 'That's kilometres by the way.'

'I know that,' she said curtly.

'Who's there?' announced Burke. His goggles seemed to be in focus now, as he suddenly picked up speed, hopping over tree stumps and zeroing in on them. 'Stop!'

Tilly and Darkus took off through the woods and down a steep incline. Darkus used one hand to secure his hat and the other to grab on to tree branches as they descended into a clearing. Tilly turned and saw Burke sprinting towards them with a demonic smile on his face. Darkus had paused to pull a compass from his inside pocket.

'Come on!' she cried out, and pulled him along with her.

Burke hurdled a fallen tree and went after the blurry infrared images in his goggles. He was gaining on them.

Tilly led Darkus under the dim moonlight, through a thick corridor of foliage. Darkus glanced at the luminous dial of his compass and pointed in the direction of an embankment that bordered the school driveway. A teacher's car drove past, headlights trained ahead, unaware of the commotion.

Darkus and Tilly scrambled across the embankment with Burke in hot pursuit.

'I don't see a car!' she shouted.

Darkus moved towards a pair of trees with a large bush in the middle. He yanked one corner of the bush, which collapsed to reveal it was only a leaf-covered tarpaulin. Underneath, almost wedged between the two trees, was the black Fairway cab, with Bogna waiting in the driver's seat, gripping the steering wheel.

'Get in,' ordered Darkus. Tilly did as she was told. Darkus got in the back seat beside her and closed the door.

'*Mój Boże!*' Bogna cried out, and flicked on the headlights, catching Burke right in the high beams.

'Argh!' Burke's night vision became a blinding snowstorm. He shielded his eyes, staggered back, tripped over a stump and fell out of sight. He would later swear that what he had seen was a London taxi.

'Floor it, Bogna,' said Darkus.

Bogna stamped on the accelerator, steering the taxi out of its hiding place and performing a wide arc, bouncing through the undergrowth, before gaining traction and rejoining the driveway.

The Fairway swerved erratically then headed for the school gate, leaving Cranston in its wake. It bounced once more as it straddled a speed bump, then it indicated left, but turned right, and was gone.

# Chapter 23
## MEANWHILE
## BACK AT THE LAB

When Miss Khan entered her classroom at eight o'clock the next morning, she instantly knew someone else had been there before her.

For a start, there was a homework assignment on her desk which clearly hadn't been there when she left the building the previous evening. It was a dozen pages thick, neatly presented in a blue plastic folder. The title page read: *'The Nature of Velocity' by Matilda Palmer.*

Miss Khan flicked through it, finding a series of well-prepared diagrams, results and conclusions, annotated with sections of ticker tape. She set it down again, flummoxed. She knew Tilly had potential, but this was most unlike her.

Then Miss Khan noticed the door to her lab annex was ajar. She slowly pushed it open and walked inside. Her white lab coat was on its hanger. Her plastic lab specs and soldering iron were carefully set out on the lab bench just as she had left them. However, the main feature of the lab was missing: a series of clamps and wires lay on the table, but the modified asthma inhaler was *gone*.

Miss Khan swallowed, feeling her throat go dry with apprehension. If Tilly had run off again, what on earth would she be doing that could require the use of pepper spray foam? And if Tilly did have cause to use it, would it even perform properly and with adequate range? It was still a work in progress. In the future, enhancements would have to be made. Perhaps other devices would need to be designed, with a wider range of capabilities. That's what her father would have wanted. 'Make the tool to fit the job,' he always said.

Against her better judgement, Miss Khan felt her brain come alive with possibilities . . .

# Chapter 24
# THE POWER OF
# SUGGESTION

The sun rose over Wolseley Close, touching the roofs of the neatly arranged mock-Tudor houses, painting a picture of suburban bliss.

Clive's Jag sat in the driveway. Jackie stood behind the kitchen window with a phone cradled on her shoulder, waiting for the kettle to boil. Clive yawned and drew the curtains in the master bedroom. His murky recollections of the previous day's events had mostly evaporated, like a long, disturbing dream that he'd thankfully woken up from. Now he was left with the recurring problem of his daughter, who had apparently escaped from school – again. Life, to all intents and purposes, had returned to normal.

He went to the bathroom, splashed some cold water on his face and looked deeply into his tired, grey eyes. Whatever he'd experienced yesterday had been a figment of his imagination, a momentary lapse of reason, nothing more. It was probably a perfectly understand-able side effect of *The Code*, part of his transformation from the 'old' Clive into the 'new' one: Clive 2.0.

He had located an 0845 number in the text of the e-book and dialled it, hoping for some reassurance, but he only got a recorded message. Not exactly great customer service. He'd left his name and mobile number as requested. He then read a bit more of the book, and was glad to report no further complications of any kind. He hadn't told Jackie about what had happened at the track. Best not to worry her, and besides, he couldn't have anyone interfering with his spiritual growth, not even her.

He believed he'd managed to convince the director and crew that the supercar's engine control unit had malfunctioned, resulting in a bout of unintended accel-eration. It could happen, he told himself.

Clive checked the e-reader was still on the top shelf of the bathroom cabinet, then zipped himself into his favourite lime-green shell suit and jogged downstairs.

Jackie was still talking on the phone when he entered the kitchen. She automatically handed Clive a mug of hot tea and finished her call: 'Well, if she contacts you, I want to be the first to know . . . Thanks. I will . . . OK, bye.' She put the phone down.

'Thanks, love,' Clive responded, sipping his tea. 'Think I might pop to Homebase. Get the thingy for the strimmer.'

'Aren't you remotely interested in where or how your daughter is?' said Jackie sharply. 'I've been on the phone to everyone we know.'

'She'll turn up. She always does,' said Clive cheerily, and poured himself a bowl of Special K.

'I can't reach Darkus or Alan either.'

'I'm sure they're just enjoying some father–son time,' Clive mused. 'Lovely day out there, isn't it?' His left eye twitched slightly as he poured the milk.

'Yes, it is,' she replied, looking at him quizzically. 'Are you all right, Clive? You've been acting . . . funny, ever since you got home last night.'

'Is it so hard to believe that I might just be – I don't know – relaxed, happy and at one with myself?'

'Yes, Clive. Frankly it is.'

'Well, get used to it, Jax,' he said. 'It's the new me.'

'I'm not sure I like it.'

The phone started ringing and Jackie leaped for it while Clive sat down to eat his cereal.

'Hello?' she said. 'Oh, hi, Bev . . . Yes, I can get to my computer. Why? What's this about?' She listened to her friend chatter at the other end of the phone. 'He what . . . ?!' She glanced at Clive suspiciously, then walked round the corner to her office nook.

Jackie balanced the phone on her shoulder, leaned over her computer, wiggled the mouse and clicked on YouTube. A list of the most popular videos flashed up. A little way down the page was a link entitled *Leaked: Clive Palmer On-Air Meltdown*. Jackie slowly put the phone down on her friend, and clicked the mouse. The video loaded up and began showing the cockpit-cam footage:

Clive was wrestling the wheel of the supercar, screaming at the rear-view mirror, dribble streaking his face. 'You wanna play?' he shouted hysterically. 'What are you?!! Huh??'

Jackie kept watching with mounting horror.

On screen, Clive stepped on the brakes, his face contorting horribly, as if it was being sucked through the business end of a vacuum cleaner. He was mumbling indecipherable words, speaking in tongues.

Jackie clicked 'Stop' and marched back into the kitchen to find the bowl of cereal half finished and Clive exiting the opposite doorway, his shell suit swishing.

'Clive? What happened at work yesterday? It's all over the web!'

'Is it?' he answered from the entrance hall. 'Must've been one of the crew. I think they secretly hate me.'

'What's going on? Do you even still *have* a job?' She turned the corner to find the front door open and Clive already getting into the Jag.

She stopped in the doorway, confused.

'Clive, I'm talking to you,' she insisted.

'That's nice, love,' he replied, starting the engine and reversing out of the driveway, then pulling away, beeping twice as he went.

Jackie watched him go, speechless.

Moments later, another car pulled into the driveway in the Jag's place, taking out an ornamental gnome as it lurched to a halt. It was a black Fairway cab.

'Alan, thank God,' said Jackie, approaching the cab only to find Bogna behind the wheel and Darkus and Tilly in the back seat, along with two laptop computers, two coffee mugs, two blankets and a half-eaten packet of chocolate digestives, which all lent the impression of a mobile headquarters. 'Doc? Tilly?' said Jackie. 'What's going on?'

'It's a stake-out,' announced Tilly.

'We've been waiting for Clive to vacate the premises,' explained Darkus. 'We need to talk. Privately.'

'Hello, Mrs Jackie,' said Bogna.

'Hello, Bogna,' she replied, confused. 'Where's Alan?'

'I'll explain everything inside,' said Darkus, as they piled out of the cab.

Jackie followed Darkus and Tilly into the kitchen, then unconsciously filled and put on the kettle. Outside the window, Bogna kept watch on the street.

'I've got a lot on my mind at the moment, Darkus,' his mother stammered. 'Clive is having some kind of . . . breakdown. And honestly, I'm starting to wonder if I'm the common factor here. First Alan's breakdown, now Clive's, Tilly's truancy, your social problems –'

'Mum,' said Darkus firmly, 'I don't have social problems. And you've got to listen to me.'

'OK,' she answered hesitantly.

'Dad's gone. He's been taken.'

'Taken? By who?'

'An organisation called the Combination,' said Darkus.

'The Combination?'

'He's talked about them before, hasn't he?'

'In passing. You know he didn't share his work with me. Only with . . .' Jackie paused and looked at Tilly, clearly referring to her mum. 'He never told me anything.'

'OK,' said Darkus. 'Then tell me what you know about Morton Underwood.'

'Morton? Your godfather? Well, Morton died. It wouldn't be right to speak ill of the dead.'

'He's not dead, Mum.'

'Well, in that case I'll tell you,' she said, wasting no time. 'I never liked the man. There was just something *not right* about him. Something dead inside.'

'Can you think of a way to find him?'

'No clue.'

'Do you have any pictures of him?' asked Tilly.

'Let me think . . .' She pondered. 'No. I don't think I've ever seen a single photo of him. Isn't that strange?'

Darkus and Tilly looked at each other.

'Have you got time for a jam sandwich?' Jackie added.

'Possibly not,' Darkus responded, then turned to Tilly. 'Uncle Bill's sedated, Mum doesn't know anything, Dad could be anywhere. It looks like this is all we've got . . .' He took out his father's scribbled note:

THE COMBINATION IS 2D75#10.

Clive left Homebase pushing a trolley with all manner of household goods protruding from it: rubber hosing, stackable drawers, a shelving unit. He didn't really know what had come over him in there. He seemed to have just bought everything. He shrugged and continued rattling across the car park.

He reached the Jag and opened the boot, realising

instantly that there was no way he was going to fit it all in. He also realised with a sinking feeling that he hadn't even remembered to get the thingy for the strimmer.

At that moment, a medium-sized man in a dark suit stepped out of a chauffeur-driven car that was idling nearby. Unbeknown to Clive, the car had been following him all morning.

Morton Underwood approached him with a smile, fixing him with the magnified stare of his glasses. 'Excuse me. Aren't you C-Clive Palmer?'

'The very same,' said Clive proudly. Afterwards he would have trouble remembering anything about this man. He would only have a vague recollection of a pair of saucer-like eyes hovering before him.

'I w-wonder . . .' Underwood began. 'Do you know *The Code*?'

'The Code?' repeated Clive.

'Y-yes. Do you *know* . . . *The Code*?' Underwood repeated again, pronouncing each word clearly. His voice was flat and mellifluous, except for that unfortunate stutter.

'Yes. Yes, I do,' said Clive, realising this must have something to do with the 0845 number that he'd dialled. 'Wow. Your customer service is . . . un-believable.'

'And do you know the *meaning of fear*?' said Underwood, trying carefully to articulate each word.

Almost at once, Clive's eyes glazed over. '*Yes . . .* yes, I do.'

'G-good,' stuttered Underwood, trying to control his impediment. But fortunately for him, the hard work was done. 'Why don't you close the boot and follow me?'

'Fan-tastic,' said Clive, and closed the boot, leaving the trolley full of household goods and following the man to his chauffeur-driven car.

Underwood opened the door for Clive, then joined him in the back seat. Although Clive's eyelids felt unnaturally heavy, he attempted to examine the car, but was unable to identify the make or model. It was as if his usual powers of perception were muted. The black leather and tinted windows gave the interior a crypt-like quality.

'Nice car,' said Clive in a monotone.

'Thank you,' replied Underwood. His words followed each other in a sort of purr: 'It was very fortunate that you c-contacted us. You see, you're in a unique position to help us.'

'I am?' said Clive, raising a heavy eyelid, still feeling as if he was falling from a great height into a dark, bottomless pit.

'Indeed you are,' Underwood continued. 'Now, I want you to do something for me.'

'OK,' answered Clive without question.

'I'd like you to murder your stepson, Darkus Knightley.'

274

'Really?' asked Clive casually. 'I mean, I know he can misbehave occasionally, but does he deserve that?'

'Yes, Clive. I'm afraid he does.'

'OK.'

'Then you'll do as I ask?'

'Of course.'

'G-good.'

A few moments later, the car door opened and Clive stepped out. As he walked back to the Jag, he quickly lost all recollection that the conversation had ever happened.

He got behind the wheel, forgetting any memory of the shopping trolley or why he was even there in the first place. He started the car and reversed it, scratching one entire side of the Jag against a lamp post, then accelerated away, leaving the shopping trolley to roll aimlessly across the car park.

# Chapter 25
# THE MISSING LINK

Jackie anxiously watched the plate of triangular shaped sandwiches that sat untouched on the kitchen table. She had just witnessed a conversation about code-breaking that was more in keeping with an episode from a forensics drama than something discussed between two thirteen-year-olds. The odd thing was just how much Darkus resembled Alan and Tilly resembled his late assistant Carol.

Tilly slid the scrap of paper with the Combination on it back to Darkus, like a chess player moving a piece across the board.

'The series of characters is too short to infer a general rule,' she said.

'That's what I thought,' he replied. 'And none of the usual cipher keys apply. Dad must have been grasping at fragments of memories, pieces of the puzzle that were left buried deep in his subconscious.'

'So we're back to square one.'

'It would appear so.'

'Perhaps a sandwich would help?' suggested Jackie. They both ignored her but she didn't seem to mind.

Tilly continued to Darkus: 'If the Combination are as powerful as your dad says they are . . . If they're in fact *evil* – I'm talking *pure evil* – well, that changes things, doesn't it? In that case, a rational solution won't be enough. Even if we find them, we won't have a hope of defeating them.'

'Everything they've done so far has been entirely rational,' argued Darkus. 'Warped, but rational. Regardless of what Dad believes, I've seen no evidence of the supernatural.'

Jackie took advantage of the ensuing silence to make a point of her own: 'Remember, evil doesn't exist unless you believe in it,' she suggested. 'If you don't believe in it, it has no power.' She took a sip of her tea and mulled it over.

Tilly shrugged then nodded, finding her and her stepmum were unexpectedly in agreement for the first time ever.

'I don't know if that's going to help, Mum,' said Darkus.

Tilly looked out of the kitchen window and frowned, seeing the Jag arrive. 'Great . . . Dad's home.'

'Look,' said Jackie, 'it hasn't escaped my attention that neither of you are exactly over the moon about

Clive and me . . . and the family situation we find ourselves in.'

Neither Darkus nor Tilly answered – their silence speaking volumes.

Jackie turned to Tilly. 'But your father's clearly having a hard time at the moment. He's . . . Well, he's just not himself. So I hope you'll try to be understanding.'

'Aren't I always?' said Tilly, and nodded to the scrap of paper in front of Darkus. 'Better put that away before the doofus starts asking questions.'

'Good idea,' replied Darkus.

Outside the house, Bogna examined Clive with sceptical curiosity mixed with outright animosity. Clive parked on the street, colliding with a wheelie bin, then got out of the Jag and walked up the driveway. The presence of the large Polish lady and the black Fairway cab parked in his spot would usually have prompted an outburst of some kind, but on this particular day he only raised his eyebrows with distaste and continued up to the house.

'Jackie? I'm home!' he said cheerfully.

He marched through the door, looking up the staircase, then glancing into the living room. 'Is that Alan's car outside? Is Darkus back?' he called out. 'Jax?'

'We're in here.' Her voice appeared from the kitchen.

Clive's face registered an odd combination of pleasure

and something darker and more determined. His eyes moved without blinking, permanently staring into the middle distance. He checked his thatch of hair in the hallway mirror, then followed his wife's voice, which sounded strangely far away.

Clive wandered through the house, still experiencing a heaviness in the brows that slackened his entire face into a gormless frown. When he entered the kitchen, Tilly instinctively retreated away from him, expecting a barrage of anger and disbelief. What she got instead was completely unexpected.

'Hello, Tilly,' he said casually. 'Didn't feel like school?'

'Er . . .' she stammered, certain it must be a trick question. 'Yeah. Well, I'm just helping Darkus with something.'

Jackie started cleaning up the kitchen, clattering plates to break the awkward silence. 'How was Homebase?' she asked tightly, barely able to conceal her annoyance.

'Phen-omenal,' responded Clive. 'And, Darkus . . .' he continued, turning to his stepson with a furrowed brow and a strangely intense expression. 'How are *you*?'

'OK.'

'Oh, that's very good to hear,' said Clive, his left eye twitching as he attempted a smile. 'Very good *indeeed*.' His face looked like it was under anaesthetic. The jaw muscles contorted but the smile failed to transpire.

Darkus noticed a small ball of spittle on the corner of Clive's lower lip. It appeared to be foaming like an aspirin dissolving in water. Strangely fascinated, Darkus couldn't take his eyes off it.

'Something's wrong,' Tilly whispered across the kitchen table. Clive didn't even hear her because his gaze was still fixed on Darkus.

'Clive?' said Jackie. 'Can I have a word in private?'

'Hut!' Clive snapped, holding up his hand to demand silence. Jackie's head spun, now supremely annoyed. Clive continued: 'First me and Darkus are going to have a little talk. Upstairs.'

'We are?' asked Darkus, finding Clive more mesmerising than he ever imagined possible.

'A little talk. Man to man,' said Clive, gently but firmly moving his stepson's chair back from the table.

Darkus stood up, not wishing to make a scene.

'What's all this about, Clive?' asked Jackie.

'I'll explain later,' he said enigmatically, and guided Darkus towards the door.

As Darkus followed orders, Tilly got to her feet, sensing something was most definitely wrong, but not having the evidence to support it.

Darkus shrugged and walked past the fridge, noticing a Post-it note stuck to the door among the various ornamental magnets and family photos. The Post-it read:

POSITIVE THINKING!

The writing was Clive's.

Darkus's nostrils flared, then he shook off the idea. Not Clive. It was too implausible.

And yet, Clive clearly required self-help, and clearly suffered from Attention Deficit Disorder. And the Combination would certainly have been very grateful to receive his call.

It was not implausible. It was suddenly very *plausible*.

Now that they were out of sight, Clive shoved him a little harder, nudging him up the staircase to the upper floor.

'Where are we going?' said Darkus.

'None of your beeswax,' Clive replied.

Darkus decided it was not in his best interests to be left alone with him. If necessary, he would have to make a scene. He turned back on the stairs and opened his mouth to shout out, just as –

The doorbell rang, drowning out his cry.

'I'll get it!' said Jackie.

Clive reacted quickly, clamping a large, sweaty hand over Darkus's face and manoeuvring him on to the landing.

281

'Wh—' Darkus shouted through the hand, feeling his feet being dragged across the carpet. 'What're you doing?'

'If you could just be quiet, that would be fan-tastic.'

Darkus struggled, trying to get a grip on the shell suit, but Clive held him in a massive bear hug.

In the entrance hall, Jackie went to the door and opened it to find a familiar figure on the doorstep.

'Inspector Draycott,' she said impatiently.

'*Chief* Inspector Draycott,' he reminded her.

'What can I do for you?'

'Funny. I was just in the neighbourhood, and I couldn't help noticing Alan's car in the driveway —'

'I've noticed you've been in the neighbourhood a lot lately,' she replied. 'I've seen you through the kitchen window. If it's Alan you're after, I'm afraid he's not here.'

Draycott glanced over his shoulder at Bogna, who was still standing guard in the front garden. 'Is that right?'

'Yup.'

'I can understand your reluctance to talk to me,' he continued, 'but I assure you I'm only performing my civic duty.' He stroked his whiskers furtively. 'If you'd just satisfy my curiosity about the rather large officer who relieved me of duty on my last visit . . .'

One floor above, Clive manhandled Darkus past his bedroom, giving a view of the street with Draycott's panda car parked outside containing two more constables. Clive's eyes went wide at the sight of it, and he steered Darkus more aggressively, towards the bathroom.

Darkus complied, realising his only chance of escape was to catch Clive off guard, when he least expected it. The catastrophiser went into overdrive, its cogs and gears engaging, churning out possible scenarios. The question was: if they'd got to Clive, what had they instructed him to do?

'You've read it, haven't you?' said Darkus, but got no response. 'The Code, Clive.'

'I know The Code,' recited Clive. 'I know the meaning of fear . . .' He pushed Darkus backward into the bathroom.

Darkus grabbed hold of the towel rack, which came away from the wall and thudded on to the bath mat, cushioning its fall and deadening the sound – downstairs they would still have no idea of the drama unfolding above them. Darkus lost his balance and fell backward into the bathtub in a parody of the unwilling bather. He scrabbled to get out again, looking for any kind of improvised weapon, until . . .

Clive grabbed the shower hose and looped it around Darkus's neck. Then he began to tighten the metal coil, pressing it into Darkus's skin, which quickly became a bright red welt. Darkus's hands flailed and grasped then they found the hot and cold water taps, and spun them to life. The shower hose expanded with water, loosening its stranglehold, and water ejected out of the nozzle into Clive's face.

'Blast!' Clive barked, recoiling.

Darkus clawed at the tub, his shoes slipping on the enamel surface, until he managed to stand up.

Clive instantly picked him up by the lapels and swung him against the mirrored bathroom cabinet with such force that one of its doors burst open and toothbrushes, deodorants and aftershave bottles cascaded off the shelves, shattering on the floor. There was no disguising *this* noise.

Downstairs, Jackie looked up from her conversation with Draycott and shouted: 'Clive? Is everything all right up there?'

Clive looked past the boy that he was now holding a metre off the ground, pinned to the bathroom cabinet. He looked past Darkus and into the mirror itself. And Clive saw himself – only it wasn't himself. It was Clive 2.0, laughing maniacally from inside the mirror, his clothes and hair on fire, flames licking up the walls behind him.

'No . . . !' he shouted at himself.

Darkus felt Clive's hands tighten around his neck; his feet kicked into space hopelessly. He could feel and smell Clive's foul breath hyperventilating out of his gaping mouth. Clive's pupils were dilated, like voracious black holes, expanding and imploding.

Darkus realised the catastrophiser was overheating, redlining, throwing valves, running on empty. The worst-case scenario had already happened. Darkus was staring death in the face. Clive's gawping features were surrounded by a halo of stars. Darkus knew this was just a hallucination because his brain was being starved of oxygen. Clive's grip had blocked his carotid artery and compressed his airway. Darkus felt his lungs burning and his limbs draining of energy. Death was probably a minute away at most.

It was at that moment that Darkus experienced a crashing wave of recollections, similar to those attributed to a drowning man. But instead of seeing his whole life flash before his eyes, Darkus's mind seemed to fast forward straight to the important parts. He saw his father looking down at him, and realised how dearly he wanted to see him again, to continue where they had left off, to solve the case, and most of all to make up for all the years they'd lost. To be together again.

That thought was quickly replaced by a more pragmatic one. If he wanted to see his dad again he had to fight this battle with his stepfather on his own. He suddenly remembered the cardinal rule of Wing Chun: to remain relaxed. He also remembered the theory of the one-inch punch: that in the correct state of complete relaxation and total focus, the fist only needs one inch to hit its target with a force equivalent to the practitioner's own body weight. In Darkus's case that was approximately forty-two kilograms. It wasn't much, but directed at just the right spot, it might be enough. Instead of struggling, Darkus went limp and slowly positioned his fist on Clive's centre line.

Clive thrust Darkus against the cabinet again, breaking the mirror. The insane image shattered, and the shards of Clive's fractured personality fell away. Amid the hail of glass and bathroom items, Clive's e-reader fell and hit him squarely on the head, then fell to the floor with *The Code* displayed on the cracked screen. Clive looked at it, spooked. His grip loosened, distracted for a moment, giving his opponent the advantage.

In a split second Darkus punched forward, rotating his fist from a horizontal position to a vertical one, connecting directly with Clive's solar plexus, the soft collection of nerves in the centre of the upper abdomen. A gale of air was expelled from Clive's mouth as he let go of Darkus, who instantly slumped to the floor.

Clive staggered backward and doubled over, unable to breathe.

At that moment, Jackie and Tilly opened the door to find Darkus on the floor, and Clive heaving against the wall by the toilet, both of them struggling for breath.

'Darkus, are you OK?' shouted Tilly.

Jackie's eyes struggled to take in what she was seeing. 'Clive! What's going on?'

Draycott appeared behind them in the doorway. 'Leave this to the professionals,' he said, politely shoving them out of the way and marching in with an air of implacable authority. 'Now, Clive. What seems to be the –'

Clive suddenly reared up from behind the toilet bowl and headbutted Draycott, who toppled elegantly, like a controlled demolition, landing in a heap at Jackie's feet.

'Clive!' said Jackie in shock.

'Sorry, dear,' he replied, looking bewildered.

Draycott groped for his walkie-talkie and mumbled into it, 'Request assistance. First-floor bathroom.' He wiped his moustache, finding blood on his finger. Through the window, on the street below, the doors of his panda car flew open and two constables ran towards the house.

Confused, Clive turned to Darkus, who was slowly getting his breath back, pushing down with his feet to slide himself back up the wall to an upright position.

'Darkus, what happened to your neck?' said Jackie, then spun to Clive accusingly. 'What did you do to him?!'

'I-I think I might be having a breakdown.'

'You think?' said Jackie sharply.

287

Clive stared at her pleadingly, as the two constables raced up the stairs and burst through the doorway.

'Inspector?' one of them asked hesitantly, finding their superior stretched out on the floor.

'*Chief* Inspector,' whined Draycott. 'Well, don't just stand there. Arrest that man!' He jabbed a bloody finger at Clive. 'And bring the whole lot of them in for questioning.'

'No . . .' Clive struggled as the constables secured him in an arm-lock and manhandled him across the landing, his feet kicking in all directions.

Jackie rushed over to Darkus and grabbed him around the shoulders. 'What happened?'

'It's not his fault,' said Darkus.

'What d'you mean, not his fault?' demanded Draycott.

Darkus nodded to the broken e-reader on the floor. 'It's *The Code*. Don't read it, Mum. Get it out of the house. Destroy it.'

Tilly nodded in agreement.

'I don't know what you're talking about,' blurted Jackie.

'There's no time to explain. Please, just do as I say.'

Darkus left his mother behind and walked across the landing towards the stairs with Tilly in tow.

Bogna was waiting in the entrance hall. 'You are OK, Master Doc?' she asked.

'Fine,' said Darkus. 'But we need to get out of here.'

As Clive was stuffed into the back seat of the panda car, Bogna hopped into the Fairway and started the engine. Darkus and Tilly got into the back of the cab and closed the door. Bogna activated the central locking and lurched into reverse.

'Halt!' shouted Draycott and stepped into the path of the reversing cab. Bogna didn't even see him, and for the second time that day Draycott was knocked elegantly to the ground, this time losing consciousness altogether.

Jackie ran on to the driveway, hopeless, only to see Darkus wave goodbye from the back of the cab.

Darkus leaned forward and slid the divider open to talk to Bogna, and for the first time realised that he had no idea where to instruct her to go. His eyes fell on a *London A–Z* street map resting on top of the dashboard. He looked at it intently. Tilly noticed his nostrils flare, and his ears lift – all the telltale signs.

'What is it?' she asked.

'Bogna, would you pass me that, please?'

Bogna passed the A–Z through the glass divider.

Darkus pulled out the scrap of paper with the Combination on it:

2D75#10.

He quickly leafed through the street map to page 75. He ran his index finger over the grid references, finding 2 on the vertical axis and D on the horizontal one. His finger arrived at the appropriate grid square, which contained a cluster of small streets in central London, just off Piccadilly.

'You cracked it!' said Tilly.

'Not yet,' he replied. 'It'll take days to search all these streets.'

'What about the number ten?' she said, referring to the last two digits. 'Maybe it's an address.'

'Number ten . . .' Darkus recited to himself. 'Number 10,' he realised.

'What is it?'

'This is Down Street,' he said, pointing to a short street in the centre of the grid square. 'It's a Tube station.'

'On what line? I've never heard of it.'

'That's because it hasn't been in use since World War Two. It's a "ghost station". Winston Churchill used it as a headquarters during the London bombing raids. He named it Number 10. Not Downing Street, but *Down Street*.'

# Chapter 26
## DOWN STREET

Bogna made the trip to central London in record time, negotiating the bus lanes with ease. By her own admission, she was starting to enjoy driving Alan's 'taxi-car'.

The meter read £1020.20 as the Fairway cab circled Hyde Park Corner and arrived on the wide swathe of Piccadilly, lined with grand stone facades and exclusive hotels. To the north, the former mansions of London's seventeenth-century elite were now home to upscale shops and private clubs. To the south, Green Park was buried under a carpet of autumnal leaves, its foliage reduced to a row of skeletal trees. The thoroughfare in the middle was awash with black cabs, one of which indicated right, but turned left, incurring the wrath of several motorists. This particular black cab then turned on to Down Street.

Compared to its busy neighbour, Down Street was quiet and residential. The classical white stone was replaced by ordinary red-brick facades, lined with black railings.

Darkus signalled to Bogna to pull over, seeing the former Tube station on their left, secreted within a row of apartment blocks. Although it was redundant and lacking any identifying signs, the station retained its trademark London Underground pillars and arches, decked out in ox-blood red glazed tiles. A drab-looking newsagent's occupied the central archway. The archways on either side of it contained an entrance to a small mews street, and a narrow grey door with a warning sign on the front.

Darkus set his phone to forward calls to Bogna's mobile and told her to stay put and wait for Uncle Bill. Darkus had phoned the hospital again on the way, and the nurses told him his uncle was *still* sleeping – but he couldn't sleep for ever, or at least Darkus hoped not. Bogna was to let Bill know exactly where they were, and request reinforcements.

'Just get Alan home in one pieces,' she said, making the sign of the cross.

'I'll do my best,' said Darkus, getting out of the cab and holding the door for Tilly to follow.

The two of them approached the station. Darkus tried the narrow grey door, which was locked tight, while Tilly checked the mews entrance.

Darkus entered the newsagent's and surveyed the walls and ceiling for any points of access. He deduced that this had once been the ticket office. Now the walls were a flat white and lined with tall shelves of canned food. There were no interior doors apart from an old one that had been painted shut and barricaded by a heavy display refrigerator containing drinks and frozen foods. The newsagent's offered no means of entry into the station.

'You want to buy something or what?' demanded the man behind the counter.

'Thank you, but you don't have what I'm looking for,' said Darkus and exited the shop.

He saw Bogna waiting patiently, parked opposite. Then Tilly reappeared from the mews street and silently beckoned him to follow her. Darkus turned the corner to find her removing a crowbar from her backpack and angling it on a small steel air vent set into the side wall of the station. The vent was circular in shape, and not wide enough for an adult – but just about wide enough for Tilly and Darkus.

At that moment, two policemen passed the archway, walking the beat. One of the officers turned, spotting them, and stopped for a closer look. Tilly quickly concealed the crowbar behind her back, while Darkus made a show of examining the old station, then tipped his tweed hat.

'School project,' he said convincingly.

The policemen nodded kindly and walked on.

Darkus and Tilly turned back to the vent to find a large black crow standing guard on the ledge above. It flapped its wings threateningly, staring at them with dead eyes and strutting on the spot.

'Not a good omen,' said Tilly.

'It's just a bird –'

Suddenly the crow squawked and hopped down on to Tilly's head, digging its talons into her hair.

'Get off!' she cried out, swatting at it.

The crow quickly hopped from her head to Darkus's, knocking his hat to the ground. Then, just as quickly, the bird flapped away under the archway and into the sky beyond the station.

Darkus grabbed his hat, dusted it off and replaced it on his head.

'Definitely not a good omen,' said Tilly, watching the sky.

'Coincidence,' Darkus rationalised.

Tilly collected herself, locating a discarded crate and using it as a step to get a better angle on the vent. She prised away the grille, and within seconds her head and shoulders had vanished into the hole in the wall, leaving only her booted feet kicking and wriggling, until they too disappeared.

Darkus looked around to check the coast was clear, then stepped up on the crate, removed his hat and slid into the vent after her.

He found himself in a cramped metal tube, with Tilly's slim outline ahead of him, slithering towards a dim fluorescent light in the distance. His herringbone coat provided relatively little friction and he slid easily along behind her, deeper into the wall of the station.

Nudging her backpack in front of her, Tilly reached the other end of the vent and used the crowbar to bash out the grille that covered it. She popped her head through to find she was approximately three metres above a wide circular floor. A dim fluorescent strip was the only light source. She dropped her backpack to the floor and it landed with a dull thud. Then she reached out with the crowbar and wedged it between two overhead pipes, to form an improvised gymnastic bar. She held on and pulled the rest of her body out of the vent, swung from the bar and dropped gracefully to the concrete below.

Moments later, Darkus threw his hat down to her. She caught it and watched as he slightly less gracefully grabbed hold of the crowbar, hauled himself out and dropped down to the station floor beside her. She handed him his hat, which he planted back on his head, and they took in their surroundings.

They were in a large, circular room, which had been gutted and was almost entirely covered in dust. Pipes and cables snaked across the walls but there were no visible doors or windows. Darkus examined the walls, then counted his strides to estimate the location of the newsagent's.

'If that was the ticket office, this must have been the lift shaft . . . originally for two lifts,' observed Darkus. 'It's been floored over.'

'So what are we meant to do now?' asked Tilly, looking slightly panicked. 'We can't get back up to that vent.' They looked up to see the crowbar still wedged overhead, useless.

Darkus roamed around the room, examining the circular floor. 'This is a reinforced concrete baffle, to defend against bombs. They would have built more of them at intervals down the shaft. Which means there has to have been . . .' He stopped, finding something at his feet. 'A door.'

Tilly caught up with him by a wooden door set into the floor at the edge of the room. Darkus pulled the rope handle and swung it open to find a rusting metal ladder, descending under the floor at an angle. Tilly fished in her backpack and took out an LED head torch, which she strapped on. She angled her head and the beam of light picked out another identical circular chamber beneath them. This one had fire escapes attached to the wall, leading down some ten metres or so to another concrete baffle. There was an overpoweringly wet, stagnant smell coming from the bowels of the station.

Without speaking, Tilly went first to illuminate the way, and Darkus followed, descending through the floor on the rusted metal ladder.

The two small figures slowly traversed the curving walls, which were dug out of the subterranean rock and secured with ribs of steel and rows of rivets. The ladder squeaked and complained, but neither one of them said anything. Darkus looked down, watching each foot carefully locate the next step. Suddenly the word 'vivisepulture' appeared in his mind, from the spelling competition. The definition: buried alive. He tried to ignore the catastrophiser, which was telling him that this was a derelict building, unlikely to be structurally sound, and even if Bogna was able to reach Uncle Bill, it would be hours before anyone could find them. Casting these thoughts out of his mind, he continued to follow the dim beam of light coming from Tilly's forehead.

They reached the floor of the second concrete baffle and found another wooden door at their feet. Darkus opened it and Tilly trained the light through it, discovering a third, identical chamber another ten metres below them.

'How far down does it go?' she asked.

'I'd guess about thirty metres in total. Which would mean there's one more baffle below that one. Then we reach subway level.'

Tilly shook her head, making their shadows dance from the light of the torch. She led the way again, descending another set of rusted fire escapes, these ones protesting even louder than the others. Finding a rhythm, they made quick progress, reaching the third baffle. Apprehensively, Tilly opened the third and hope-fully final door in the floor, and saw a rickety ladder descending another ten metres to a short landing and a narrow metal footbridge. Beneath the footbridge was a gaping chasm that was too wide and deep for the head torch to shed any light on.

They performed the same procedure again, finding the walls were covered in an even thicker layer of dust and grime.

'Did you know that dust is seventy per cent human skin and hair?' remarked Darkus.

'Not helping,' Tilly replied. Then a breeze tousled her hair. 'What was that?' she whispered sharply.

Darkus felt it too. The breeze was becoming stronger by the second, rapidly swelling into a gale-force wind.

'It's a draught,' said Darkus over the growing noise.

'A draught from what?'

'A train.'

'A *what?!*'

The blast of rank air was accompanied by a massive rumbling that reverberated through the entire station, shaking the walls. The rivets whined, quickly reaching screaming pitch. The ladder began jolting and rattling uncontrollably under their feet, trying to shake them off. Darkus lost his footing, the tails of his coat dangling over the abyss as he held on for dear life. He shifted his weight, regaining his balance.

'It's travelling at full speed,' said Darkus over the roar. 'Only another few seconds.'

As quickly as it had arrived, the rush of wind went into reverse, as the air was sucked down the tunnels by the departing train. A second later, it was deathly quiet again.

'You said the station wasn't in use?' Tilly whispered accusingly.

'Yes, but the tracks are,' replied Darkus, as if the assumption would have been obvious. 'The trains run straight through.'

They reached the narrow metal footbridge. Below it was another drop into the lift well: a circular sump that contained the remains of a giant fan that looked like the propeller of a sunken ship.

Tilly trained the light ahead and they crossed the

bridge to the opening of a large semicircular tunnel, dug deep into the rock. ⟨t⟩

'This is the exit for the lifts,' whispered Darkus. 'It should lead to the platforms.'

'So?'

'That's where Churchill's HQ was. It had its own power and phone lines. If the Combination's here, logically that's where they would be.'

They walked softly down the length of the tunnel, the torch picking out the familiar cream and maroon London Underground tiles. Pipes snaked idly along the walls and over their heads. Reaching the end of the tunnel, a faded sign still read: TO THE TRAINS. Darkus followed an artistically rendered arrow around a corner to a steep descending staircase with a tubular railing down the middle and curving walls on either side. At the base of the steps was a small pool of fluorescent light.

Tilly switched off her torch and they crept down the stairs, arriving at a T-junction between two platforms. To their right, the eastbound platform had been walled off to create a narrow corridor that ran the length of the track. To their left, a metal grate covered the entrance to what was once the westbound platform. On cue, another rush of air hurtled through the tunnels, followed by a seismic rumbling that shook the whole station.

In a flash, a westbound train sped past the metal grate, appearing only as a blur of grey and red with a row of lit windows. Passengers on the train would later recall seeing what looked like two children watching them from inside the tunnel, but no one would report it, for fear of being labelled either drunk or delusional.

A split second later, an eastbound train sped along the opposite platform out of sight, obscured by the walled corridor.

As the tail of the westbound train flashed past the grate, the air was sucked after it and the rumbling subsided.

Tilly opened her mouth to speak, until Darkus held up his hand.

They heard the unmistakable sound of a woman's laughter echoing through the subway. Then the distinct sound of footsteps approaching quickly along the corridor on the eastbound platform. Darkus deduced from the sound that they were stilettos, and from the rhythm he deduced who they belonged to.

Darkus and Tilly retreated up the staircase as the glamorous figure of Bram Beecham's assistant, Chloe, walked straight past the T-junction without a second glance. They prepared to move again, until a second set of footsteps followed Chloe's. Darkus recognised these footsteps too, and signalled to Tilly to wait. They stood motionless on the staircase, Tilly holding her breath for fear of being heard.

Mr Presto marched past the T-junction, then came to a halt, his equestrian boots swivelling to inspect the cross passage. His nostrils twitched under the low brim of his hat, almost smelling their presence. Darkus and Tilly pressed themselves against the wall of the stair-well, exchanging a glance. After an agonising few seconds, they exhaled as the booted footsteps continued down the eastbound corridor after Chloe's. Moments later, a door opened and closed, blocking out any further sound.

Darkus peered around the corner of the stairwell and gave the all-clear. They crept out of the cross passage and into the eastbound corridor, which was lined with doors and curved on one side, conforming to the shape of the tunnel. The entire platform had been crudely converted into a row of dormitory rooms, resembling the cabins of an ocean liner. Dim light bulbs dangled from the ceiling.

Darkus began checking the door to each dormitory, quietly but systematically. Tilly shadowed him, providing additional light with the head torch. They found an old switch room lined with levers and heavy-duty fuse boxes. The entire room and all the machinery was painted grey to indicate it had been decommissioned. Next door was a bathroom, complete with toilet bowl and sink, all covered in several decades' worth of dust.

They entered the next cubicle along and found a telephone exchange with tall banks of relays, wiring and plugs hanging disconnected. The entire room and all its contents were also painted grey. Darkus quickly dismissed it and moved on.

As Tilly turned to follow him out, a shadow moved from behind the operator's switchboard and grabbed her.

'Darkus!'

He turned back to see Tilly wincing as Chloe held a long thin blade to her throat.

'Move. Now,' instructed Chloe.

She manoeuvred them both out of the telephone exchange, using Tilly as a shield.

'Where's my dad?' demanded Darkus.

Chloe shooed him down the corridor, marching them towards a door at the end. 'Someone wants to see you,' she said.

Without warning, Tilly started coughing and clutching her throat.

Darkus turned, alarmed. 'Are you OK?'

'My asthma,' she wheezed, pointing at her backpack.

'Help her. It must be the dust,' said Darkus, genuinely concerned.

'Should've thought of that before,' said Chloe.

'It's me you want,' he reasoned. 'You don't want her death on your conscience.'

Chloe trained the blade on the nape of Tilly's neck and allowed her to shuffle the backpack from her shoulders to the ground. Tilly unzipped the front compartment and went to fish inside.

'Ah-ah,' Chloe warned, pricking her with the knife.

'Ouch. All right,' said Tilly impatiently.

'Allow me,' said Chloe, and dipped her hand into the compartment, removing the asthma inhaler and passing it to Tilly.

'Thanks.' Tilly gave the inhaler a shake, then subtly angled the mouthpiece to point backward over her shoulder, directly at her assailant.

'Hurry up,' barked Chloe.

'OK.'

Tilly pumped the inhaler and a spurt of foam shot out of the mouthpiece, hitting Chloe dead in the forehead, but producing no apparent effect beyond a comic one.

Chloe burst out laughing. 'What a genius toy!' She giggled, not noticing the foam expanding in all directions and sliding down her forehead. 'What . . . ?' She felt the pepper burn her skin, the foam expanding to cover her eyes, gluing her eyelids closed. She clawed at her face, finding the substance stuck to her fingers. It progressed down her face like a custard pie, only this one was accompanied by scalding pain, which within ten seconds had reduced Chloe to an unconscious pile of rangy limbs.

Darkus looked at Tilly incredulously.

'School project . . .' she explained.

'Come on.' Darkus pushed through the next door along to find a disused kitchen, complete with sinks and counters. 'He must be here somewhere . . .' Darkus moved from room to room with increasing speed and desperation. Tilly followed, helpless to slow him down.

Darkus reached the last door at the end of the corridor and pushed it open to find a frail figure bound to a grey metal chair, overpowered by his own shadow.

'Dad . . . !'

# Chapter 27
## FATHER AND SON

Knightley tried to peer through the mist of his own dulled consciousness. In the past twenty-four hours he'd endured hypnotic suggestions that would have turned lesser men insane. And now, through the soup of his addled mind, he actually thought he saw his son's face. But it wasn't possible. It couldn't be. Even if Darkus had deduced the location from the scrawled piece of paper, he couldn't have found his way into this cave alone. Not without Uncle Bill's assistance. And in that case, where were the officers? Where was the back-up?

Knightley blinked helplessly, trying to focus, but the room was swimming. He couldn't move.

Darkus abandoned any attempt to be covert and ran to hug his father, nearly knocking him off his chair.

'Dad . . .'

Knightley felt his son's arms shivering around him. 'Doc, it *is* you . . .'

'Of course it is,' said Darkus.

'It's OK. I'm OK.'

'I'm sorry I let you down.'

'Of course you didn't – you're the best son in the world.'

Darkus smiled, hardly believing what he was hearing. 'I thought I'd lost you again.'

'I haven't gone anywhere –'

Someone snapped their fingers loudly to interrupt them, and Knightley's head instantly lolled.

Darkus spun around to see Morton Underwood with his right hand in the air. His saucer-like eyes gazed out from a dark hat and raincoat.

'Hello, Doc.'

Darkus studied him for any trace of the person who'd allegedly been his godfather, but any connection that might once have existed had been drained from his features by time and bitter experience. Now it was simply the face of a dangerous stranger.

'What do you want?' said Darkus. 'We'll drop the case. Just let us go.'

'Speak for yourself,' Tilly interjected. 'We're all here for our own reasons.' She took Chloe's stiletto knife from her belt and pointed it at Underwood. 'You know who I'm here for.'

'Your mother's death was a sad necessity, Matilda. She

was halfway to pinpointing this l-location when we found her out,' Underwood explained. 'I'm sorry she never made it to pick you up from school that day.' Tilly listened with clenched fists, her teeth digging into her lip and her eyes streaming. 'It was a relatively quick death,' he added.

Tilly ran at him, but Underwood swung open the door to a switching box mounted on the wall, which stopped her progress dead, cleanly knocking her out. Tilly fell to the ground, unconscious, the knife skittering away.

Darkus got to his feet, assessing the room. It was larger than the others, and he deduced it was at the end of the platform where the eastbound and westbound tracks converged, and a siding would have been laid to accommodate parked and disused train carriages. There were two doorways in the room. One was occupied by Underwood, who was motionless, scarecrow-like; the other was located in the centre of the far wall, its door firmly closed.

'This, Darkus, is the end of the l-line,' said Underwood, as if reading his mind.

Darkus noticed that the man was now holding a pistol in his hand, and it was pointed directly at him.

'You shouldn't have c-come here,' Underwood went on, his eyes floating in the twin whirlpools of his lenses. 'This is grown-up business.'

'I came to get my dad,' insisted Darkus.

'I warned you that if you proceeded with this investigation, it would mean losing your father all over again. And yet you chose to proceed.'

Knightley looked up, as if to say something, but his head lolled.

'Alan was perfectly safe until you chose to interfere,' added Underwood.

Darkus blinked. Inside his head, theories were flaring and exploding. Reason had abandoned him. He struggled to recalibrate his mind. 'You took him because he got too close to cracking the case,' said Darkus. 'To cracking *The Code*.'

'No,' answered Underwood. 'It was *you* who cracked *The Code*. *You* who resurrected his ailing career, and remembered the Knowledge he so badly needed. *You* are responsible for his current situation – no one else.'

Underwood walked forward to allow another figure to enter through the doorway behind him. It was Presto, balancing something in his hands like a ritual sacrifice. It was a heavy, bulky manuscript, bound in some indeterminate animal skin. For a moment Darkus wondered whether it was in fact *human* skin. The stiff cover had come away from the spine, which was in tatters. The pages were barely held together, warped and worn by age. Darkus realised this was the original text that the Order of the New Dawn had talked about.

'*The Code* was my offering to the Combination,' Underwood went on. 'My way in. You see, there was a boy under my care —'

'I know all about it,' said Darkus.

'You don't know everything,' Underwood corrected him. 'The boy came to me with behavioural problems, lack of f-focus, that sort of thing. During the course of our sessions he told me about a book he'd discovered. His family were wealthy and powerful. They were collectors. They had come into possession of a certain manuscript . . .' Underwood nodded to the burden in Presto's hands. 'I asked him to bring it to me. The manuscript had no effect on me, but it had the most unusual effect on the boy: he tried to k-kill me. I defended myself, and he fell to his death. I did some research, and realised what I'd stumbled upon. And so it set me on my path, and afforded me entry into a very exclusive organisation.'

'A criminal organisation,' said Darkus.

'The judicial system found me guilty, so I used the manuscript to gain access to an alternative system. One that doesn't rely purely on reason.'

'Without reason there's only madness,' argued Darkus.

'We're *beyond* reason. The Combination doesn't

exclude anyone, or anything, however extraordinary, or supernatural. You might say, we use a *combination* of everything to succeed.'

'That still makes you a criminal,' insisted Darkus.

Underwood didn't blink. 'Crime is only another form of justice. And *The Code* is the perfect recruiting tool.'

'You're endangering innocent people.'

'I'm inspiring the weak-minded, giving them something to believe in.'

'That doesn't explain what you want with my dad.'

Underwood nodded, continuing his story. 'Alan *f-found* me . . . several months after I was presumed dead. But by that time it was too late. We were on opposite sides of the law. The truth is, I never wanted to harm him. It was Alan who told me about the existence of the Combination in the first place – or his suspicions of it. One day he might have been an asset,' Underwood explained. 'So when he found me, I didn't want to kill him, and I couldn't risk him talking. And that's when I came up with a solution.'

Above ground, Bogna's phone was ringing off the hook and she was starting to regret her choice of ringtone – a Polish folk dance was hardly appropriate for the grave circumstances she now found herself in.

Uncle Bill had called as soon as he woke up, and was now, against doctor's orders, making the trip to Down Street, with every available officer.

Bogna watched as several white vans pulled up outside the abandoned Tube station. She crossed herself as officers entered the newsagent's and the mews, and started testing the strength of the grey security door.

Inside one of the vans, Bill's wheelchair was positioned at a control desk, his right arm in plaster, his left leg, also plastered, extended out in front of him. He peered at a large monitor as a technician worked the keyboard.

Bill picked up a walkie-talkie with his good hand. 'Let me know when we hae contact.'

# Chapter 28
## THE OPEN BOOK

Darkus was hanging on his godfather's every word, and Underwood knew it.

'I used hypnosis to make Alan believe he'd never found me. Alan returned to his former life none the wiser, but deep down he knew he had the answer . . . he just couldn't find it. It made him even more obsessive, even more determined to crack the Combination. It drove him away from Jackie, and away from you. And one day his mind locked up, and he couldn't handle it any longer. And that's when he had his episode.'

Darkus felt a throbbing in his temples as the catastrophiser struggled to process what he was hearing. 'It was your fault.'

'A coma was the safest place for him. While he was asleep, nothing bad could happen to him. Then something woke him up. We may never know what that was,' said Underwood. 'He was perfectly safe until you helped him remember.'

Darkus turned to his father, who was now completely still.

'He's in a deep, post-hypnotic trance,' Underwood went on. 'When he wakes up he won't remember a thing: not this case, not your budding partnership. You, on the other hand . . . You're the only one left with the Knowledge. Which means you'll have to be consigned to history along with it. You were last seen entering a disused Tube station. No one will be surprised when an accident befalls you on the tracks.' Underwood nodded to the manuscript in Presto's hands. 'You know, there is something to that book. In the last few minutes, I haven't stuttered once.'

Darkus lifted his father's chin, looking into his eyes, but they remained defiantly, terminally closed.

'Dad,' he said, his own eyes welling up. 'Talk to me.' He shook him, but Knightley wouldn't wake up. Darkus sank to his knees, resting his head on his father's arm, detecting the familiar smell of his shirt cuff, feeling the familiar rhythm of his chest heaving and falling – but his father was as lost to him as he'd ever been. 'Please . . .'

All of a sudden, Knightley's body seemed to sense the proximity of his son, as if Darkus had an even stronger gravitational pull than the hypnosis. Knightley's nostrils flared, his brows knitted and his ears lifted – all unbe-known to Darkus, whose face was buried in his father's argyle jumper. Yet these subtle facial movements were as significant as a drowning man fighting his way back to the surface.

Darkus heard the whistle from his father's nose get quicker and looked up, daring to deduce what it might mean. 'Dad?' he whispered.

'Yes-yes,' Knightley answered, as if something deep inside him couldn't refuse his son's wish.

At that moment, an announcement crackled over the station's public address system: 'This is SO 42. We have ye surrounded. Release the Knightleys and exit the station with yer hands in the air.' Bill's voice went on, 'Ah repeat: we have ye surrounded . . .'

Underwood turned in the direction of the announce-ment. Presto frowned and exchanged a glance with him.

But neither of them noticed the manuscript in Presto's hands. The pages began to riffle from top to bottom, like a wave breaking. The leathery cover creaked and flew open. Presto looked down, his eyes widening, as the book appeared to tremble.

Darkus stood up, feeling a vibration moving through the ground, affecting the whole station, pushing him off balance.

'It's just a train,' said Presto, trying to convince himself.

Knightley looked up, his eyes trying to focus. 'No . . .' he said. 'It's the *book* . . .' He turned to Darkus. 'We have to get out of here, Doc.'

'We're not finished,' said Underwood, raising his pistol, but the vibration made it impossible to aim.

'The book's more than just a trick of the eye. The Order was right – it brings death and damnation,' Knightley rattled on, as if to himself. 'Don't you see? It always does!'

'It's a train,' repeated Presto, a little too vehemently.

'You're only its custodian, Morton,' shouted Knightley. 'It's an ancient evil. Can't you see? It's protecting itself!'

The curved station walls started shaking. The grey switching box came off its hinges and fell to the floor, narrowly missing Tilly, who was sleeping soundly from her concussion. A gust of wind crept in, tousling clothes and hair. Underwood spun around. The door in the centre of the wall flew open, exposing the train tracks beyond the platform, where the eastbound and west-bound tunnels met side by side. The gale picked up strength, whirling dust and tearing grey paint flakes from the walls.

Darkus shielded his eyes, picked up the stiletto knife and cut through Knightley's bindings.

Presto looked down at the book, which was now thumping and bouncing in his hands. Without warning, his fingers went rigid, as if the manuscript was on fire. 'Ouch!'

He dropped it with a dull thud, and started blowing on his hands, in a parody of a man searching for a bucket of cold water. He screamed and kicked the book towards the open door.

'No . . .' shouted Underwood.

The manuscript seemed to fly out through the doorway, picked up by the wind, which was swelling into a tornado.

Knightley staggered to his feet as the chair was knocked over and blown clattering across the room. Presto didn't wait around to witness any more. He dashed for the side door and vanished through it.

Underwood stared into the central doorway, entranced, his eyes bigger than ever. The wind rippled his clothes, as if something inside him was tearing and struggling to get out.

'N-no . . .' he muttered, and went after the manuscript, descending a short set of metal stairs on to the tracks.

'Morton!' Knightley shouted after him.

But his old friend didn't listen. Underwood's face was that of a man possessed. He had the same slack-jawed expression that characterised the faces of miners during the gold rush, or politicians eyeing the seat of power. It was an age-old expression of greed and avarice, and it made Darkus realise that Underwood was deeper under the book's spell than anyone else.

The manuscript bounced lightly along the tracks, like a paper bag in the breeze. Underwood stumbled after it, crossing from the siding on to the main track.

The seismic rumbling through the earth reached a deafening climax as an eastbound train sped through the tunnel, past the room and within inches of Underwood . . . decimating the manuscript.

Underwood was thrown to the ground by the force of it, the lenses in his glasses shattered, and he began crawling along the opposite set of tracks. He struggled to his feet, hopelessly grasping at the strewn pages.

Knightley shielded Darkus's eyes as the rumbling continued unabated – they both knew full well what was coming next. Darkus peered through his father's fingers.

A split second later, the Knightleys flinched in unison as a westbound train sped past in the opposite direction, running over the book a second time, and soundlessly swallowing up Underwood – leaving no trace of him in its wake.

The manuscript pages flew around the tunnel like a crazed flock of sparrows, soaring and diving. The tails of both trains vanished into the tunnels, leaving a whirling tower of paper, like the column of a storm. For a moment, it seemed to take on the appearance of a gaping skull.

The Knightleys stood together, braced against it, their clothes and hair windblown. Darkus pinned his hat on his head with one hand. The rumbling died down, and the wind abated, only to go into reverse, like the thrusters of a jet engine on landing.

'Hold on!' shouted Knightley over the mounting roar. 'It's not over yet –'

Darkus's hat took flight and billowed through the doorway on to the tracks.

Knightley held Darkus tight as the air was sucked out of the room and down the tunnels by the departing trains, threatening to take them with it. Their shoes slid over the concrete floor, carrying them towards the doorway and the same fate as Underwood.

The dust and paint flakes dislodged by the first gale were now swirling around them as debris was vacuumed into the tunnels. The switching box clattered and rolled across the room, then took flight. Tilly regained consciousness as she began to travel across the floor after it. She immediately extended her feet and wedged herself into a corner.

The Knightleys weren't so fortunate, finding themselves in the eye of the storm, drawn towards the doorway, deprived of oxygen and unable to breathe.

'Dad?'

'Close your eyes, Doc,' Knightley shouted over the din.

Darkus obeyed him without question and clamped his eyes shut. It was at that moment – in the reddish blackness of his closed lids – that his mother's words returned to him.

*'Evil doesn't exist unless you believe in it.'*

He heard her voice clearly. He could almost see her holding her mug of tea.

*'If you don't believe in it, it has no power.'*

Darkus repeated the phrases over and over in his head above the roar. He felt his father's arms around him, and his mother's words in his head, and although they were being pulled towards certain doom, he felt safe. In his world, at that moment, there was no room for evil.

At the same moment, the signal lights over the train tracks flicked from green to red. With a series of loud mechanical clicks, the same thing happened all along the line. The tunnels that stretched into the distance were suddenly bathed in a warm glow. The rumbling receded to an eerie stillness; the wind reduced to a soft breeze.

Tilly got to her feet, rubbing her head, unsure of what had just happened. Darkus opened his eyes to find the tracks empty. There was no sign of the manuscript, or of

Underwood. The station was deathly quiet once more. He looked up to his dad for confirmation.

'Let's go home,' said Knightley, taking Darkus's hand in one of his, and Tilly's in the other, and leading them out.

They made their way to the end of the platform, and followed a faded sign that read: TO THE STREET. An artistically rendered arrow led to a tall spiral staircase with a well-preserved cartouche that read: WAY OUT. After one hundred and three steps, they reached a doorway to the outside world.

# Chapter 29
## QUALITY TIME

The remaining half of the school term proceeded without incident. The hooded tops continued to lurk at the back of the room, making disparaging remarks about Darkus's name. Darkus continued to deflect them, practising peaceful engagement. It was as if the recent events involving shadowy crime organisations, and possibly supernatural forces, had never happened.

And so, with the inevitable pomp and expectation, Christmas rolled around. Despite heavy snowfall, buses and trains were still running, and most people had forgotten about the freak tornado that affected parts of the Piccadilly line several weeks earlier. The phenomenon was put down to an air pressure problem in the Underground rail network, and the relevant transport safety organisations assured the public that repairs were under way. Rumours of passengers seeing people, including children, playing by the tracks around the time of the incident were put down to urban myth, although one of Darkus's female classmates happened to be on the Tube at the time, and swore she caught a glimpse of someone matching his description. Darkus laughed off the idea, but wasn't sure how convincing he'd been.

Meanwhile, consumers who were scouring high street and online stores in search of the popular bestseller *The Code* were disappointed to find that stocks had inexplicably dried up. Even e-book readers found only a dead link. A week later a newspaper reported that a lawsuit had indefinitely suspended publication of the book due to a copyright issue. Ambrose Chambers could not be reached for comment. However, the publisher would not rule out the possibility of a sequel.

On the home front, Darkus tried to return to some semblance of 'normal'. His father was living at his office on Cherwell Place, being well fed and cared for by Bogna, who was also doing a self-defence course in her spare time. Darkus wasn't happy about being returned to his former domestic situation and had the nagging suspicion that the investigation with his father was a one-off that wouldn't be repeated. They had never spoken about the case again. They had never discussed whether the book was responsible for the disturbance in the tunnel, or whether it was just the trains. (Darkus already knew what his father's answer would be, and there wasn't suffi-cient evidence to prove it either way.) They also hadn't talked about the fact that Presto and Chloe were still unaccounted for. Nor the fact that Tilly would not stop until she found every member of the Combination and exacted her punishment. More than ever, Darkus under-stood that this was less the end of one case than the beginning of another.

He could at least relax in the knowledge that his father was alive and well, and only an hour and a half away by London cab.

Clive continued his efforts at self-improvement, this time from a court-ordered stay at a trauma clinic in Staffordshire, practising what Jackie diplomatically referred to as R & R. A junior presenter was standing in for him on *Wheel Spin*, and the official reason for his being off-air was a cranial injury sustained during a high-speed test drive.

Tilly willingly returned to Cranston as a day pupil, and completed her coursework with flying colours, defying her teachers' expectations. She was even rumoured to be in the running for form captain. Miss Khan never reported the theft of the asthma inhaler, fearing accusations that she had inadvertently put her pupils' welfare at risk. Instead, Tilly reached a plea-bargain, where she apologised to Miss Khan for the theft, suggested future improvements and they agreed to keep it their secret.

Without consulting each other, Darkus and Tilly returned to keeping a safe distance between them, which seemed easier than reliving the disturbing events of the case ad nauseam.

At noon on Christmas Day, a fully laden black Fairway cab pulled up outside Clive and Jackie's house.

Darkus, who had been watching the street for most of the morning, quickly deserted his vantage point at an upstairs window and raced down the stairs to greet their guests. He reached the front door, took a breath, straightened his blazer and opened it.

'Hello, Dad.'

Knightley stood on the doorstep in an immaculate tweed ensemble. 'Hello, son.' He gave Darkus a hug, as Jackie appeared in the entrance hall.

'Hello, Alan,' she said, fixing her hair a little.

'Jackie.' He nodded, and took something from behind his back. 'Merry Christmas.' He handed her a hand-woven wreath made of cones, bark and mistletoe.

'Still got the old magic,' she said, accepting it.

'It didn't take too long,' he explained. 'You know, I find it quite relaxing.'

'Well, you'd better come in . . .'

Jackie looked over Knightley's shoulder to see Bogna helping the somewhat reduced but still significant bulk of Uncle Bill out of the back of the cab. One of his legs was still in plaster, but it was hard to tell which because both legs were wrapped in thick cream-coloured socks with tartan garters. Bill appeared to be wearing a traditional Highland kilt that ended at the knee, which wasn't the most flattering garment on him, and as Bogna loaded him into a wheelchair for the trip up the driveway, it bordered on undignified.

As Knightley stepped into the entrance hall he saw the back of Clive's head, crowned with a red party hat, watching a Christmas special on TV.

'Hello, Clive.'

Clive raised a limp hand by way of reply. Knightley glanced at Darkus, who shrugged, then continued into the kitchen.

Tilly looked up from stirring a large punch bowl. 'Hi, Alan.' Her hair was dyed a particularly festive red, with what appeared to be green lowlights. 'Drink?'

'What's in it?' he asked.

'That would be telling.'

'I'll chance it,' said Knightley.

Jackie automatically put the kettle on and got a new packet of chocolate digestives from the cupboard for

Uncle Bill, who, judging by the creaking, shuffling sounds, was evidently approaching the kitchen. She marvelled to herself how much it felt like old times.

As is customary, everyone ate and drank too much, particularly Uncle Bill, who even sneaked a turkey leg in his pocket when he wheeled himself out to 'get some air', then promptly returned and slept for the rest of the afternoon. Bogna put a blanket over him and confided in Tilly that she found the Scotsman extremely 'charm ings', but admitted the language barrier could be a problem. Clive ate mechanically without saying a word, except to compliment Jackie on the stuffing. Tilly helped Jackie lay and relay the table.

Darkus looked at his father sitting across the dining table from his mother, and he couldn't help wondering. Between the formal affair of Christmas dinner and the polite requests for salt, pepper or gravy, there was an unspoken communication going on between Knightley and his son. There were many unresolved issues, on the domestic front and the professional one. Knightley had refrained from even a passing reference to what he might be working on, or whether he required Darkus's assistance. Darkus found himself feeling hurt that whatever it was, he clearly wasn't going to be included.

Finally, although it was childish, Darkus wondered whether his father had brought him a Christmas present.

He'd been too polite to ask, and his father didn't appear to be carrying anything concealed on his person. Everyone else had brought him something – including Tilly, who gave him a customised multifunction pen that she promised to explain in private – but his father's gift was the only one that mattered.

As everyone retired to the TV set, Knightley took Darkus aside. 'Got a moment?' he asked.

'Of course.'

'Shall we go to your room?'

Darkus led his father upstairs and across the landing to his bedroom. He was glad he'd taken extra care to tidy it up.

'Looks just like my office,' said Knightley, smiling.

Darkus shrugged, a little embarrassed.

Knightley fished in his inside jacket pocket, removed a slim package and handed it to Darkus.

'Merry Christmas.'

Darkus unwrapped the green paper to find a stainless-steel business-card holder. He opened it up to find a stack of perfectly off-white, watermarked cards that read:

# Knightley & Son

Underneath was an 0845 number.

Darkus looked up at his dad, speechless, then took the top card and turned it over in his hand. On the reverse side there was a small, embossed symbol: an eye with a blue iris, a black pupil and a tiny mirror in the centre.

'The evil eye,' said Darkus, recognising the symbol with surprise.

'Not to the person holding it,' Knightley explained. 'It's *protection*. Like the gargoyles they put over doors and windows to keep out malevolent forces. Not all self-defence is physical; sometimes it's mental, or even psychic.'

'If you believe in that sort of thing, yes,' Darkus said, doubtfully.

'My father, Rexford – your grandfather – was in the same profession as us,' Knightley continued. 'So you see, a lot can be predicted by cause and effect. He believed in myths and legends long before I did. Back then I thought there was a rational explanation for everything. You see, we're not so different after all.'

Darkus replaced the card in the holder and put it in his inside pocket. 'Thanks, Dad,' he said with a mixture of affection and fear.

'There is one more thing,' said Knightley, almost as an afterthought.

He led Darkus downstairs again, through the kitchen door at the back of the house, towards the shed at the end of the garden. Darkus was once again at a loss. He hadn't noticed his father – or anyone else for that matter – transporting anything to the back garden. This forgotten outhouse was only home to Clive's jet washer and a small assortment of car cleaning accessories. Knightley undid the catch and slowly opened the rickety wooden door.

Darkus heard a small whimper, but mistook it for the quick breath of his own anticipation. Then he saw two bright eyes watching him from waist height in the depths of the shed. They were surrounded by a soft halo of fur, two bat-like ears and a long pair of whiskers. A small bone lay chewed in a corner. So this was where Uncle Bill had disposed of the extra turkey leg. A wet, black nose approached cautiously from the darkness.

'His name's Wilburforce,' announced Knightley. 'But you can call him Wilbur. He's a former police dog.'

Darkus immediately identified him as a German shepherd, and not a puppy either. This dog looked long in the tooth, and was already greying around the temples. Darkus reached out to stroke his head. Wilbur's tail wagged once, uncertainly.

'I thought you could use some company,' said Knightley. 'I haven't told Clive yet. Best we break it to him gently.'

They heard a heavy car door slam, and Wilbur started.

Knightley gently shushed him. 'Post-traumatic stress disorder,' he explained. 'He's a bit jumpy . . .' He slowly attached a lead to Wilbur's collar and handed Darkus the strap.

Darkus led Wilbur across the patio and up the alley to the front garden. They spotted Bogna carrying an odd-shaped duffle bag from the back of the black cab to the house. Moments later, a strange, discordant sound wound to life. Wilbur's ears pricked up, then cowered. Darkus and his father looked at each other, unsure what to make of it.

They approached the front windows of the house to find the whole party gathered in the living room around Uncle Bill, who was now balancing a set of tartan bagpipes on his lap. He nodded in time, popping the blowpipe into his mouth and puffing out his cheeks. He and the instrument appeared to inflate as one, accompanied by a mounting drone. After a couple of wrong notes, his large fingers found the familiar strains of *Amazing Grace*. When the chorus of pipes ascended, Tilly nervously bit her lip and Darkus thought he saw Jackie wipe away a tear.

As heavy snowflakes began to fall outside, Wilbur sat obediently, Knightley put a hand on his son's shoulder, and they listened together. And old worries were, for the time being, forgotten.

# Knightley & Son

## WILL RETURN . . .